BOOKS BY

Edward F. Droge, Jr.

IN THE HIGHEST TRADITION (1974)
THE PATROLMAN: A COP'S STORY (1973)

In the Highest Tradition

IN THE HIGHEST TRADITION

Edward F. Droge, Jr.

ATHENEUM

New York

1974

The characters in this novel are
fictitious and any resemblance to
real persons is entirely coincidental.

*To Joanne, Chris,
Cheryl and Kim*

The author wishes to thank the following for the special help that made this book possible:

Abigail T. Droge
Joe and Ann Marcello
Richard Gilmartin

In the
Highest
Tradition

CHAPTER 1

A HEAVY rain covered New York. At five minutes to midnight Willie O'Brien, sheltered by the fancy marquee of the Corinthian, waved to the passing radio car and the two patrolmen inside smiled and waved back. Scanning Fifth Avenue for at least the twentieth time since six o'clock, first to his left, then slowly to his right, Willie looked for signs of life. There were none. He amused himself watching nearby puddles swell. Across the street, even Central Park was empty in the downpour. Only occasionally would someone, umbrella or newspaper raised above his head, scurry from the 59th St. BMT subway exit by the park wall, across the avenue, and into one of the luxurious apartment buildings to either side of the hotel. In twenty-three years as a doorman, in fact, in sixty-four years as a resident of New York, never had Willie witnessed a more violent rain or a more desolate Fifth Avenue.

Rising six hundred twenty-seven feet, forty-nine stories of handsome grey brick, the Corinthian ranked as one of the tallest, most spectacular building in the distinguished Upper East Side. Renowned for its perfection and flamboyance, the hotel hosted the upper echelon of every major industry and profession in the world during their stay in the city. It was not uncommon to see movie stars, television personalities, socialites, visiting dignitaries, and other illustrious people arriving or leaving at all hours of the day and night.

Willie, humble blue eyes set shallow in a kind face, looked at his watch, a little more anxious this night than usual to get off work. At one thirty Channel 2 was showing "The Petrified Forest," with Humphrey Bogart and Bette Davis. The constant abuse he absorbed as a doorman made him relish the opportunity to sit back and relax every chance he could. And Bogart to Willie was synonymous with relaxation. He would have a half-hour to get out of his uniform and drive home to lower Manhattan. If he hurried, he figured he could just about make it.

The idyl was interrupted by a chocolate-brown Continental splashing to the curb. The rear door opened just as he stepped to it and a middle-aged man, dark complexion, thick, wavy hair, smartly dressed in an expensive black topcoat, emerged quickly, darting under the marquee to stay dry. Close up, he had a cold and vicious look about him, tough skin, sloping forehead covering sinister eyes, two parallel, three-inch scars on the right side of his jaw.

"Good evening, sir," Willie said perfunctorily. "Welcome to the Corinthian."

[4]

"Good evening," came the curt reply. Willie was used to the caustic tone.

Another, similarly dressed, but much younger and taller than the first, slid off the back seat and leaned quickly to the protection of the canopy. In his late teens, he, too, had hard piercing eyes under wavy, raven hair. A uniformed chauffeur, exiting the street side, walked in the pouring rain directly to the trunk and opened it. Willie stepped to the edge of the curb, accepted two pieces of luggage and turned to lead the guests to the front desk. Stopping by the entrance, he set down the suitcases and swung open the glass door. "This way," he said, motioning inside with his free hand. The two men entered. The driver, his black jacket soaked through, removed two more suitcases from the trunk and followed behind closely.

The lobby of the plush hotel exemplified the luxury to be found throughout. Palace-deep, rose-colored carpeting cushioned the sole from wall to wall. To the left of the front door a massive, glittering chandelier, hand made of the finest crystal, hung conspicuously over a long, cardinal-red velvet sofa, fronted by a rectangular marble-slab table. To the right, flanked by exotic plants twisting their way to the ceiling, a stairway led down to the Dominican Room, a well-respected, successful nightclub, temporarily closed for a facelift. Two elevators stood farther back and beyond them was a door marked "Exit." Ornate mirror covered nearly every inch of the walls, making the lobby appear much larger than it really was.

[5]

Facing the front desk, an executive type with neatly combed grey-streaked hair sat on the sofa reading a newspaper. Absorbed in a book, the night manager, a peculiar sort with an obvious toupee and a constant grin, stood at ease behind the desk, while on a bare wooden chair beside him dozed the bell captain, a Puerto Rican, in his mid-forties. By the elevators an elderly couple patiently waited to return to their room.

The two newly arrived guests, followed by Willie and the driver, walked directly to the desk. The bell captain remained napping.

"Good evening, gentlemen," the manager said, a bit flushed. "Do you have reservations?"

"Yes," replied the elder of the two as the other looked around the floor, apparently impressed by the elegance. "Reynolds."

Mouthing the name, the manager looked down at the list in front of him. "Ah, yes, Mr. Reynolds, a suite for a party of two."

"That's correct."

"Very good, sir." He slid a registration form across the desk and pointed to the bottom line. "If you'll kindly fill this out and sign here . . ."

Roused by the conversation, the bell captain rose from his chair and padded from behind the desk. The driver, meanwhile, set down the bags, turned, and briskly walked the length of the lobby, out the front door. Willie stalled for a tip by the luggage.

The elevator arrived and the elderly couple stepped in. Mechanically, the man sitting on the sofa laid the newspaper down, stood up, and walked across the floor toward the rear exit, reaching it just as the elevator doors met with a metallic clunk. He turned to gaze at the new guests still at the front desk. Willie watched him and was puzzled. Also watching was the younger of the two gentlemen registering. There was no uncertainty on his face; he was aware and alert. Sliding the registration form toward the manager, Reynolds glanced toward the rear exit, then at his younger companion, who responded with a wintry smile. Simultaneously they reached within their coats, the younger producing a revolver, which he pointed at Willie, his scar-faced partner a .45-caliber automatic that startled the manager and the bell captain. Cued, the man at the exit pushed open the door and in ran two more men, both in their thirties, one dressed in a doorman's uniform similar to Willie's, the other in a blue, waist-length jacket with a zipper up the front. The former strode to the front door and stepped outside, while the latter withdrew an oversized screwdriver from his back pocket and forced it into the crack of the elevator nearest him, prying open the doors. When they were far enough apart he stooped and placed a wooden block on the metal runner between them. After repeating the procedure on the other elevator, he stationed himself by the rear exit and opened his jacket. A gun handle protruded from his belt.

The executive-looking accomplice carried two pieces of luggage to the marble table. Laying them flat, he opened one and removed a rubbery mass that he placed on the bright red sofa cushion to his left. He opened the other suitcase and removed a like blob, setting it down beside the first. A heavy, three-inch cord hung from each, and one at a time, as he braced the rubber with his left hand, he jerked the cord with his right. A hissing sound broke the silence as the rubber lumps filled with air and took shape. In seconds, two inflated dummies, a man and a woman, sat with their backs to the front door, so amazingly lifelike it would have been difficult for anyone more than a yard away to suspect they were not real people; for someone outside it would have been near impossible. Closing the empty suitcases, the man with the streaking grey slid one out of sight under the sofa and returned to the front desk with the other, handing it to his youthful confederate. He hoisted one of the others from the floor to the counter. From within he removed a machine gun, a menacing sight, the black metal glistening in the light. He closed the bag and pushed it to the floor behind the desk. With his free hand he picked up the remaining piece of luggage.

The three hoods hurriedly herded the trio of employees behind the mail-slot board in back of the desk and through a door designated with a plate, "Employees Only."

Stationed just outside the lobby entrance, the doorman glanced through the glass now and then to make sure all went smoothly.

In the Twenty-first Precinct sitting room, Chris Chamber and eleven other patrolmen waited for roll call. A transistor radio blasted away on the huge oak table in the center of the room. Some men sat in the iron-frame chairs scattered about, a few sat on the table, the remainder stood. The talk was free and easy.

"Cousin Bruno comin' your way," blared the disc jockey. "At the chime the correct time will be eleven fifty-five. Bong."

"Turn that thing down a little will you, Lou," said one of the patrolmen. "It's making my brain hurt."

"Sure, brother," said Lou Washington, a black cop with a modified afro. "It's a white station anyhow. Ain't no good music on there." A few of the men chuckled. Chamber, sitting on the other end of the table, glanced at him for a second, then returned to the conversation with his new partner, Joe Hummel, an eighteen-year veteran of the force. They would be riding together that night for the first time.

Twenty-eight years old, just under six feet, Chris Chamber was built powerfully. Light brown, neatly parted hair and intelligent blue eyes complimented his strong face. His uniform was neatly pressed and an array of bravery citations glistened above the shield.

The room buzzed with four unrelated conversations until all were interrupted by the sergeant, Harvey "Hoot" Gibson. "Fall in," he shouted as he entered. No one in a particular hurry, the better part of a minute passed before all lined up in two ranks, facing him.

"Golumbiewski."

"Here."

"Lewis."

"Yo."

"Adam-Boy. Special attention Eighty-second and First: they've been complaining about their cars getting broken into. The captain's giving a day for the guy who catches somebody up there."

"We'll keep our eyes peeled, sarge," said Lewis.

"I'm sure you will," the sergeant said with a smirk, apparently dissatisfied with this particular radio-car crew. "Just how many collars do you two have this year anyhow?"

"Same as we had last year, sir," Lewis replied. "None."

"Just two goddamned good on preventive patrol, Hoot," Golumbiewski chimed in. "Everybody out there knows better than to try anything while we're on patrol."

"Yeah," said the sergeant sarcastically, "just don't let Inspector Haynes catch you while you're on patrol behind the gas station between three and five this morning." Everyone laughed except Chris Chamber. He didn't think sleeping on the job was so funny. Naturally, the taxpayers suffered, but, more important, the other police officers working that shift suffered by having to answer the sleeping sector's jobs. And he certainly didn't feel it was right for a superior officer to let it go on, let alone joke about it. Unfortunately, Sergeant Gibson was just like one of the boys.

"Washington."

"Here."

"Conrad."

"Here."

"Sector Charley. Mail run at five o'clock."

"Hummel."

"Yo."

"Chamber."

"Here."

"Sector David. Special attention Fifth Avenue hotels."

And as roll call continued, Chris Chamber's thoughts drifted. The loose handling of the men by Sergeant Gibson—the first-name basis, the unrestrained, lackadaisical attitudes—reminded him of the Eight-O. Granted, the disregard for rules and regulations was nowhere near as flagrant here as in his old command, he thought, but the relationship between the patrolmen and the majority of bosses was identical. It was nice for the men to be close to the sergeant, but he wondered if the lack of discipline that resulted was worth it. God, in the Eight-O some men were turning out missing half their equipment. The sergeants didn't seem to mind much, but they should have. That was their duty. Moreover, the patrolmen themselves should have cared more. Their very lives, never mind their self-respect, depended on some of the equipment they lacked or carried in disrepair. But in the slums of the Eight-O, it seemed that everything and everyone fell into disrepair after a while. He thought about the Eight-O. About Brooklyn. About Bedford-Stuyvesant, undoubtedly the worst black ghetto in the nation. About the filth, the danger, the crime, the lack of respect, the militant black attitudes, the rats, the roaches, the drugs, the degradation, the corruption. And about how he was glad to be away from it all.

What a difference it was, working in East Manhattan. Another world. Respectable people most of the time, exquisite homes, comparatively clean streets, less crime, less chance of getting killed. O.K., so the bosses were a little stricter here, some complained. That didn't bother Chris at all. In fact, they weren't strict enough to suit him. To think that Bedford-Stuyvesant and East Man-

[11]

hattan were both part of the same city; and that the cop who worked in the luxury of the Two-One was paid exactly the same as the cop who fought to stay alive and to keep his dignity in the decadence of the Eight-O. That's what bothered him most for six long, miserable years in the Eight-O; and what he enjoyed most for two good years in his new command. As long as the inequity existed and there was nothing he could do about it, he was happy to be on the better side.

The new team of Hummel and Chamber was a calculated coupling. Changing partners was nothing new for Chris Chamber. Hummel was his fourth one in the eighteen months he had been steadily assigned to a radio car. No one liked to see his name next to Chamber's on the roll call, even as a fill-in, let alone as a steady partner. And although most of the men fraternized with him during working hours, in two years Chris had not once been invited to a social gathering at another officer's home nor, for that matter, had he much of any contact with the men of the Two-One after a day's tour. It wasn't because he wanted it that way. It was the price he had to pay for his refusal to participate in any form of corruption.

Whether a ten-dollar payoff from Joe the Juke on York Avenue to overlook his illegal gambling activities —a weekly contract that had been set up and honored by the last generation of Two-One patrolmen over fifteen years earlier—or a free meal at any one of the numerous cafés, restaurants, nightclubs or coffee shops, Chris had made it known in the precinct right from the beginning that he would not take part. He had turned spectator only. His position surprised a few men, for all it took was a couple of phone calls to reveal that he had participated in venal activities in the Eight-O. It was the rare bird who didn't go along with the crowd; the very rare bird who changed his colors entirely. Still, not one man felt jeopardized. The unwritten code of silence that tied down a policeman's tongue prevailed and it was unthinkable that anyone would break it.

Chris Chamber had made up his mind that things for him at least would be different in his new command. He chalked up his previous participation in corruption to experience and more than once thanked God he had never been caught. Young and naive as a rookie, he had been indoctrinated by older patrolmen, and like most rookies he had gone along for the ride. At first he had been too green and dependent to do anything except what the more experienced men did. After a while it just grew on him. Taking a few bucks here and there wasn't that bad, he had rationalized; everyone was doing it. And most of the time in the beginning it had involved the supposedly good citizens of the community—to beat a traffic summons or to keep a special watch on their place of business when it was closed. Before long it became gamblers looking to avoid arrest, lawyers looking to get some cases steered their way, tow truck drivers looking for a private call to an accident scene, and many, many other offers for various police services.

Though he hadn't gone out hounding, Chris had taken what came his way and after a while he was up to his neck. But he discovered that it was against his nature. Deep inside he had wanted to get out and waited patiently for the opportunity. That opportunity came with his transfer to the Two-One. If it hadn't come along, there was a good chance he would have left the force to escape the corruption. But now with a new surrounding and a new crew of men, he was willing to start all over again. This time he knew how to handle himself. It wasn't going to be easy, bucking the system, the tradition, but he was intent on finally being the kind of police officer he had wanted to be since he was seven years old. That meant absolute honesty. Being a good cop in every sense of the word had become more important to him than being one of the boys. It meant he'd be treated like an outsider, but he was willing to pay that price. Ridding the department of corruption was not his problem; keeping himself clean and maintaining his self-respect would be.

It was no surprise then that no one looked forward to riding with Chamber. Thus, the four steady partners in a year and a half. Thus, the new assignment for Joe Hummel.

The captain of the Two-One, Otto Varing, was repaying Hummel for infringing on one of his private contracts. The patrolman had disregarded warnings and had put the squeeze on a personal friend. Assigning him to a foot post on the outskirts of the precinct was not as harsh as putting him in as a steady partner with Chamber, Varing figured. He knew that working with Chamber would considerably curtail Hummel's movement and, he hoped, make his last two years on the force as miserable as possible.

In the relatively short time that Chamber had been stationed at the Two-One, Captain Varing viewed him with mixed feelings. He led the precinct in activity: number one in arrests and more summonses issued each month than any two other patrolmen combined. But recently he had been treading on dangerous ground, summonsing local businessmen, threatening them with arrest, even after they had informed him they were paying the captain. Then, to make things worse, he ignored the captain's warning to lay off and the threats to have him shipped back to Bedford-Stuyvesant. He was carrying his personal code of honesty too far and Varing was determined to make good his threat, notwithstanding the fact that his loss would mean a drastic dip in the activity of the precinct as a whole and ultimately cast a bad reflection on the commanding officer.

When the roll call was complete, Sergeant Gibson looked up at the platoon. "Anybody here whose name I haven't called?" No response. "O.K., take your posts." He paused a second and as the men began filing out of the room he called to Patrolman Conrad. "Hey, Bart." Conrad approached. "Listen, see if you can pick up a quart of milk for the coffee, huh. And some cake."

Chris heard him and was glad he hadn't asked Hummel. Though he hadn't ridden with Hummel before, he knew that such time-wasting errands would appeal to him. He had met a hundred Joe Hummels in the Department. If his partner stopped back at the stationhouse for a cup of coffee, it would be a real job to get him back out on the street again. Hummel had sat on his ass for eighteen years in the Two-One, going through the motions, and the two years left before he retired promised to be no different. Imagine, Chris thought, twenty years on the

[15]

job and he won't even know what it's like to be a real cop. One good year in Bed-Stuy and he would never have been the same man. Attaché case in hand, Chris shook his head with an artificial smile and a disgusted sigh as he walked past the desk officer on the way to the street.

"What the hell are you grinning about?" Hummel asked in a friendly tone, pulling up alongside at the front door of the stationhouse. He was stoop-shouldered, bald in front, thinning brown on the sides, and looking older than his forty-two years.

"Oh, nothing," Chris replied, looking around for the radio car. The rain was heavy.

They spotted the car and ran to it. Drenched, Hummel entered the driver's side and Chris, only slightly drier because he had held his attaché case over his head, entered the shotgun side. Senior man always drove the first four hours, while the other recorded any messages the unit might receive.

"Feel like coffee?" Hummel asked. He knew about Chamber and had decided to feel him out as he went along to see just where his new partner stood.

"Brought my own," said Chris. "There's enough for two."

"Oh . . . Well, I need cigarettes, anyhow," Hummel said. If this guy brought his own coffee with him to a precinct like the Two-One, where you could get a steak dinner for nothing in any one of a hundred places, all the rumors must be true, he thought.

"I'll tell you what, Joe. Why don't we take a run down Fifth to check out the hotels first. We can put it in our books and get it out of the way. Then we can have our coffee without having to worry." Chris was easy and polite. He certainly didn't want to give the impression that he ran the show, but at the same time he wanted Hummel to know where he stood.

"Worry!" said Hummel. "Worry about what?"

"Well, we are responsible for the hotels. I think it'd be a good idea to cruise by every now and again."

"You take this job pretty serious, don't you?"

Chris eyed him quickly. Either you took your work seriously or you didn't. It was rather disconcerting riding with a police officer who didn't feel that way. Life and death was the name of the game and life and death was a very serious business. He smiled. "It'll only take about five minutes. And Louie's is right up there. He sells cigarettes." As if Hummel had any intention of buying them.

Hummel smiled, too. He turned on the windshield wipers and pulled away from the stationhouse, heading for Fifth Avenue.

At night in Manhattan Chris was always struck by how quiet the radio was. At this time of night in the Thirteenth Division in Bedford-Stuyvesant the radio would have been blasting out job assignments nonstop to every available car.

"What the hell are you grinning about now?" Hummel asked. "You fuckin' cracking up?"

"No. Just happy to be working in Manhattan, Joe. That's all. Just happy to be out of the jungle."

"Yeah. I know what you mean."

But Chris knew Hummel could never really know.

Driving past some high-priced apartment buildings,

Hummel continued. "How long you here now?" The rain pounded the car and the wipers were too slow and too old to keep the windshield clear.

"About two years."

"You use a hook to get out of Brooklyn?"

"Believe me, Joe, if I had a hook I wouldn't have been happy just to come to the Two-One. I would've gone all the way and landed a real tit detail."

"Like what? The Equipment Bureau? The range?"

"Nope. Close, though. The academy pool. Swimming instructor in the Police Academy pool. That's where I'd like to be right now."

"Tired of working in the bag?"

"No, I don't mind the uniform that much. I just can't see myself enjoying anything more than teaching water safety to recruits. And getting paid for it!"

"You've got a point there. That's a tit job all right. You a good swimmer?" He swung a left on to Fifth Avenue.

"I like to think I'm good," Chris said, looking into the lobby of the Saint Marceau as Hummel slowed to twenty miles per hour. "I swam in high school. Even landed a scholarship to Saint John's, but I didn't really want to go to college then. The only reason I went for a year was 'cause my parents wanted me to. They figured that was what you were supposed to do right out of high school if you ever wanted to get anywhere. Looking back, though, I wish I would've stayed. The way it looks now, I might never get back to school. I swam in the Marines, also."

"So how'd you get out of the Eight-O° Just put in for a transfer?"

[18]

"Yep. Once a month for a year and a half. Somebody finally must've gotten the message I wanted out."

"What reason did you give?"

"Travel hardship. I bought a house in Queens, right on the Nassau County border, three years ago. Without traffic on four to twelves and late tours I can make it here in about three-quarters of an hour. It only saves me ten minutes, but I couldn't very well put 'I just want to get out of this shithole' on the transfer."

"Yeah. I know what you mean."

They approached the Corinthian. The rain gave not the slightest hint of letting up and Chris had difficulty seeing anything outside the car. When he spotted the doorman's uniform under the hotel marquee he raised his hand to wave hello to Willie. Chris liked Willie; he reminded him a bit of his father. The doorman saw the friendly gesture and waved back.

"Hey, wait a minute," Chris said as they passed. "That's not Willie." He strained to get a clear view of the lobby.

"Must be off tonight," Hummel said. He drove on.

"He's only off on weekends." Chris caught a quick glimpse of the man with the blue jacket by the rear door, the unmanned front desk, and the back of the couple's heads sitting on the couch.

"Maybe he's sick," said Hummel.

"I hope not." The lobby picture registered in Chris's mind. "Strange," he said.

"What's strange?"

"Maybe my imagination, but I've got a feeling everything's not kosher back there."

"Why?"

"There was a guy standing by the exit door in the back. It was open. And the desk. There was no one at the front desk."

"So."

"No one at the desk of the Hotel Corinthian? It's strange..."

"A coincidence," Hummel said, dismissing it.

"Let's have a look."

"All right. Give me a second to get some smokes."

Chris was uneasy.

"If the place is getting ripped off, by the time we get back there they'll be gone."

"Take it easy, Chris. It'll only take a few seconds."

Hummel made a left off Fifth Avenue and pulled to the curb outside a restaurant in the middle of the block. A neon sign flashed above, intermittently illuminating the raindrops. With the "u" and "e" not lighting, it was still possible to tell the sign said "Louie's." Springing the door open, jumping off the seat into the rain, and slamming the door behind him, Hummel dashed the width of the sidewalk into the restaurant.

"Damnit," Chris said aloud to himself. The lobby again flashed to his mind.

A minute passed. Two minutes.

Hurry up, you mother.

Sliding across the front seat, Chris wiped the door window clear. Through the fogged restaurant window he could see Hummel with his arm propped on the counter and his left leg propped on a stool. He was talking to Louie, the owner, all in white behind the counter. I should have known, Chris thought. Without hesitation he pushed down on the horn rim and held it for a few seconds until Hummel looked out toward the car.

"C'mon," Chris mouthed as he motioned for his partner to return. Slowly Hummel stood erect, said a few more words to Louie and turned toward the front door of the restaurant. He ran through the rain to the car and swung open the door. Chris slid back across the seat as Hummel sat down.

"What's up?" Hummel asked.

"The Corinthian. Remember?"

Hummel smiled as he pulled away from the curb.

Chris wondered if there were trouble how long he would last with this imitation cop.

Hummel was silent and Chris checked his equipment to make certain he was prepared.

At five minutes to midnight in room 2320, Stuart Pierce stepped from the shower. A young, light-skinned, handsome Negro, Pierce took a fluffy white towel from the rack and held it to his silken body. He closed his eyes and drifted into space, caressing himself for a few seconds with the soft, smooth cloth, before proceeding to pat his slender frame. Starting from the shoulders, he worked his way down, lingering longest in the genital area. Comfortably dry, he dropped the towel to the blue shag and stepped to the sink for a cup of water. Tilting forward the Roman handmaiden, a faucet affixed to every sink exclusively at the Corinthian, he spilled water from the jug she held, filled the cup and took a drink.

Pierce stared into the mirror of the medicine cabinet

and ran his fingers through his thick black hair, un-naturally straight. Beautiful, he thought. You're beauti-ful. His face was young. He pursed his lips, then gapped them to inspect his teeth, pearl white and magnificently even. Satisfied, he leaned forward and kissed the mirror.

Sixth son of Alabama poor blacks, Stuart Whitman Jeremiah Pierce, at the age of twenty-two, had suc-ceeded in amassing a small fortune, though hardly via conventional means. More amazing, just four years earlier to the month he had been sitting in a dingy South-ern detention cell with not a penny to his name, arrested for sodomy and male prostitution, the only trade he knew. He had decided that when he was released he would head North, where life was a little easier, not only for a Negro, but also for a homosexual.

An uncle from New York City had written him several times, telling him how simple it was to "hop on the wel-fare wagon." Why work for a living if the government will give you a check for nothing, he figured. And so it was he moved to New York and, as easily as his uncle had said, he lived off the city. The taxpayers took care of his bills, bought his clothes and put food on the table, while he wasted his days watching television and his nights visiting gay bars.

But he was not happy with that. He wanted wealth, his childhood dream, and the checks, though substantial, were nowhere near enough. It was inevitable that he re-turn to his trade, and to his delight he found business booming in this new location. A ripe Negro boy of his youth and good looks was always in great demand.

Initially he walked the streets. The more he worked,

the more he realized that it was indeed possible to make the kind of money he had dreamed of: in addition to a steep cash fee in advance, it was the customer's responsibility to pay for the hotel and any other expenses incurred in a half-hour of pleasure. Of course, there was no limit to the amount of time spent with each "client," but, naturally, the longer the evening, the more it cost. He chose his prospects carefully, with an uncanny knack of determining who was right and who wasn't; not once did he get beaten by a freak or collared by the law.

Pierce was aware that his customers would return again and again for his service if they got what they paid for and on every occasion satisfaction was utmost in his mind. He was good and it paid off. He built up a sizable clientele and in a short time he was deriving enough income from it so that he no longer had to walk the streets. He set up appointments and kept records. He had a head for organization and was never late. His business thrived on convenience for the client. Customer after customer referred his friends to him. His clientele steadily developed and before long consisted largely of respectable men with plenty of money. He cultivated it. He could well afford to choose only the cream of the crop. Bankers, stockbrokers, attorneys, politicians and the like filled his schedule daily. Not surprisingly, many asked him for assistance in satisfying family and friends who required female bed partners and soon he was supplying breathtakingly beautiful prostitutes and lesbians for the private and public affairs of some of the most prominent names in the city. Pierce himself serviced the mayor's brother monthly.

[23]

But success was not without its drawbacks and an organization the size of Pierce's could hardly have expected to go undetected and untouched by the Police Department for long, despite his influential clientele. This obstacle was overcome neatly by an arrangement whereby all members of the force concerned, a total of thirty-three police officers, were paid in either cash or service every month to look the other way. Those receiving payoffs ranged from the very top to the very bottom: the police commissioner to the public morals division to the cop on the beat. The deal was set up personally by the police commissioner's own representative, First Deputy Commissioner Lawrence Stephens, who assured Pierce that no action would be taken against the organization as long as the payments were met. With enough foresight to know that he would be unable to function without police cooperation, Pierce reluctantly agreed to the exorbitant fees. Ironically, the department proved to be a new source of income, since the policemen wanted sex as much as anyone else, and the revenue more than made up for the money being spent to make payoffs. Many men chose to be paid off in service and the girls they were provided with were instructed beforehand to stretch the evening if they could, thus raising considerably the cost of the service. As a result, instead of having to pay out protection money on those occasions, Pierce received payment for the overtime incurred.

"Come on, Stuart," came a male voice from outside the bathroom. "Are you going to stay in there all night?"

"I won't be much longer," said Pierce, politely. "Relax."

From the floor he retrieved a brown suede pouch, fringed with rawhide, and removed a pencil. Again he turned to the mirror and, with a skilled hand, penciled his eyebrows to perfection. Next came the shadow, then the mascara, and in moments he had accented his eyes to be the envy of any woman. A slight touch of rouge and white lipstick and his face was complete. He smiled in narcissistic delight. He stepped back a pace and, still staring into the mirror, stroked his flesh from the chest to the loins, slowly covering his smooth womanly curves, writhing to the tingle caused by his own touch. From within the pouch he took a quarter-ounce bottle of imported perfume and dabbed his body generously with a flowery fragrance. A few strokes of a comb through his hair, one more look to the mirror, and he strode naked into the next room.

The lights were dim. Well-placed, marblelike mirrors echoed original paintings by contemporary masters and talented reproductions of Renaissance prints, each with an elaborate gold frame, in itself a piece of art. Blue, wall-to-wall shag complimented a white, chandeliered ceiling.

Clad only in a white terrycloth knee-length bathrobe, Harold Windsor sat patiently on the enormous brass-posted bed. "Oh, God, you're beautiful," he said, his eyes affixed to the shimmering, walnut body before him.

"That's what I like about you, Harry, you know a good thing when you see one."

"You conceited bitch."

"Tsk, tsk, tsk. And I thought you loved me," Pierce said in a soft, mocking tone.

[25]

Windsor stood. Near bald on top and grey on the sides, he looked every one of his fifty-three years. A large, overly pointed nose protruded from a milk-white, freckled face. His one hundred seventy pounds barely covered a six-foot frame.

"I do love you," he said, starting toward Pierce. Untying the sash, he slid the robe from his shoulders, uncovering completely his pale, underdeveloped body. Inches apart, the two stared at each other. Windsor outstretched his arms and the youth responded. They embraced for a few seconds. Windsor pulled back his head and looked into the eyes of his soulful mate. "I do love you," he whispered. They kissed.

In a few moments they were making passionate love to each other: Pierce, the twenty-two-year-old homosexual, king of the big-town pimps, and Windsor, the police commissioner of the City of New York.

CHAPTER 2

THE room marked "Employees Only" reflected the full
opulence of the lobby outside: regal paintings, fashionable mirrors, expensive, deep-pink carpeting and three
walls lavishly adorned with a red velvetlike material.
The fourth wall, the far wall, was taken up entirely with
safety-deposit boxes, three hundred fifty in all, large and
small, containing jewelry and cash of the hotel guests.
Nestled in the near right-hand corner of the room, an
antique, lanternlike lamp sat atop a table covered with
floor-length red satin. Actually, the red satin was poor
camouflage for a safe containing over one hundred
thousand dollars in cash, on hand to accommodate out-
of-town guests with traveler's checks and personal checks
of regular guests. A large, rectangular table and four
wooden chairs, elaborately carved, dominated the center
of the room.

Sal Napola walked to the near corner, pulled the satin off the grey-metal safe and threw it to the floor. He ignored the crashing lamp. "What's the combination?" he demanded of the night manager, sitting at the table, palms down and handcuffed, twitching his fingers. He sat between the bell captain and Willie O'Brien, also handcuffed.

"You've got exactly ten seconds." Napola's eyes were cold and ruthless, and the manager feared for his life. Willie, too, was terrified as he gazed upon the scarred face. The thief, with streaking grey machine gun under arm, and his tall, youthful confederate, a revolver in his hand, stood side-by-side near the door.

A few minutes earlier Napola had identified himself at the front desk as Mr. James E. Reynolds, real estate investor. In reality he was a part-time bookie, part-time loan shark, part-time bank robber (three successful jobs in the past four years), and now a hotel thief. He owned and operated a bar in the Red Hook section of Brooklyn, his residence for forty-seven years. Because he had been convicted of gambling violations four times and, according to the State Liquor Authority, was "not of sound character," the bar was licensed to a relative. It was a hangout for many members of one of New York's foremost Mafia families, to which Napola was affiliated in his bookie and loan-sharking activities. But the bank robberies and the hotel robbery now in progress were freelance projects, organized and controlled by Napola himself. He had recruited a band of five local small-time hoods who took orders from him and who each would receive ten percent of the total haul. That would leave him with a comfortable fifty percent for running the operation. All were hoping the Corinthian job would bring close to a million, to make the risk worthwhile. Little did they know there would be over three million on hand that morning.

Napola's nature was sadistic. Absolutely nothing would stand in his way of successfully executing the robbery, including a life, a number of lives if need be. In the past he had murdered twice.

"What's the combination?" he again demanded.

The night manager was perspiring. "Please . . . please give me a few minutes . . . my mind is blank."

Napola withdrew a knife from his pocket, pushed the button springing a six-inch blade and leaned against the table. The manager felt the point prick the skin beneath his right ear. "You better remember real quick."

Seconds passed and the manager remained terrified in silence. Napola withdrew the blade from his neck area and in one swift and unsuspecting motion, lunged toward him, bringing the knife downward to the table with all his might. It penetrated the manager's right hand, pinning it to the wood. He screamed inhumanly. Napola's cuff was quickly hued a crimson red. The manager looked with disbelief from the knife, into the eyes of his tormentor, then back to the blood flowing from his hand onto the table. He screamed again, but this scream was silenced by a brutal slap from Napola.

Napola seemed to be enjoying it. He released his grip on the knife, grabbed the manager by the throat and squeezed his Adam's apple. The manager rasped, trying to pull away from the table, but was thwarted by

Napola's firm grip and the deeply imbedded knife. His left hand was helplessly shackled to the right. Involuntarily, he rose sharply, knocking away the chair beneath him. His eyes bulged from the sockets and his face turned a deathly purple. He rasped a weak plea for his life.

The other hoods were silent, showing no emotion toward an impending death, as Napola fixed a maniacal stare on his prey. The bell captain sat transfixed in horror.

Willie O'Brien could not sit by and watch a murder. "You're killing him," he shouted. "Let him go. You're killing him." Though he had little power left in his frail body, he jumped forward from his chair and thrust his handcuffed hand around Napola's neck. "Let him go, damn it. Let him go."

Napola released his grasp and spun toward the doorman. The manager, unconscious, dropped forward on the table, then slid back toward the floor. The falling weight of his body dislodged his hand from the steel that had impaled it. Napola easily overpowered Willie and smashed a right fist to his face, knocking him to the floor. The accomplice with the machine gun bent over the fallen old man and battered his head repeatedly with the butt of his weapon. Willie lay motionless.

Napola smoothed his clothing and walked around the table to the manager. He picked up the limp bundle by the collar and shook him to his senses. "My friend, there is a distinct difference between the role of a hero and the role of a fool. What's the combination?"

Still groggy, the manager answered weakly. "Thirteen left, thirty-seven right, twice around to twenty-one, back to thirty-three."

Napola smiled, dropped the manager to the floor and moved to the safe. The man wielding the machine gun moved away from Willie and circled the table. Placing his weapon in the open suitcase in front of him, he withdrew two rolls of wide, white adhesive tape and tossed one to his confederate near the door. Working together, they covered the eyes and mouths of the bell captain and the manager in a minute, winding the tape completely around their heads.

The accomplice with grey-streaked hair retrieved the machine gun and motioned toward Willie O'Brien, sprawled on the carpet, dark with his blood. "He's not going anywhere. No need to tape him." The tall, nervous youth nodded in agreement.

"Bingo," said Napola as the safe door swung open. The two others strained to get a good look as the leader riffled through stacks of twenty- and one-hundred-dollar bills. "Get working on the boxes," he said, heaping the bills neatly into a suitcase. The hood with the machine gun took a crowbar from the table and laid the gun on a chair. He stepped to the safety-deposit boxes. Systematically, starting in the middle row, he inserted an end of the bar into the left side of the box, ripped it open with a powerful, jerking motion and moved on to the next. Following, his young accomplice plucked the jewelry and cash from within and placed it in another suitcase.

"God *damn!*" the young man exclaimed. "Almost every box is loaded." His face glowed in satisfaction as his nervousness disappeared. "Take a look at this stuff." He held up a necklace, a brooch and a bracelet, all glittering of diamonds in the light.

[31]

"Just keep moving," said Napola, still at the safe. "We've gotta get the hell out of here."

Chris Chamber was preparing for the worst. As his partner maneuvered the radio car through the torrential rain toward the Corinthian, Chris checked to see how many rounds of ammunition he had. Unsnapping the top of a pouch on the right side of his holster belt, tilting it forward, he accepted into his palm six .38-caliber bullets. One by one he dropped them back into the pouch, making certain each faced the buckle, that when they came out they would be ready for loading. He was well aware that the few seconds saved by having the bullets lined up properly for reload might be crucial. Fumbling around with them would break the concentration that would have to be directed elsewhere. He resnapped the pouch and repeated the procedure with the one next to it. Satisfied, he slid his thumb along the top of the bullets attached to the rear of his belt: eighteen in a row, all in place. He gripped the handle of his revolver, slipped his thumb down the inside of the holster, twisted the gun and lifted. The twist was necessary with regulation holsters to bypass a stiff leather ridge, designed to prevent removal by anyone but the officer. He opened the revolver to see that it was properly loaded, closed it and returned it to his hip, moving the holster back about an inch on the belt for comfort. He was content with thirty-six rounds of ammunition.

The Corinthian was now only two blocks away. The rain pounded the car and made the going slow. They stopped for a red light. Hummel smirked as Chris inspected his equipment.

"You're unbelievable. Where the hell do you think you're going? To a war?"

Chris was silent.

"For Christ's sake, there's a different doorman at the Corinthian and right away you suspect the worst."

"It's always good to be prepared. You work over here in an atmosphere like the Two-One for a while and you tend to relax. It only takes that one time that you're not ready when you should have been. I figure if you're ready all the time, you cut the odds of your getting hurt quite a bit."

"The odds'll never be in your favor."

"No, but the odds in the Two-One are a helluva lot better than in a place like Bedford-Stuyvesant. And if you're always on guard, your chances of getting a pension some day are pretty good."

"I've got a little less than two years to go. I've done O.K."

"When's the last time you fired your gun?" The traffic light turned green and they started moving again.

"About two years ago at the firing range."

"A lot can happen in two years, Joe." Chris thought immediately of rust, and of the men he knew who had gone to the range to fire their guns and found them inoperable after a year's disuse.

Hummel slowed up the car as the Corinthian marquee became visible between alternate swipes of the windshield wipers. With the bottom of his trousers soaked from the windswept rain, the doorman stood motionless by the glass doors. Chris hoped that Hummel knew enough not to pull up right in front of the hotel, just in case there was something wrong: God, eighteen years on the job, he had better know, Chris thought. The element of surprise could be invaluable at times: his years in the Marine Corps had taught him that. Chris was relieved when Hummel stopped just shy of the marquee, far enough away to be out of view of anyone inside. He studied the doorman. It was obvious to Chris he was aware of the radio car, yet he made no overt recognition; no waves or smiles this time. He stood rigid, his back flush to the entrance, glancing over every few seconds without moving his head.

"What do you think?" said Hummel.

"I'm not really sure, but I've got a feeling something's wrong." The rain was driving.

"How do you want to work it?"

"Why don't I just check him out. No sense in both of us getting drenched. If I think we should go in, I'll wave for you."

"O.K. by me."

Chris pushed open the door and jumped out into the pouring rain. Immediately the doorman turned about face, opened the glass door and stepped inside. Chris ran to the side of the entrance and put his back to the wall. In seconds he was soaked through to the skin. He inched his way to the door and stuck his head under the marquee to peer inside. Aside from the couple sitting on the bright red sofa, the lobby was empty. The rear door was open, but the man with the blue jacket was nowhere in sight. And there was still no one behind the desk. A large potted plant blocked his view of the open elevators. He looked at his watch: twelve twenty-three. There was supposed to be a man at the desk at all times. Where was he? Where was the bell captain? And the security man? And where the hell did the doorman go? Chris turned to wave Hummel out of the car, but his partner had already gotten out and was dashing through the rain.

"What's up?" Hummel asked, now standing beside Chris.

"The doorman disappeared. The guy with the blue jacket's not by the exit anymore and there's just nobody around except a man and a woman on the couch."

"What do you think?"

"Could very well be a ripoff."

"Let's go in."

"O.K., but be careful."

Chris wished he were with someone else. He didn't feel that he could rely on Joe Hummel as he could other men he had worked with in the past, especially men in the perilous Eight-O where anything could happen and usually did. Hummel's attitude was cavalier. He was not prepared. Chris knew what it was like to face danger—both in Vietnam and Bedford-Stuyvesant—so he twisted his revolver and lifted it halfway out of the holster as he led the way through the glass doors.

All was silent and still. The officers stopped just inside the entrance to survey the lobby. They stared at the couple on the red velvet sofa. Both men felt the strangeness but couldn't define it. Chris turned his attention to the front desk. Everything looked in order; only there was no one to man it. He glanced to the right at the open

[35]

exit. If there had been a robbery, he thought, the thieves no doubt left through that door. Then the elevators! Both doors were cracked a few inches. Noting the blocks of wood at the base of the openings, he tapped his partner. "Look," he whispered, pointing. He didn't have to tell Hummel that this was the real thing.

Hummel said in a soft voice: "These two on the couch haven't moved since we came in. I think they're some kind of mannequins."

"Better radio for another car to back us up. I'll wait here till you get back."

Hummel agreed and suddenly, as he turned, a series of loud explosions filled the air. Chris dove for cover behind the sofa as glass shattered all around. Hummel ran for the stairs to the Dominican Room. A cracking, piercing thunder in a staccato tempo combined with the crashing of glass as the mirrored walls fractured and smashed to the ground. Chris well knew the awesome, bone-chilling blast of a machine gun. A small table in the far corner was chopped in half, and a wooden bench beside it split from end to end, as the gunner swept the lobby.

Chris had instinctively unholstered his revolver and pinned himself as close to the sofa and as near to the floor as he could. He looked over to Hummel who had made it to the safety of the stairs. His hat was askew on his bald head. He, too, had his gun out and was hugging the iron railing, hoping he was out of range. The fire was coming from the front desk area. Glass splattered in all directions as huge chunks of ornate

[36]

mirror fell to the floor. Paintings had fallen and furniture splintered.

The shooting stopped. The ear-splitting outburst had lasted only a few seconds, but to the men under fire it had seemed much longer. Chris removed his cap and peeked from the lower right side of the sofa. The man with the blue jacket who had been stationed by the exit was running out the door with a suitcase. Close behind was the phony doorman. Immediately in back of him was a tall, younger man, no more than nineteen, and he, too, had a suitcase. It struck Chris, for no apparent reason, that he was well dressed. Behind the front desk, with a machine gun smoking under his arm, was a man with grey-streaked hair.

Chris raised his gun. Instinctively he knew it was too late to try for the first two, so he quickly sighted in on the tallest and youngest. He placed his left hand over his right to reinforce the grip and pulled the hammer back swiftly, squeezing the trigger evenly. The revolver exploded and jolted his hands backward. The third in line fell to the floor, his hand over his temple. The suitcase slid forward to the elevator. Chris, swinging to his secondary target, fired again toward the exit, but the two men had made it through the door and were out of sight. The man with the machine gun knew where the shots had come from. Crack-crack-crack: a spurt of three aimed at the sofa. All flew wild high and smashed the mirrored wall behind Chris. He lowered the muzzle and depressed the trigger, unleashing another barrage. A thunderous flurry of lead assaulted Chris's protective sofa. The inflated dummies were struck repeatedly and

[37]

air gushed from their bodies. The powerful blast continued, and the sofa was hit again and again. Chris held himself to the floor as the bullets burst out the back, cutting massive uneven holes in the velvet. The smell of gunpowder was stifling.

Chris looked to his partner. Hummel was lying on the stairs, farther down, with only his head showing. His eyes reflected the fear and frustration of the situation. If he were to expose himself to take a shot, he would be shielded only by the iron railing. The machine gun rattled on, no longer concentrating on the sofa, indiscriminately ripping apart the entire lobby. Chris knew his work. He waited until the concentration was away from him and rolled to the opposite side of the sofa. He caught the gunman's stare as he quickly squeezed off two rounds. They weren't well aimed and missed. The barrel of the machine gun swung toward him. Chris fired another. And still another. He rolled back toward the sofa to the sound of rapid fire. Then silence. Chris knew he had hit his mark. He peered from the right side of the sofa and saw the body slumped forward over the desk. On the floor in front lay the automatic weapon.

Chris coiled back behind the bullet-ridden sofa and opened his revolver. He struck the ejector rod sharply with his thumb, and six spent cartridges fell to the carpet. He unsnapped one of his belt pouches and six fresh rounds dropped to his palm, all in line for loading.

While Chris filled his gun, Hummel poked his head up to see what had happened. He saw one body sprawled on the floor by the door and his accomplice draped over the desk. The machine gun lay harmlessly on the rose-colored carpet, as the outstretched arm of the gunner swayed limply above it. A cloud of blue-grey smoke hovered overhead. Hummel, assuming it was over, climbed the steps and started toward the front desk.

Chris had unloaded and reloaded in eight seconds and was ready once more. He looked up to see Hummel emerging from the safety of the stairs. "Get down, Joe," he shouted. "For chrissake, get down."

Hummel scarcely had time to register surprise.

From behind the mail partition in back of the desk a figure emerged. In his joined hands was a .45-caliber military hand weapon, raised and extended toward Joe Hummel. In the army for four years, Corporal Salvatore Napola had been an expert with the forty-five. After discharge it had not been very difficult to buy one for a price on the streets of New York City, and at this moment there was no way he could miss such an easy target as a uniformed police officer less than thirty yards away. He squeezed.

Hummel turned as the hammer struck. The sound was overpowering. A shock of fire streaked from the muzzle of the forty-five. The officer's mouth was agape in utter surprise and confusion as the bullet ripped into his body. He was struck in the chest, but the lead ricocheted down to the lower half of his back and tore away six inches of flesh in its exit. At the exact second the bullet hit his body, Hummel instinctively pulled the trigger of his gun. It fired, but the shot was wild high and cut through the air toward the chandelier, smashing the crystal into pieces. For an instant his eyes caught Chris' and there seemed to be satisfaction, Chris thought, that his gun had indeed fired. The impact of the forty-five turned him and reeled him backward with great force, slamming him into the wall, which in turn shoved him forward to the floor.

Chris was horror-struck. An emptiness gripped his insides. He knew his partner was dead; his rage and his senses told him that, but he remained calm. This was not the first gun battle he had been in that claimed casualties.

He moved his head slowly away from the left side of the sofa to locate his opponent. He saw nothing. Still behind the desk, he thought. A stalemate at this point would be to Chris' advantage, since someone must have heard the shots by now and phoned the stationhouse. He would sit and wait for help.

Sal Napola squatted behind the desk, reloading and checking his forty-five. This was not his first gun battle either. He clicked the magazine home. He was ready. Now, escape. He would leave behind the suitcase filled with cash and take only the money stuffed in his pockets. He knew police officers carried 38's; he had an advantage in firepower and hoped to take advantage of it by keeping the cop pinned while he raced to the door. There would not be much time. More police would be already on their way to the hotel. Then he heard it. A faint, distant sound. Sirens! It was time to move.

Chris heard the sirens, too, and knew the killer behind the desk would be forced to make an immediate move. He listened intensely for the first sound of stirring, guessing that his adversary would make a mad dash toward the door, firing the forty-five in his direction as he did so. He was determined to prevent his escape.

Napola made his way to the edge of the desk and peered out at the lobby: paintings destroyed; furniture splintered everywhere; shattered mirrors clinging to the walls; glass fragments strewn about the carpet; the dead police officer lying in a heap by the far wall. The only thing that stood between Napola and escape was the cop crouched behind the shattered sofa. He jumped out from behind the desk and fired at the red velvet, hitting the mark dead center. He ran for the door.

Lying on the floor the length of the sofa, Chris swallowed hard as the forty-five slug ripped the cushion above him. But he was ready. He took a deep breath, rolled himself to the right, then sprang to his knees in combat-ready position. He outstretched his revolver hand and let three rounds go at the moving target. All missed, all high and to the right. Napola swirled and, with his left hand bracing his gun hand, fired the forty-five. Then again. Both shots hit the arm of the sofa with such force, the first tilted it backward, the second knocked it over. Chris fired two more and his bullets found their mark. Napola spun around and dropped to the floor. The carpet darkened quickly with blood. It occurred to Chris that one of the two rounds must have severed Napola's jugular.

Chris rolled back behind the fallen sofa, opened his revolver, pushed the ejector rod with his thumb, and reloaded from his second pouch. He closed the revolver and took another deep breath. The sirens were loud now; maybe a block away. He got up and in a crouch moved quickly to the desk, still ready for action if there was more to come. He glanced at the two bodies on the floor to his right and knew they were both dead. He poked the man lying over the counter. The man did not move. Chris stepped behind the desk and moved to the edge of the mail partition. He stretched his neck, peering into the room marked "Employees Only." Three bodies, two of them taped around the head, lay motionless on the floor. All were handcuffed. Willie O'Brien was bleeding profusely from the scalp, his head resting face down on a red-stained carpet.

Chris surveyed the room quickly: the grey-metal safe was open in the near corner; numerous safety-deposit boxes were ripped apart on the far wall. Convinced it was safe, he ran to the trio at the base of the table. He bent over Willie, examining closely the wounds in his crushed head. Grabbing his wrist, he felt no pulse. He pressed gently on his neck. He knew the doorman was dead. As callous as anyone could be from eight years as a police officer, seeing the city at its worst, familiar on a daily basis with physical sickness, gore, mental depravity, all forms of death, still Chris was sickened.

The bell captain squirmed a few feet from Willie. Chris stepped over the night manager and unraveled the adhesive tape.

"Thank God," said the bell captain, indentations across his Puerto Rican face. "Thank God. For a while I thought for sure it was my last night on earth."

By now the sirens were wailing in front of the hotel and the lobby was flooding with police. Chris turned

[42]

his attention to the night manager, toupee to one side. He removed the tape from his head.

"My hand," he moaned with shackled hands between his legs, his pants hued a deep red. Chris reached for his arms and gently pulled them toward him. The flesh from the back of his hand was shredded and minced. Chris took a handkerchief from his back pocket and applied direct pressure to the wound.

Glass crumpled underfoot. "In here," Chris yelled. In an instant the room filled with police officers. They all had questions, but for a few minutes Chris heard them not at all. His knees were shaking, as were his hands. His brow beaded with perspiration. He was reacting physically to the fear which he had had no time to feel before. And he couldn't stop thinking about Joe Hummel and Willie O'Brien.

CHAPTER 3

THE brass-posted bed was still. A majestic spread of blue silk stretched beneath a smiling Renaissance madonna, squared off by an eighteen-carat, hand-engraved frame. Through the picture window, the moon shone on the blue shag. Side by side under the spread, two bodies lay motionless. One twitched, rustled, then rolled over and threw back the covers. Sitting up, Harold Windsor looked at his young bed partner and decided to let him sleep. He stood, put on his robe and padded to the bathroom. Closing the door, he drew back the shower curtain and turned the lever marked "cold" a full revolution, the "hot" halfway. He stepped to the sink, tilted the handmaiden-faucet forward and spilled water into his cupped hands, splashing his face repeatedly, stopping only to stare at his image in the mirror. He stared and smiled. Stuart Pierce was just about the best bed partner he had ever had, he thought. Better than any fair-haired boy or busty woman. He savored in his mind the moments of pleasure he had had with Pierce in the past, then splashed his smiling face once more. He dropped his robe to the shag and stepped into the shower.

Harold Windsor had been enjoying both male and female sexual relations since he was fourteen years old. In fact, his first shared sexual experience had been with another boy as they sat in a movie theatre one afternoon. He never could remember the name of the movie, nor what it was about, for that matter, but he remembered very well how his closest friend had reached over and laid his hand on Windsor's lap. He was momentarily stunned. And embarrassed. But it felt sort of good, and when his friend pulled down the zipper and slid his hand inside, Windsor made no attempt to stop him. He just sat back and enjoyed it. It was great, he thought when it was all over. It was the best physical thing that had ever happened to him at that point in time, for he had not known the warmth and depth of a woman, nor had he the experience of anyone but himself touching that most sensitive organ. And, by far, the thrill of *being* masturbated was many times the thrill of self-masturbation.

After that initial experience Windsor and his friend reciprocated sexual favors at every opportunity. Almost every week they went to the movies and sat in the last row. They slept over in each other's house many, many times, never once hinting at their well-kept secret to unsuspecting parents. They stole moments together in

[45]

the park bushes, in public men's rooms, even in school if they were certain they were alone. Girls never bored Windsor, nor was he discouraged by them any more than were his classmates or friends. He was just having more fun as a homosexual for a while. It was great for both boys until his best, most trusting friend moved away after six months. It was at this time that Windsor had his first female experience. Funny, he always thought, but he could never remember her name. Not much reason to. Although she was the first, she certainly wasn't the best. She just spread her legs and lay there, while he did all the moving. He might just as well have been poking at a mushy sponge. But it was fun and he did go back for more; more with her and more with other girls. Right up to college.

It was at the University of Maryland in the freshman year that Windsor met Billie. William "Billie" Doan was a sophomore from Southern California who seemed to stay tan the year round—a neat trick in Maryland—with blonde hair, green eyes and a fairly good build on a medium frame. Most important, however, Billie was a homosexual. He didn't walk or talk like a fag, nor did he shun the many girls who threw themselves at him, but Billie liked his own kind and it was inevitable that Windsor and he would hook up. They became very good friends and enjoyed each other's company constantly for three years in Maryland. It was a strange relationship. They dated girls often and even double dated. To most, Billie and Windsor were simply very good friends, no more. And to those few who had their doubts, that's all they ever amounted to were doubts, never convictions.

[46]

There was just something about each man that wouldn't encourage an observer to be convinced that either went to bed with the other to have sex. Billie seemingly was too masculine. And Windsor acted straight at all times. But they did go to bed, off and on for three years, until Billie graduated and moved on to a good job in San Diego.

After Billie, there were only three more male partners that Windsor found himself attracted to and they were simply one-night affairs. He was never possessed with the idea of visiting gay bars, looking for a pickup. He merely enjoyed a homosexual relationship if the opportunity presented itself and if there was a rapport.

He was graduated from the University of Maryland with honors and went on to Harvard Law School, where he did remarkably well. He was admitted to the Maryland bar and promptly took up a post with the Baltimore district attorney's office. He learned the ropes there for seven arduous years at a poor rate of pay before moving on to the United States attorney's office in the same city—where the pay scale was not too much higher. He stayed there for twenty-two years, during which time he married and raised a family. However, twenty-two years of low-pay government service was not without its rewards, for it was through his affiliation with the United States Attorney's office, as chief of the rackets bureau, a post to which he had ever so slowly progressed, that Windsor met the people who would be influential in his next move. With the election of John Claridge to the mayorship of Baltimore came the sure bet that Harold Windsor would be appointed police commissioner, and he was. He built neither a reputation for being a hard-nosed, crime-fighting leader of men, nor the reputation of being a weak-kneed puppet of the mayor, though the latter description was certainly closer to reality. The fact of the matter was that he simply built no reputation at all. He innovated no policies. He made no fancy speeches, nor did he hold weekly press conferences or seek publicity in any other manner. "He's just there: he don't bother us, we don't bother him, and everything seems to work out fine," was how one of his charges had put it and that about summed it up the best. He served in the post for three years and two months before being tapped as one of the many candidates for the office of police commisioner in New York City, the most prestigious job in the law-enforcement area.

The newly elected mayor of New York City was eager to run things smoothly and he needed someone in the Police Department who could be manipulated. The obvious choice was the passive nominee from Baltimore. Windsor was interviewed and told that if he were appointed he would be expected to cooperate fully with the office of the mayor. The new mayor had great plans for the police department and he wanted someone in charge who would implement his ideas and maintain a good rapport with the men. Windsor nodded his head throughout the interview and made it perfectly clear without serious damage to his self-respect that certainly he could be manipulated. The mayor knew he had the right man for the job. But, because Windsor's service record as Baltimore police commissioner was mediocre at best, it was not without a few political strings being pulled before finally Windsor's appointment was confirmed.

Windsor lived in a midtown Manhattan hotel and commuted on the weekends to his wife and children, who had opted to stay in Maryland. He was happy with the arrangement, for after twenty-six years of marriage he was glad to have a little freedom. Not that he was out to find a new love of whatever sexual persuasion. His family meant much to him. But he was glad that he could move around more easily, not have his wife on his arm at all times, enjoy the New York nightlife without worrying about what time he got home or what excuse he would use because he was late. Two of his three sons were unmarried and lived at home. Both in their early twenties, they were not overly disappointed in their father's absence. Nor was Mrs. Windsor crushed because her spouse lived away from home five days a week. Twenty-six years of marriage had taken its toll on her, also, and she very easily accepted a weekend husband. Besides, she, too, had diversions: civic affairs and the like. The mayor thought the arrangement a bit odd, but he was so happy to have a puppet on a string that he never gave the commissioner's living expenses a second thought.

Windsor ran a loose ship. As in Baltimore, the men under him for his nine months in New York were hardly aware he was around most of the time. There were no new rules or regulations set forth when he was appointed. There was no drastic shakeup in command. But most important to the majority of the thirty-two thousand members of the Department, there was no declaration of war on inactivity or vow to root out corruption, as was often the case with a newly appointed commissioner attempting to gain the confidence of the citizenry. Of course, when questioned specifically by members of the press, the commissioner staunchly supported those ideals and spoke ambitiously of new programs in the planning stage, but, in fact, the climate under him was lackadaisical. Corruption and inactivity permeated the Department, thriving as much as it always had.

Corruption was not considered a problem. It simply existed and was dealt with as it was uncovered. There was no effective preventive training provided in the Police Academy and the naive, unsuspecting rookie, almost completely dependent on the more experienced officer to show him the ropes, was an easy prey for the unchecked monster. The more experienced policeman, himself participating in venal activity, taught the rookie not only the ropes of good policework, but also the ropes of corruption. In a real sense, the two were not mutually exclusive. One could be a "good" policeman and still be on the take. The attitude was free-wheeling: the majority of men were taking and the best advice was just don't get caught. Whenever someone was caught he was quickly labeled to the public as a rotten apple in the barrel and by no means indicative of the rest of the Department. But the men knew differently. It was a rare case indeed that called for dismissal from the force when someone was caught. Most often a stiff loss of pay or a shaved vacation would suffice, or, perhaps, a transfer to an undesirable precinct. So, understandably, the majority of members of the Department participated in corrupt activities of one form or another, some minor, some major, since the system and the tradition dictated it and since the penalties for getting caught were not all that severe. Those who did not participate were ostracized and the peer pressure was upon them to change their ways.

The new commissioner made no effort to change the order of things and for this reason was not hated by his men. He never would be loved, but because of his policy of laissez-faire he was not despised as were some of his predecessors who had chosen to innovate and tackle the unenviable task of cleaning up the corrupt system, the tradition.

Windsor's career record was ostensibly unblemished. Thirty-two years in law enforcement and not a bad mark against him; notable achievements and accolades conspicuously absent, but not a blot on his past. The record obviously did not reflect the years of corruption tolerance and participation. Windsor was not unaccustomed to shady deals and money passed under the table. On many occasions as an assistant district attorney in Baltimore he had accepted money from defendants or their lawyers to throw a case or to be satisfied with a guilty plea to a lesser offense. Occasionally a judge had been included in the bribe. More than once the judge himself had suggested it. As an Assistant United States Attorney Windsor had received payoffs at various times to refrain from prosecuting certain people, mostly those linked to organized crime. As police commissioner of Baltimore he had shared in many payoffs for many reasons: money had filtered into his office from criminals and politicians alike to squelch investigations, from narcotics dealers and gambling rings to minimize pressure, even from his own men for promotions and transfers. The prices had varied according to the services and they ranged in scope from harmless to despicable. For thirty-two years in law enforcement Harold Windsor had played the game and won—he had not been caught.

And so it was when the new commissioner was gradually introduced to the system in New York City, not only was he not appalled, he participated. The man who coordinated all his transactions was First Deputy Commissioner Lawrence Stephens, a member of the force for more than thirty years and personal liaison for the past two commissioners. Stephens was second in command and let no one forget it. Windsor gave him a free hand, which Stephens used to his full advantage. He made policy decisions and granted favors to friends in key positions without bothering to check first with the commissioner. As a matter of formality, he would submit a written report after the action had been taken. Windsor was content to sit back and let the department be run for him, with the mayor and First Deputy Stephens making most of the decisions.

Once a month Stephens presented to the commissioner an envelope containing regular payments for various established contracts and whatever spontaneous windfalls of money—called "scores"—had been received for distribution to the staff. For obvious reasons, only cash was acceptable for money payoffs (as distinguished from those involving goods, favors or services) and only cash was ever placed in the commissioner's envelope. The envelope's existence was never acknowledged, even to the staff, though it was obvious to them that the commissioner received payments. The only person who knew for certain that the corruption in the New York City Police Department went right to the top, who actually witnessed any transaction, was Stephens. In that way the chances of being uncovered were infinitesimal. In a court of law the only person who could testify effectively against Windsor was the man who paid him, Stephens, himself on the take. It was a good arrangement.

To Windsor, Stephens' efficiency was surpassed only by his quality of judgment. The deputy commissioner would brief him on all contracts and all transactions, informing him of the circumstances surrounding each payoff. Not all offers to bribe the police commissioner were accepted and it was this uncanny ability of Stephens to discern what was safe and what was dangerous that Windsor admired. It created a minimal risk for him to share in a lucrative conspiracy.

Away from home five days a week, with New York City almost literally in the palm of his hand, it was inevitable that Windsor with his bisexual background would look for a little sensual pleasure and come in contact with a Stuart Pierce. Windsor was receiving a healthy sum for protecting Pierce and he was well aware that some of his own men paid often for a night with one of his curvaceous, accommodating young women. The fees were exorbitant, yet no one complained that the night had not been worth every cent. Deputy Commissioner Stephens himself indulged occasionally and reported personally to Windsor that it had been indeed a worthwhile investment. So it was not too surprising that when the commissioner sought a little extramarital activity, he asked Stephens to set it up through Pierce. As a gesture of good faith, Pierce volunteered to personally introduce his sexiest, most valuable women. But with young Pierce's good looks and Windsor's weakness, it was not too surprising either that the commissioner was more impressed by the pimp than by the shapely prostitute. He took the girl the first night, but opted for Pierce on several occasions after that. Pierce was instructed explicitly by Deputy Commissioner Stephens to keep quiet about the fact that Windsor was a switch-hitter. Aside from the trio, no one had even a remote notion that the police commissioner was a part-time homosexual. This knowledge, however, strengthened to a great degree Stephens' position in the Department and, in effect, what little power had escaped him before fell completely into his hands with the secret. What little separated Windsor from being simply a figurehead was dissipated and Stephens became the number-one man.

Harold Windsor stepped from the shower, grabbed a towel from the rack and dried himself. He put on his robe and padded into the bedroom, reflecting on the unmistakable police sirens he had heard a little while earlier. He knew it had to have been something big to warrant so many cars. There must have been at least a dozen far below on the street beneath his window, he figured, but he did not know where they were headed or why. His first impulse had been to call his twenty-four-hour office number, but he had decided to wait until he was out of the hotel. It would wait until then. Moreover, it might have been nothing to begin with: maybe an unfounded call. He stared at the bed for a few seconds. Pierce was still asleep. He went to the closet to retrieve his clothes and dress. What he had failed to realize was that it was the Corinthian to which all the radio cars, sirens blasting, had responded.

Chris Chamber sat disheveled on a chair in the corner of the lobby, watching the chaos that usually followed a shooting. A shooting with no injuries and only one or two shots fired was bad enough, but an armed robbery with a machine gun topping the arsenal, resulting in five deaths, one of those a police officer, created havoc. Uniformed patrolmen, twenty-two in all, were literally bumping into each other as they waited for further instructions. Not half that many were needed and most of those only for crowd control outside. The atmosphere was electric, but only to Chris. Two sergeants stood by the elevators talking over their golf games. Two ambulance attendants administered first aid to the night manager while three detectives questioned him. A captain and an inspector stood by the rear exit door discussing a recent mass promotion which had bypassed them both. The three dead thieves and Willie O'Brien, each covered with a grey blanket, lay side by side in front of the register desk.

Glass was shattered everywhere. Chunks of mirror hung precariously from the wall near the front door, and the splintered red velvet sofa, laying on its side, had been pushed in front of the staircase leading to the

[55]

Dominican Room. The body of Joe Hummel had been removed already. Through the glass doors Chris could see a large crowd cordoned off by police stanchions. The torrential rain had stopped. Every time someone entered or left the hotel the noise from the street became distinct. A radio car team from Manhattan North left the hotel to resume patrol. Fifteen seconds after they walked out, in walked a radio car crew that had been assigned on the other side of the precinct during the melee. They were curious. The second ambulance attendant on the scene and his driver walked out after refusing to transport a body to the morgue, emphatically stating that their job was taking care of live bodies, not dead ones. Guests of the hotel who got out of the elevators were aghast and immediately escorted to the street by a police officer. Guests returning to the hotel, after proper identification procedures, were likewise escorted through the lobby. A faint scent of gunpowder still hung in the air when the morgue wagon men finally arrived.

Also in the lobby were detectives from the Photo Lab and Fingerprints Bureau. Outside the hotel they had parked a special evidence van that could store blood samples in refrigerators and accommodate fingerprints, plaster casts, vacuumed samples and other evidence to be transported eventually to the main laboratory downtown. Three newspaper reporters questioned everybody in the lobby, trying to piece together the story. Two photographers snapped flashbulbs constantly, concentrating on the dead bodies heaped on the floor. Chris had been approached by all three reporters and had refused to comment until he received permission from his superiors.

A few feet from Chris, Lieutenant Jack Kilkenny and Detective Paul Krausse, best of friends and the two men Chris felt closest to in the precinct, methodically obtained a description of the two escaped holdup men from the Puerto Rican bell captain. It seemed to Chris, who could overhear the questioning, that this was the most organized action, the procedure most free of confusion, taking place in the lobby.

". . . He was about thirty-five, dark hair . . . ," said the bell captain.

The lieutenant interrupted. "A lot of hair? Bushy? Thinning? Parted on the side?"

"Like yours, I guess," he replied, pointing to Kilkenny's neatly combed shock of brown, parted on the left side. "Pretty much like yours, I guess."

"Same color as mine?"

The bell captain nodded.

"How tall was he?"

He shrugged. "About your height, I guess."

The lieutenant turned to Krausse who was writing down all the information. "Six-one," he said. Krausse kept writing without looking up. Kilkenny turned back to the Puerto Rican and continued the questioning. "How much did he weigh, Mr. Rodriguez? Was he fat? Skinny? Medium build?" The bell captain closed his eyes in thought for a few seconds. "Take your time now. Try to remember. Picture him in your mind if you can. We'd like you to be as accurate as possible. A good description of this guy might be instrumental in his capture."

"He was about average build," Rodriguez said, opening his eyes. "You know, not fat, not skinny. Just average."

[57]

Krausse looked up from his pad, then put his head down again.

"Now you say he had a light blue jacket, dark pants and black shoes. How about his shirt? Do you remember the color of his shirt?"

The bell captain shook his head.

"How about the style? Did it have a small collar, or a large one? Did it have a collar at all?"

"I'm sorry, lieutenant, I can't remember his shirt. You know how it is."

"Yes, I know how it is. You've done a fine job in remembering all that you have already, Mr. Rodriguez."

"Yeah, I'm pretty good at rememberin'."

"Just one more question. Were there any distinguishing marks that you remember . . . on either man? Scars? Tattoos? Anything about them that sticks in your mind?"

He shook his head.

"Okay. Thanks, Mr. Rodriguez, that's all for now. We'll be in touch."

The bell captain walked away, toward the center of the lobby, and was immediately approached by the reporters as the photographers flashed away.

Detective Krausse finished writing in his pad and stuffed it into his inside jacket pocket. "Where were you when you got the call to respond here, Jack?" he asked the lieutenant.

"On patrol," Kilkenny answered. "Why?"

" 'Cause you fit the description of the second guy perfectly." The lieutenant laughed. Krausse smiled and in a voice meant to imitate the Puerto Rican intonation of the bell captain, he added: "I guess." They both got a good laugh from that.

Chris, too, smiled at the pair as they approached him. He rose from the chair. "How'd you make out?" he asked.

"Well," the detective responded, "all we've got to find are two males, white, brown hair, average height and average weight—whatever that is. But it shouldn't take too long, even though that description fits a half-million people in New York, 'cause one's wearing a doorman's outfit and the other one has on a light blue jacket."

"Yeah," the lieutenant added, "that ought to cut it down to only a couple of hundred thousand." They all chuckled.

"Did you find out what happened to the security man?" Chris asked.

"Called in sick," Krausse answered. "He picked a good night."

Chris nodded.

"How do you feel?" Krausse asked in a more serious tone.

"I'm okay. Just a little rubber-legged at first, but I'm okay now."

"Good."

"The brass get you yet?" Kilkenny inquired.

"Not really. I gave the inspector a brief description of what happened, but he said he'd be back to me later."

"I feel sorry for the one-twenty-four man who has to type this unusual," Kilkenny said, referring to the precinct clerical man whose duty it was to type "Unusual Happening" reports. "This one'll take all day."

"My report's not going to be any piece of cake, either, you know," said Krausse. "I've got to find out what was taken, who owned it, how much it was worth . . . I've got to get a full description of each piece of jewelry . . . and to make things worse, half the owners are probably scattered all over the world. The people registered here only use this hotel as a home base. The 'beautiful people' are the ones who rent those boxes—to keep the jewelry they don't want to carry with them as they traipse around the globe. I'll be tied up for months just trying to find out what was taken and who owns what we've already recovered."

"I'll give you a hand, Paul," Chris said. "It'll keep me busy and as long as I've got to finish the tour, I'd just as soon not go back on patrol."

"Great," Krausse said. "Think we can swing that, Jack?"

"No problem," said the lieutenant. He looked at Chamber.

"You might as well stick around here for the rest of the tour, Chris. If I need you, I can send somebody to pick you up."

"Okay."

"Wait a minute," said the lieutenant, remembering, "there'll be a ton of paperwork for you to fill out on this."

"Shit, Jack," Krausse said, "can't you hide that stuff till tomorrow night?"

"No way." He pondered for a few seconds, then turned to Chamber. "But I'll tell you what I will do. Stay here till about seven. I'll have Adam-Boy pick you up and bring you in. If you run overtime, you'll make a little extra money." He smiled. Krausse and Chamber followed suit.

"Thanks, Jack," Krausse said.

Kilkenny nodded. "Just make sure you're available when Inspector Haynes is looking for you."

"Ten-four."

"Okay then, I'll see you back at the house this morning," said the lieutenant. He turned to Krausse. "And I'll see you Saturday night at my place."

"Still on?" Krausse asked.

"Yep."

Krausse nodded as Lieutenant Kilkenny walked toward the front door, motioning for his driver to follow.

Chris turned to the detective. "Where do we start?"

In his best W. C. Fields voice, Krausse put his hand on Chamber's shoulder and said: "At the beginning, my boy, at the beginning." Chris smiled. "Seriously, though, the best thing for you to do would be to try and get descriptions on the stolen jewelry."

"Okay."

"Hang out here till I get a list of the boxes that were broken into and who they're registered to. The owner's agent's in the back getting that for me now. If any of them are supposed to be in the hotel you can interview them." Chris looked at his watch. It was 1:15 A.M. "Fuck 'em," Krausse said. "If they're in, wake 'em up." Chris nodded. Krausse turned toward the room marked "Employees Only." "I'll be right back."

"I'll be here," Chris said. He glanced around. The

chaos was still present, though the lobby had thinned out a bit. The newspaper men had hustled back to their offices to write the stories. The ambulance attendant had early on taken the night manager, with his hand in bandages, to the hospital. A few more police officers had left to resume patrol and one of the sergeants was just leaving. A middle-aged couple with their teen-aged son, craning their necks to get a better view, were led through the front door and ushered to a waiting elevator. The crowd in the street had also thinned.

Chris focused his attention toward the front desk. The morgue wagon attendants had removed the blanket from Willie O'Brien and were placing him in a grey plastic sack. His face was milk-white, except for streaks of red. His hair was matted with dried blood. Chris asked God to have mercy on his soul. His thoughts turned to Joe Hummel's expression just before he had been hit. He had been careless and it had cost him his life. Chris recalled a Cong ambush in the rainy north of Vietnam. His patrol was passing through a small clearing when the trap was sprung. The man directly behind him, a machine gunner, was killed. Then others. They all had worn the same expression worn by Joe Hummel when he was hit. Chris's thoughts returned to the present, where a hotel lobby ironically resembled a patch of Vietnamese jungle. Two isolated moments in time and space joined together by the common bond of violence and death. The Lord only knows what was running through Hummel's mind, Chris thought, but the simple fact was that he would still be alive if he had not been so careless. Chris's thoughts were interrupted by a voice.

[62]

"How do you feel, Chamber?"

Chris turned. It was Inspector Haynes, his uniform neatly pressed, his shoes and cap brim shining mirror-like in the light. Scrambled eggs decorated his cap and a gold eagle, signifying his rank, decorated each shoulder. His angular nose was set between brown, inquiring eyes. The captain assigned to cover the division that night stood a foot or so behind.

"Excuse me, sir?" Chris said.

"How do you feel?" the inspector asked again.

"Oh, I'm okay, sir."

"Good. I'd like you to start from the beginning and tell me what happened."

"Yes, sir."

"Did you receive a call to respond here?"

"No, sir. We passed by and noticed that Willie O'Brien, the regular doorman, wasn't on duty. There was another man out front. We'd never seen him before." The captain took notes. "We weren't really sure if anything was wrong, but a little while later we decided to come back just to make sure."

Chris did not want to bring up Joe Hummel's attitude and decided not to mention the cigarette stop unless he was asked specifically where they had gone before returning to the hotel. And even then Chris would say they'd only stopped for a moment. Hummel was dead now, and Chris wasn't about to dishonor him. When he explained how Hummel was shot, he never once said his partner had been unprepared. The man had given his life in the performance of his duty, and there was no greater sacrifice, Chris figured, so why throw any shadow on

[63]

that performance? When Chris finished, the inspector smiled.

"It's just amazing that you're alive. It's men like you and Officer Hummel that make me very proud to be a part of this department."

"Thank you, sir."

"I'll probably be wanting to talk to you again before the week is out. I'll be in touch."

"Yes, sir."

The inspector, with the captain on his heels, turned and walked toward the front door. He waved the sergeant over, told him where he would be if something came up, then continued on to the street. The captain followed.

Detective Krausse approached Chris.

"What'd he have to say?" Krausse asked.

"Nothing much. He just wanted to hear it again."

"You'll probably wind up repeating the story a hundred times in the next few weeks. Maybe you should talk into a tape recorder and play it for whoever asks what happened." Chris smiled.

"You're a hero, you know." Krausse added. "The story'll be in all the papers tomorrow. You'll be king of the precinct."

"Where does it get you?" Chris said. "I'm no hero."

"Who's to say what makes a hero?" Krausse said. Chris shrugged and they were both silent for a few seconds.

"Well, listen," Krausse said, holding out a sheet of paper, "here's the list of guests whose boxes were hit. The ones with checks are supposed to be here, but the owner's agent says you can't be sure who's here and who's not. They pay for the year and come and go as they please. How about checking some of them out? Like I said before, I'm not going to be the least bit surprised if half or more of them are on their yachts in the Mediterranean, but we've got to start somewhere."

"Okay."

"If you do get any in, get a description of the contents of the box and try to get a number we can reach them at other than the hotel. When we sort out all the jewelry in the suitcases and on the floor in the back, we're going to have to call them in to identify their property. Some of that stuff goes for a couple of hundred thousand dollars. We wouldn't want to go giving it away indiscriminately."

"I've got you." Chris walked toward the elevators. The list was in numerical order according to the box number. The first one read: "Box Number 17, Julius E. Fagan, Room 2701." He took the elevator to the twenty-seventh floor and walked down the hall a few feet to the room. The carpets were as plush up here, he thought, as they were downstairs, but the lighting wasn't as good. He knocked. No answer. He knocked again. He waited a few minutes and still no answer. He looked at the list to see if there were any other persons to be interviewed on the twenty-seventh floor. There were none. He strolled back to the elevator.

Next on the list was: "Box Number 34, P. F. M. Incorporated, Stuart Pierce, Room 2320." The elevator opened, he got on and pushed the button for the twenty-third floor. On the way down it occurred to him that a lot of effort could be saved if first he called each room on the list to determine exactly who was in and who wasn't. As the doors opened he decided to check out the twenty-third floor, then return to the lobby to call the remaining rooms. The sign in front of him showed 2301 to 2320 to the right, 2321 to 2340 to the left. He stepped from the elevator and walked right. The hall stretched out before him. At the end of the straightaway he had passed room 2315 and the hall turned left for another one hundred feet. There were four doors, two on each side. At the end there appeared to be another passageway to the right. He started down the corridor.

He heard a door open in front of him. Two people were talking, but he missed what was being said. The door slammed closed. He kept walking and had reached room 2317 when up in front of him, coming from the passageway to the right, a figure appeared. It was a man in a black raincoat with the collar pulled high around his face. He seemed startled when he saw Chris, but kept walking and in a few seconds they were abreast. There was something vaguely familiar about the man that Chris could not quite place. It appeared, too, that he was purposely hunching his back to raise the raincoat collar around his face a bit more, that he would not be recognized. When Chris could have gotten his clearest view, the man put his hand to his mouth and bent forward with an exaggerated cough. Bald on top, grey on the sides, he kept walking and was past before straightening up again. Chris could not get a very good look, but was certain he had seen him before. Damn it, he thought, where? The man's features flashed to his head: the eyes; the nose; the cough; the hair; the raincoat. He kept the picture clear in his mind. He concentrated intensely.

Then it dawned on him. He turned quickly, but the hall was empty. He was sure it had been New York City's own police commissioner, Harold Windsor. No wonder he was so familiar. He turned back to look for 2320. *What the heck was he doing here? Had he responded to the scene because a police officer had been shot and killed? If so, then why didn't I see him downstairs? Why would he be on the twenty-third floor? And why would he want to avoid being seen?* Chris was curious. He was certain it was the police commissioner who had just passed.

He came to the passageway on the right. At the end of a short corridor was a door. It was the only door left—2320. And it was the room from which Commissioner Windsor had just come. He looked at the sheet once more. "P. F. M., Incorporated, Stuart Pierce, Room 2320." With his inquisitiveness triggered, with numerous questions mounting in his mind and with a legitimate excuse in his hand to satiate his curiosity, he approached the door and knocked.

CHAPTER 4

THE office of First Deputy Commissioner Lawrence Stephens was highlighted by a huge mahogany desk, equipped with a high-back swivel chair tufted in dark-brown leather. Directly behind the desk a picture window afforded a stagnant view of the Franklin Delano Roosevelt Drive, the Brooklyn Bridge and the East River. Across the river, Brooklyn was barely visible on a smoggy day. Massive wall-bookcases, rising from the floor on each side of the desk, shelved thick texts of law and administration. A high ceiling was fitted with sound-absorbent tiles, the walls paneled in mahogany a shade darker than the desk. To the left, a simple, white-faced clock hung conspicuously near the door. Five brown, vinyl-covered chairs were placed around the room, filling the spaces between two file cabinets and two small tables, one with a tape recorder atop, the other a radio. A sixth vinyl chair sat directly in front of the desk. The floors were covered with a rust-colored carpet from wall to wall. A musty odor of cigarette smoke lingered faintly.

Stephens sat at his desk reading a twenty-two-page report on the investigation of one of his men. As he turned the pages he unconsciously toyed with a ballpoint pen. Covered with a green blotter, the top of the desk was impeccable, with an "In" box at one corner and an "Out" box at the other, all papers inside each piled neatly. Between the boxes a cream-shaded lamp contrasted with a black telephone sitting to the right, in front of the "Out."

Cold, narrow eyes under bushy, white brows offset the mean, rotund face of Lawrence Stephens. At first glance, with a horseshoe of white hair and a double chin, he appeared older and flabbier than he really was, but at fifty-nine he was in very good shape, much better than most men his age. He worked at staying that way. Twice a week he visited a health spa for a calculated workout. His hands were huge and he depended on them often when he talked. His reputation was that of a martinet and he looked every bit the part.

Stephens had been raised in the violent Park Slope section of Brooklyn with two younger sisters and a brother two years older. To help support the family he left school at twelve and worked on an ice wagon from five in the morning to seven at night, carrying heavy chunks of ice on his back, up and down as many as six flights of tenement steps. With a quick-triggered temper, he was not an easy guy to get along with and wound up in a fist fight at least once a week in the rough neighborhood. He never lost. He was solid when he was young—carrying ice every day didn't hurt—and he fought by only one rule: win in any way you can. He never thought twice about slamming a baseball bat across an opponent's skull or kicking him in the groin. Winning. That's all he cared about in a brawl and he would not accept defeat. At fifteen he went to work for a moving and storage company where he developed a lot of strength. At eighteen he joined the Army. For the first time in his life he had it easy, wasting four years pushing papers around on a clerical job. He settled down and got into very few fights, but he hung on to the principle of winning and followed it in everything he attempted. His major achievement in the service was the earning of a high school diploma.

He left the army as a staff sergeant at the age of twenty-two and, influenced by a friend, took the test for the Police Department. Having a good mind, Stephens had no trouble with either the written exam or the physical. His fist-fighting days notwithstanding, he had never been arrested and passed the character background investigation without a hitch. He was appointed to the Department two years, almost to the day, after taking the written test. He really never gave thought to why he wanted to become a police officer; there was no idealism involved. It was more a case of why not. At least he wouldn't have to carry heavy cakes of ice or living room chairs on his back.

He was fairly active in his early years as a police officer, working primarily in the Williamsburgh and Bensonhurst sections of Brooklyn, averaging about two arrests a month—nothing spectacular, but above the norm. He had been a patrolman nine years before he had any inclination to take the sergeant's exam, and he passed it on the first try. It was six more years before the lieutenant's test came up. He studied hard and passed that, too. Three years later he wrote the highest mark on the exam for captain. That was as far as he could advance relying on civil service tests, for the ranks above captain were attainable only at the discretion of and appointment by the police commissioner. His promotions were few because positions were few. Stephens was not inclined toward bootlicking and therefore never fell into any one commissioner's favor. He attended John Jay College, where classes were set up to fit a police officer's schedule and, ten years after starting, he received a bachelor's degree in police science. He enrolled in Columbia University and labored for three years on a master's. By that time he had been asked by the incumbent police commissioner to leave the uniformed ranks and serve as first deputy commissioner, a prestigious, high-paying position that he gladly accepted.

But Stephens had hardened in his maturation and remained unyielding. The lessons he had learned in those early years in Brooklyn were ones he'd never forget. He would not hesitate to smash somebody's skull if it meant winning. He was educated, he was cagey, he was tough, and he was corrupt.

[71]

Before joining the Police Department, he had had little to do with crime, outside of sporadic shoplifting as a teenager, committed only when he needed something he had not the money to buy. He followed his Catholic parents' example and went to church nearly every Sunday.

As a rookie he was quickly initiated into the system of the New York City Police Department, which encouraged participation in corrupt activities. In his stay at the Police Academy corruption was never mentioned. None of the naive recruits thought to ask about it and none of the instructors considered it a problem. The attitude was simply that you were old enough to know the difference between right and wrong; if you were going to take, like most men did, the main objective was to avoid being caught.

On his first tour of duty in the street, he was assigned with a more experienced patrolman who took him to a restaurant for a free meal. That day he was told which other restaurants were good to policemen and he never paid for a meal again. Before his first week on the job had ended, he had taken money. He and a more experienced patrolman—the fourth different "teacher" in as many tours—responded to a past burglary. The owner was on the scene and asked the officers to accompany him throughout the premises, to make sure the burglars had gone and to take a quick survey of what had been stolen. As was their duty, Stephens and his partner accompanied the man and when they had finished, he gave them five dollars as a token of his appreciation. Stephens received two dollars and fifty cents for simply doing his job and he was flabbergasted. He learned that little bonuses like that were common to policemen and that the majority of the men accepted them. There were tips from city marshals for police presence at evictions, from merchants for police presence when taking their receipts to the bank, payoffs from grocery store owners who broke the anachronistic Sabbath law, from motorists to avoid summonses; the list went on and on. Stephens participated and soon was not satisfied to accept only what was offered. He took full advantage of his gun and shield and shook down everyone he could. Gamblers, prostitutes, drug dealers, traffic violators and merchants, working or traveling through the area he patroled, paid varying amounts. He even went so far as to release a man he knew to be a murderer for a payoff of five hundred dollars. If there was money to be made, nothing was too sacred. If he was first on the scene of a D.O.A., he stuffed his pockets with anything and everything of value. Though most men in the department participated in corrupt activities of one form or another, not many were as compulsively avaricious as Stephens.

When he was promoted to sergeant, the shakedowns increased. He pressured construction companies working in the precinct to either pay him or be inundated with summonses for petty infractions of ridiculous laws. Violators of the State Liquor Authority laws also proved a source of income. He established regular contracts with juice joints and after-hour clubs, usually basements or apartments where liquor was sold by unlicensed entrepreneurs, and every weekend he visited each one to collect a predetermined amount for protection from arrest.

Lieutenant Stephens, when assigned to desk duty in

[73]

the stationhouse, charged plainclothes policemen two dollars to book a prisoner. There was never a gripe by the arresting officers since the money was eventually reimbursed through their expense accounts under "miscellaneous." Flashing his rank he also continued to shake down construction sites and State Liquor Authority violators, only then he demanded and received more money.

With each change of rank there came a change of command, but the graft was basically the same in each precinct of the city.

As a captain, Stephens received a cut of everything the sergeants and lieutenants under him pulled in. A personal representative, a greedy sergeant he had taken under his wing, collected his contracts for him on a monthly basis. If a certain business, or even a place of worship, wanted special police attention, they had to pay for it. Most of the time the patrolmen stationed in front of a synagogue or department store for their entire eight hours had no idea they had been bought and paid for. At Christmastime the custom called for most men in every precinct to make their rounds, stopping in on each merchant to receive a gift of liquor or cash for services rendered during the past twelve months. Even if the merchant had never laid eyes on the police officer during the year, he readily offered, knowing if he refused, the following year he would pay the consequences. The higher the rank, the more money there was to be made at Christmas and Captain Stephens took full advantage.

Above the rank of captain, the opportunities to take

money were not as great for Stephens as when assigned to a precinct, for often he found himself confined to an office, having little or no contact with his usual sources. Even so, above the rank of captain he commanded not just one precinct, but many precincts and when there was a score the amount of money involved was sometimes three times greater than that which he had received as a captain.

He charged the men beneath him in rank for help in transfers or promotions. He rarely did favors for anyone but old friends where there was not a price involved, and even with old friends he would remind them they owed a favor in return. He was hated by the majority of men he came in contact with and was feared by all as a ruthless mercenary who would not be crossed.

Stephens lived in a very comfortable, one hundred thousand dollar home in the exclusive Garden City section of Long Island. His neighbors saw little of him, yet most considered him a devoted police officer and family man. His wife of twenty-five years knew differently, however, and was often the victim of his rage. She also knew, as only a wife could, that he was up to his neck in corruption, though he never talked about his work. A twenty-three-year-old son, his only child, had moved away from home at eighteen. Rumor had it that the son's hate for his father was so intense that he had not so much as spoken to him since leaving, though he visited his mother occasionally when he knew she was alone.

The office of the first deputy commissioner was often responsible for crucial policy decisions in the Department and when the commissioner himself was on vacation or out of town, the first deputy filled his shoes. The police commissioner was supposed to have the final word on all matters, but as far as Stephens and Windsor were concerned, most policy decisions emanated from the first deputy's office without the police commissioner's knowledge, let alone his approval.

Stephens first learned of Stuart Pierce from the mayor's brother, also a homosexual. That he was a homosexual was well known, for he made no effort to hide it. At an informal dinner at the mayor's mansion one evening he mentioned Pierce and his stable of beautiful women. He had assumed that everyone had at least heard of the pimp, for his reputation was fast spreading, but Stephens had been unaware of the operation.

Not wanting to let anything lucrative slip through his fingers, the next day the first deputy called into his office the head of the Public Morals Division, Assistant Chief Inspector Frank Costello, and asked him for a rundown on Stuart Pierce. Costello said he knew little of Pierce, since he had only been in operation a short while, but informants had told him that he jumped around quite a bit. Word was that his girls were spread all over town and never moved until they heard from him personally. They never turned tricks in their own apartments. Most of the time they met the "John", as the customer was called, at his office, where they just closed the door for a half-hour. That made an arrest extremely difficult. The public morals unit had not been able to get too much on Pierce yet, but knew his clientele was top shelf and included corporation executives, attorneys, judges, bank presidents, politicians, and so on. He concluded that Pierce was probably becoming the number-one pimp in the city.

Stephens paid Pierce a visit that very same night. In the palatial setting of his apartment, the homosexual pimp listened quietly to the deputy's demand for one thousand dollars a month if he wanted to remain in business. Pierce played dumb; he was not willing to pay the price and insisted he was not involved with any prostitutes. Stephens warned him that he would pay one way or another. Pierce failed to recognize the violent nature of the first deputy commissioner and feigned ignorance again.

At 6 A.M. the following morning Pierce was awakened by three detectives who bulled their way into the apartment and slapped him around. They tore the place apart, overturning priceless furniture and smashing everything they laid hands on, stating they had received a tip and were looking for the gun used to murder a police officer a few months earlier. Pierce denied any knowledge of the murder and told them he did not own a gun. They weren't listening. They hit him in the mouth repeatedly until he was unable to speak. Bloodied, in a state of shock, he was taken to the Twenty-third Precinct in handcuffs. He was brought before the desk officer, whereupon one of the detectives produced a revolver that he said had been found in the apartment. The lieutenant behind the desk was told that the bleeding prisoner had resisted arrest.

Pierce was taken to the detective's office upstairs and thrown to the floor of a detention cage. He was told not to move. He laid there for hours. His body ached from the beating. Most of his teeth had been knocked loose and blood trickled from one corner of his mouth. It was a nightmare. He could not understand where the gun had come from. He could not understand what had made the police believe that he had been involved with murdering an officer. He dared not ask for water or to make a phone call, for fear of being beaten again. He laid on the floor, handcuffed behind the back, and, moaning softly, did not move.

Finally, after six hours that seemed an eternity, a detective knelt down beside the cage and talked to Pierce through the grating. He told him that he didn't know if the gun really belonged to Pierce or not, or whether he was actually involved in the police officer's murder, but that it wasn't too uncommon for a man to be sent to prison for a long time for something he did not do. The word of a police officer was twice as strong as the word of a civilian in a court of law, he told him, and the judges and juries most often accepted it as gospel. Pierce simply lay motionless, his eyes fixed in astonishment on the detective's. He did not want to go to jail at all, especially for something he had nothing to do with. But why was he being tortured this way he wondered. Why? The answer was forthcoming.

The detective said that it was funny how certain things about a case could work in the defendant's favor. If the arresting officer was not very convincing, for instance. All it would take was a reasonable doubt to make a judge or jury dismiss. It seemed, the detective said, that most of the time the fate of the prisoner—

whether or not he rotted in jail half his life—was entirely dependent on the police officer's testimony. Pierce began to understand.

The detective said he had been talking to First Deputy Commissioner Stephens, who had wanted him to convey his good wishes. He had also asked if Mr. Pierce was willing to cooperate.

Pierce understood very well now. It was a simple choice: pay Stephens or go to jail. He was filled with impotent rage. He lay there bleeding, brutally beaten and accused of murder because he had refused to pay Stephens. But there was nothing he could do. He did not doubt for an instant that the first deputy was entirely capable of making good his threat. He was at the mercy of this depraved being and resigned himself to defeat. He nodded his head.

The detective smiled and said that Deputy Stephens had also mentioned that if there was anything he could do, not to hesitate to call. He had indicated he wouldn't be surprised if the charges against him were dropped. An hour later Pierce was driven home.

The following week the premier pimp of Manhattan received directions on how to make his payments, which also included additional money for the Public Morals Division. He thought of his painful experience and did not complain.

Now before him on his desk Stephens read with interest the report concerning one of his men. On the front of the report was the heading: "To: First Deputy Commissioner Lawrence Stephens; From: Captain William

[79]

Cunningham, Internal Affairs Division; Re: Investigation for Bribery of Patrolman Ronald Woods, Shield Number 46290, 29th Precinct."

Patrolman Woods had been a member of the department for seven years. He had been assigned to the 29th Precinct in Harlem right out of the Police Academy. He was black and the captain of the Two-Nine had received two letters in the past three years from local community organizations commending his work in the area and praising him as an ideal representative of the department. However, the captain of the Two-Nine, when asked for his appraisal, had labeled him a "black racist, an instigator, and potential trouble." Woods was married and the father of five children. He had received four departmental recognitions in his seven years on the job, three for excellent police duty and one for bravery. In truth, he was not a racist nor an instigator. He wore his hair in an afro and when the captain demanded he change the style, he declined, thus the unfavorable evaluation.

The report concerned a charge of bribery. Two months earlier the Internal Affairs Division had received an unsigned letter alleging that Patrolman Woods had shaken down a tow-truck driver for ten dollars because the driver had passed a red light. A cursory investigation followed and the letter of complaint was routinely pigeonholed. Two weeks later another letter was received alleging that Woods was shaking down grocery stores on Sundays, pressuring them into paying five dollars apiece to avoid a summons for violation of the antique Sabbath law. A new investigation was undertaken and Officer Woods was placed under surveillance during his working hours. Over the course of one and a half months he was observed on various occasions taking payoffs from gamblers, prostitutes and motorists. He was suspended from the force, charged with bribery. The departmental trial was to begin at the end of the week.

Stephens read the report charging Patrolman Woods with some of the very same crimes he had committed when he was a patrolman. He reminisced about some of his old payoffs, some of his old contracts, some of his old scores. He was rather surprised that the collection procedures had not changed over the years.

The main difference between Woods and himself, Stephens thought, was that Woods had been caught. Not once in all his years on the job was Stephens even accused, to his knowledge, let alone caught. He could not overlook the actions of Patrolman Woods. He could empathize, and he knew full well that Woods had merely fallen prey to the system and the tradition, but the patrolman had been accused, investigated and caught in the act. Stephens in his official capacity could not condone the crimes.

He picked up the phone and dialed. A few moments passed, and a woman answered.

"Commissioner Stanley's office, Officer Heywood speaking."

"Commissioner Stanley, please," Stephens said.

"Who's calling, please?"

"Commissioner Stephens."

"Oh, yes sir. Just a minute, sir."

There was a pause, a click to "hold," another pause, then another click.

[81]

"Hello, Larry," came a man's voice, "I was about to call you."

"Hello, Bert," Stephens said to Trial Commissioner Bertram Stanley, who sat as judge and jury on all important departmental trials. "I just finished reading the report on Woods." Stephens spoke in an accent characteristic of his Irish immigrant background.

"Right," said Stanley. "I've got the case on for Friday."

"How does it look?"

"Airtight. There's no way he can beat it."

The outcome of the case had been decided before the trial had even begun. Woods would not stand a chance for acquittal.

"According to the report," Stephens mumbled, glancing at the papers in front of him, twitching his wiry, white brows, "he's got over thirteen thousand in a savings account, he owns his own home . . ."

"What do you want me to do?"

Naturally, the determination of what to do with a corrupt policeman was supposed to be decided only after conviction, after it had been proven beyond doubt that he was indeed corrupt.

"Dump him," Stephens said. "This guy's up to his neck now. If we hold on to him, we might be sorry."

"Okay."

"Give me a call next week and let me know how everything went."

"Okay. It'll probably last till Wednesday or so. I'll give you a ring Thursday or Friday."

"Good. Meanwhile, tell Lou Murphy to have a press

[82]

release ready to go when the trial is over, saying that the commissioner is determined to crack down on these rotten apples in the barrel who discredit the uniform. Or something like that. Maybe we can get some of these assholes to wise up." And to himself Stephens added "and at least be a little more discreet."

"Okay, Larry."

"So long," Stephens said and he hung up. He reflected a minute on Patrolman Woods. He tried to think how he would have felt if he had been caught and thrown off the force. He shook his head and sighed in relief that he had not. He threw the report on Woods in the "Out" box and picked up a handful of papers from the "In." On top was a message that there was a meeting between the police commissioner and all his deputies scheduled for the following Monday. He crumpled the notice and threw it in the wastepaper basket under the desk. Next in the pile was a folder marked "Transfers." He opened it. On the left was a packet containing some of the printed orders of the week that had been distributed to the field. The heading on top of the packet read "Transfers: Approved and Ordered." On the right was another packet, this containing a thick batch of letters with official department headings. Above the packet was the caption: "Transfer Requests." These were from commanding officers. Other requests reached his desk only after they had been approved up the chain of command. He removed the letters and perused them, one by one, in order. There was a request from the Internal Affairs Division for two more men to cover a special assignment, a request from the police laboratory for three more men to assist "an overloaded staff and to unclog a back-load inventory of drug evidence," a request from the Organized Crime Control Bureau to transfer thirteen temporarily assigned men back to their permanent commands, and so on. He turned them face down on the desk as he read them. Halfway down the pile he reached a request of apparently particular interest. He removed it from the stack and slid the folder and the requests he had already looked at away from him. The form heading stated that the letter was from the commanding officer of the Twenty-first Precinct, Captain Otto Varing, and regarded a request for transfer of a member of the service for disciplinary reasons.

The interest generated by this particular request was because of Otto Varing, an old friend of Stephens. They had been sergeants together in Brooklyn and had joined in raping their precinct for every cent. They were two of a kind and both had made captain about the same time. But where Stephens had seen the potential rewards of going to college part time to earn a degree, Varing never bothered with school. As Stephens was promoted, Varing remained a captain, floating around from assignment to assignment, until eventually receiving his own command, the Two-One. He was content in the Two-One, for, indeed, it was the fashionable East Side, but more important to Varing, it was ripe, ready to be squeezed for all its worth. The captain before him had estblished only a few contracts. When Varing was assigned he put nearly every business in the precinct on the payroll, and applied a constant pressure to the vulnerable spots of those who did not cooperate. Having been a captain

[84]

for over five years, he was now drawing pay equivalent to that of an inspector, in accordance with his position on the seniority chart. A combination of salary and untaxed, tainted income afforded him a very comfortable life style.

Stephens read the request from Varing, smiled and picked up the telephone. He dialed the Two-One Precinct and asked the switchboard operator for the captain. A strong, healthy voice answered on the second ring.

"Captain Varing," came the voice.

"Good morning, Otto. Larry Stephens."

"Larry," Varing said, obviously glad to hear Stephens' voice, "how the hell are you?"

"Good."

Varing and Stephens hadn't talked in three years, and they recalled the last time they'd seen each other: it was at a murdered patrolman's funeral in Maspeth.

There was a pause. "I was just looking at your transfer request," Stephens said.

"Yeah, I've got a problem with this hump Chamber."

"What's up?"

"This fuckin' guy's been breakin' my balls for the last couple of months. He's not takin' a nickel on the street."

"You can't transfer a guy 'cause he's not taking money."

"I wouldn't mind if he just did his job and didn't take. You've gotta admire a guy that's got the balls to be different. I sometimes wonder if I could ever do it. But it's not that simple with Chamber. He's not happy at just being clean, he's knockin' the jock off every fuckin' joint

[85]

in the precinct. Last month he turned in thirty-five summonses for Administrative Code and Health Code violations on twenty-two places. Can you imagine? Thirty-five summonses in one month. The rest of the command put together hasn't turned in that many violations in the past five years. The owners are calling me up every day."

"You've got contracts with these places?"

"Every one of them. They want his ass out of the Two-One."

"Have you talked to him?"

"I warned him twice now. I've threatened him with a transfer, and I know it bothered him, but he hasn't let up."

"Why don't you just stick him out in the corner of the precinct? Don't you have any synagogue fixers?"

"Sure, I've thought of that, but there's two things that make me hesitate. He's the most active man I've got. I put him on a fixer and I not only lose his activity, but I've also got the Patrolmen's Benevolent Association on my ass. I can do without that."

"If you get him transferred you're going to lose his activity anyway. What the hell's the difference? You that worried about the P. B. A.?"

"I'm just fed up with the aggravation. And a transfer will serve as a good example in case anybody else decides to fuck around with me. As long as I'm going to lose his activity, I'd like to lose it under the best circumstances."

"Why don't you just try a fixer for a while and see what happens. Maybe he'll come around."

"You don't know this fuckin' guy, Larry. He's crafty. He'd figure out some way, a legitimate way, to screw up the fuckin' synagogue and get them pissed off. I'd just as soon get rid of him altogether. He's stepping on too many toes. And he's hurtin' me where it counts . . ."

". . . In the pocket," Stephens said.

"Right."

"What's with him, anyhow? Does he say why he's not taking any money, or at least cooperating?"

"He doesn't say shit. He just says he's doin' his job. I can't figure the fuckin' guy out. The strange thing is that he came here from the Eight-O. I called them up and they swear by him. He was on the take over there. In fact, he even collected for the commanding officer last Christmas. It's just my luck he comes to the Two-One and decides to go straight. It burns my fuckin' balls everytime I think about it."

"I wonder if he's gone outside of the Department."

"I don't think so. Some of the other men say it's just a personal thing. They can't figure him for sure, either, but they're sure he's not giving anybody up. Still, nobody wants to work with him."

"Understandably."

Stephens picked up the request in front of him and looked at it through half-squinted eyes. "Chamber," he said. "Where the hell have I heard that name before?"

"Probably on the radio this morning," Varing said. "Or in the papers. He was in that shootout at the Corinthian last night."

"You're shitting!"

"I wish I was. Now the fuckin' guy's a hero; to everyone outside the Two-One, anyhow."

"Sure, that's where I heard his name. That was some deal last night."

"You should have seen the lobby. They blew the fuckin' thing apart. I was down there this morning. It's just unbelievable."

"I saw the pictures in the paper. Too bad for you Chamber didn't catch a slug, too, huh?"

Sitting at his desk in the precinct, Varing recoiled when he heard that. Obviously he hated Chamber. He wanted him out of the Two-One, as far away as possible. He wanted to show him that he was just the guy that could do it, too. He cursed him for the aggravation he had caused the past few months. But he didn't want him dead. He cringed at the thought of a police officer wishing death to another police officer, another police officer that he didn't even know. His avaricious ambitions notwithstanding, after thirty years on the job he felt a compelling allegiance to the force. There was a common bond that united all police officers in a close-knit fraternity. If you cut one, they all bled. His stomach tightened at the first deputy's statement, because he knew he meant it. He had forgotten the man's nature. To Stephens, nothing was sacred. If the only solution to a problem meant that a fellow police officer had to be eliminated, then that was the course to take. Varing realized ever so clearly at that time just what a callous, violent, ruthless man Larry Stephens really was.

"Okay, listen, Otto," Stephens said, "I'll take care of this for you. How do you want me to handle it?"

"I want him to know it was my doing," Varing said.

"Where do you want me to send him?"

"Can you fit him in Bedfort-Stuyvesant? That's the shithole he came from. I'm sure going back there will bother the shit out of him."

"No problem."

"Great, Larry, I really appreciate it."

"You know this is going to cost you a favor, don't you?"

"Anytime you want. Just give me a call."

"Okay. You know, with this shootout in the Corinthian last night and the front-page splash, I'm going to have to hold off on it a little while. It might set something off if we transfer a hero."

"Understood."

"When I think it's okay, I'll put the papers through."

"Thanks a lot, Larry."

"I'll be talking to you, Otto." He hung up. Leaning back on his chair and lighting a cigarette, he reflected on the conversation for a moment, then leaned forward and wrote "APPROVE" across the top of the request.

CHAPTER 5

LYING shirtless, face down, across his bed, Chris Chamber woke to a noisy truck rumbling past the window. Gold, frilly-bottomed shades drawn shut, the door opposite the bed admitted a small ray of light from the hall. To the left of the door sat a contemporary walnut highboy and to the right a matching mirrored dresser. A drab painting of a bowl of fruit, artist unknown, hung squarely above the highboy. Doily-covered night-tables flanked the bed and at the foot, a portable television rested on a tin-tube cart. Reddish-brown linoleum contrasted pleasantly with beige, flowered wallpaper and a white Celotex ceiling. Faintly audible from outside the room, a transistor radio played the number-one tune.

Chris rolled over on his back and stared for a few seconds at the ceiling, sat up and reached to turn on the television. Placing one pillow on top of another, lying straight back, he clasped his hands behind his head. His pants were wrinkled from top to bottom; he had been too tired to remove them. A moment passed. The television grew bright, slightly illuminating the dim-lit room.

". . . At the small, Middle Eastern airport," said the newscaster in a baritone. "The blast tied up air traffic for seven hours." Chris wasn't really listening. "In Japan today . . ."

Chris' mind wandered to the Corinthian, reflecting on the police commissioner in the hallway. He flashed him passing, bending down, exaggerating a phony cough in an effort to hide his face. He smiled. He remembered the walk down the rest of the corridor, the right turn, the approach to room 2320. His thoughts were interrupted by the television.

"Here in New York early this morning," the newscaster reported, "a blazing gun battle at the elite Corinthian Hotel on Fifth Avenue resulted in five deaths, one of them an eighteen-year veteran police officer. Shortly after midnight, police say, at least five men held at bay three employees of the hotel while rifling safety-deposit boxes containing an estimated three million dollars in cash and jewelry belonging to a long list of illustrious patrons, half of whom, reputedly, are spread out around the world at this time and unaware they have been robbed. In the middle of the robbery, two alert police officers of the Twenty-first Precinct, Patrolman Joseph Hummel and Patrolman Christopher Chamber, noticing a new doorman acting suspiciously, decided to check out the hotel. The doorman, actually one of the thieves, darted inside and tipped his accomplices. When the officers reached the lobby they were met with a hail of machine-gun bullets and the battle had begun. Before it was over, two robbers had escaped and Patrolman Hummel lay dead."

The picture on the screen switched to film clips of the Corinthian.

"The lobby was virtually cut to pieces by the barrage of gunfire. These pictures were taken a short while after the incident. In addition to the police officer, three holdup men and one hotel employee were also killed, while Patrolman Chamber came away uninjured. Although it is extremely difficult to gauge at this time, because so many of the hotel's guests are not available, it is believed the thieves got away with well over one and a half million dollars worth of jewelry. Two suitcases crammed with cash and jewelry were left behind at the scene."

The picture on the screen switched back to the newscaster.

"This afternoon Police Commissioner Harold Windsor held a press conference at police headquarters to expound on the incident. Matthew Stanton reports."

On the screen appeared the commissioner, standing at a podium in a crowded room, surrounded by police officials. To his immediate right stood First Deputy Commissioner Stephens. Commissioner Windsor's lips were movng but the voice on the television was that of the on-the-scene reporter.

"In the aftermath of the incredible Corinthian shootout, where robbers used an arsenal of weapons that included a machine gun and a forty-five caliber automatic pistol, Police Commissioner Harold Windsor went before the cameras today and demanded federal legislation on gun control. New York will not be safe, he said, until we are able to rid the city of illegal guns and the only effective way to accomplish that is through national cooperation and a federal law rigidly restricting firearm ownership. New York has the most stringent gun control law in the country, he added, but it is ineffective because other states allow gun sales over the counter and there is no way to stop the flow across state lines. In a fifteen-minute, prepared speech he outlined the holdup attempt and said that twenty-three men have been assigned to track down the two escaped bandits and the stolen jewelry, believed to be valued at close to two million dollars. In his closing statement he reflected on the police officer who was fatally wounded in the shootout."

When Commissioner Windsor moved his lips again, his voice was audible.

"Without a doubt," he said, "the most difficult part of being a police commissioner is trying to cope with the news that a police officer has been killed in the line of duty. In the past two years in the United States, two hundred and fifty-two policemen have died protecting life and property; forty-eight of those were slain in outright ambush. Each one is a devastating blow, but when it's one of your own men, the feeling is indescribable. All New York will miss Patrolman Joseph Hummel. He was not only an outstanding police officer, he was an

[93]

outstanding man and a credit to our city."

Chris lay on the bed listening as the original news-caster came back on to comment about the story. Funny, he thought, how everybody remembers only how good you were when you're killed in the line of duty; to judge from speeches and eulogies after every police officer's death, there is no such thing as a bad cop. It's better that way, he figured. Why let the truth come out about a man who is no longer alive to defend himself.

He thought about the police commissioner. He looked at him now in a completely different light. Again his mind flashed back to the twenty-third floor of the Corinthian ...

Chris approached room 2320 and knocked. A moment passed. He knocked again. The door opened and Stuart Pierce, dressed only in a white terrycloth bathrobe, stood before him.

"Good morning, officer," Pierce said in a soft tone. "What can I do for you?"

Chris eyed the makeup on his face. "Mr. Pierce?"

"Yes."

"I'm Patrolman Chamber. I wonder if I might come in and talk to you for a few minutes. There's been a robbery downstairs and a safe-deposit box registered to you was involved."

"Certainly," Pierce said, swinging the door open wide, stepping aside to let Chris pass. "Do come in."

As Chris walked by, he was hit with the fragrance of a strong perfume. It struck him that the police commissioner had just left. He couldn't quite believe it. There was no question that Pierce was a homosexual—but the commissioner? Could Harold Windsor be a homosexual? he wondered.

"Make yourself comfortable, officer," Pierce said. "Can I get you a drink? Or is that a no-no while you're working?"

Chris moved farther into the suite, and noticed the luxury.

"No, thanks just the same." He noted the ruffled covers on the bed.

"Oh? Well, I hope you don't mind if I have one."

"Not at all."

Pierce strutted to a grey-flecked marble table in the corner of the room and poured a drink from a crystal bottle. He motioned Chris over to the sofa. Chris complied, and they both sat down.

Pierce put down the glass and smiled. "Please, officer," he said, "make yourself comfortable. I promise I won't tell anyone if you take off your hat."

Chris smiled politely, though he was uncomfortable. He had come in contact with homosexuals before in his years on the job, but he had never enjoyed their company. There was just something about a man wearing mascara and lipstick that turned his stomach, and it was indeed a strain to act unbothered when talking to someone so made up. He was impressed, however, at Pierce's skill. His face was flawless and rather attractive. It made conversing with him a little easier.

"You do rent box number thirty-four, don't you, Mr. Pierce?" Chris said, looking at the list in his left hand, removing his hat with his right. His healthy shock of light brown hair was slightly tousled, but still neat.

"That's right," said Pierce, surveying Chris. "Have I been robbed?"

"Well, sir, there has been a robbery involving many boxes and we're not quite sure yet what's missing. Some of the contents has been recovered already and we're trying to find out who owns it."

"I see."

"So what I'd like to know is what exactly, if anything, you had in your box."

"A gold watch and a pinky ring."

Chris opened his jacket and withdrew a small white pad. From his belt he removed a pen. "Can you describe the watch?"

"Certainly. It was a Baccardi, twenty-four jewel. It had a calendar and the numbers on the face were roman numerals."

Chris wrote everything down. "Anything else?" he asked. "Any inscription?"

"No. No inscriptions. Nothing else that I can think of."

"How about the band . . . gold? Leather?"

"A gold expansion band. Not very fancy, I'm afraid."

"Any special design?"

"No, just an ordinary gold expansion band. You know."

"Yes, sir. Now, how about the ring?"

"A gold pinky ring with a full carat setting, right in the middle. Again no inscription or initials. No elaborate design. Just plain and simple."

Chris looked up from the pad. "What would you estimate the value of the watch?" he asked.

Pierce mulled it over for a few seconds. "About fifteen hundred dollars, I'd guess. It's not even a year old."

"And the value of the ring?"

"About the same. On second thought," he added, "it might be a little higher."

Chris marked $1500 next to each description on the pad. "Is that all that was in the box?"

"That's all. I don't use it much, but I like to know it's there if I need it."

Again Chris thought of the police commissioner having just been in the room with Pierce, and he smiled without realizing it. They probably had a good tumble in the bed, he figured. Pierce saw the upturned corners of Chris's mouth and made his own interpretation. There was something about Chris that appealed to him. He returned the smile.

"Is this your permanent address?" Chris asked.

"Oh, heavens, no. I keep this place strictly for business and convenience reasons."

"May I have your permanent address and a phone number where you can be reached, Mr. Pierce? The detective division will be wanting to get in touch with you."

"Certainly. I'll give you my card." He got up and walked to a closet near the bed. In a moment he was back and placed his business card on the table.

"What business are you in, sir?" Chris asked, glancing at the card, curious that it did not say.

"P. F. M., Incorporated is my own firm," Pierce said, a wry smile on his face. "It's a consulting firm."

"Oh. And what do the letters P. F. M. stand for, if I might ask?"

"Personal, financial, managerial: the three areas of consultation for which I am available. I like brevity in business matters, so I simply abbreviated. It makes things much easier for me. Besides, P. F. M. has a certain mystique to it, don't you think?"

Chris nodded. He wasn't quite sure why.

"You'd be surprised how much business I have come by as a result of people asking me what the letters P. F. M. stand for, just like you did. At one time or another most everyone can use my services." He smiled at the policeman's unknowingness. "Pleasure for money" was more apropos for the initials, but Pierce kept his joke to himself.

There was a pause while Chris tried unsuccessfully to comprehend.

Pierce got up again. "How long will it be before I find out if I have, in fact, been robbed?"

Chris rose, too. "That's very difficult to say. Investigations are hell. It could be a couple of days. It could be a couple of weeks."

They walked to the door.

"I'm sorry to have bothered you at this hour, Mr. Pierce," Chris said, "but it is imperative that we find out as much as we can as soon as we can. You understand."

"You haven't bothered me at all," Pierce said. His tone was flirtatious. "On the contrary, I rather enjoyed your visit. I get very lonely sometimes and relish the company of someone as pleasant as you. Do you know what I mean?"

[98]

Chris knew exactly what he meant. "Well, I'm glad I haven't disturbed you." He saw a chance to throw a dig at the police commissioner. After all, he thought, that bastard had been up here jerking off while he was downstairs dodging machine-gun bullets. "Your other guest couldn't have been very good company if you were lonely when I arrived." He wondered if Pierce would comment on the commissioner's role as love-maker. It would make a great kicker when he told the story to his friends.

"What guest?" Pierce said. "I've been alone all night."

Chris was taken aback for an instant. This guy had to be kidding, he thought. Surely Pierce realized he and Windsor must have passed in the hallway. It didn't make sense to flaunt your homosexuality, then deny you just had been balling with another guy. Or did it? But why make a pass at someone and forego the chance to show him you were experienced? Or was that a silly thing to do? Chris was confused and decided not to press the issue.

"Oh, okay, Mr. Pierce . . . my mistake."

Pierce moved to open the door and as he passed, brushed Chris's genital area with his hand. "I'm very serious about enjoying the visit, you know," he said, standing very close. "I'd love it if we could get together again sometime real soon."

Chris was tempted to crash his fist into Pierce's mouth. The perfume, the mascara, the lipstick were suddenly very disgusting. But he controlled himself and stepped into the hall.

"The detective division will be in touch," he said politely. He turned and walked away.

Pierce called to him, and Chris heard a clear note of

frustration present in his voice: "You know where to get me if you ever need any more information, Patrolman Chamber."

Chris kept walking. So the police commissioner of New York City was a fucking queer. The leader of men. The fearless chief who has so much criticism about how his men act, who all too often transfers, fines or fires men who have been caught fooling around with women. He wondered if their fate would be the same if they were caught fooling around with men. He wondered what the commissioner's nickname would be once the word got around. The irony was too much. He reached the elevator and pushed the button. By the time it came he was chuckling.

His wife's voice snapped him back into the bedroom.

"Supper's almost ready, hon," she said as she leaned into the doorway, her left hand on the doorknob, her right hand braced against the wall. Long blonde hair and blue eyes, shapely, Sandy Chamber was enticingly attractive, even in the simple house dress she wore.

"Oh, okay," Chris said, "I'll be right there. I just want to watch this." He was staring at the television set but was not aware at all of what was on. His wife looked at the cat food commercial on the set, then to Chris. She shrugged her shoulders and went back to the kitchen.

She had barely left when Chris's thoughts were back on the Corinthian elevator, coming from the twenty-third floor. He was amused over the fact that the police commissioner was a homosexual and that Chris was probably the only member of the force who knew it, but suddenly it was no longer funny. It occurred to him that maybe it was better that only he knew.

The lobby was comparatively empty. Most of the guests and the people who had not belonged there in the first place were gone. Only two uniformed officers were on duty, and they stood by the front door facing the street. Between them Chris could see that the crowd outside had dispersed. Three men in overalls were cleaning up the mess as best they could. Detective Krausse was not in sight. Chris walked past the front desk and into the room marked "Employees Only." The carpet was still stained with Willie O'Brien's blood. Krausse was talking to another man in civilian clothes by the table as three detectives dusted for prints on the safe and on the boxes. The room was covered with a milky powder from where they had already dusted.

Krausse saw Chris and excused himself. "Finished already?" he asked as he approached.

"No," Chris said, "it just occurred to me that it would be a whole lot easier if I first called all these rooms on the list to see if there's anybody in them, rather than knock myself out hitting every one in person."

"Good thinking," Krausse said. "Use the phone at the front desk. It's been dusted already."

Krausse paused and said softly: "See the guy I'm talking to?"

Chris nodded.

"He's the owner's agent. I'm setting up a good deal for the guys in the precinct."

"What kind of deal?"

"Moonlighting, keeping an eye on things. Roaming the halls. We figure about four or five hours a night, per man. Say till about eight or nine if you're finishing up an eight to four and starting about seven or so if you're doing a late tour. If two guys overlap, he don't care. He's looking for all the off-duty cops he can get. And at four bucks an hour, off the books. Not bad, huh? Interested?"

Chris laughed. "You're unbelievable," he said. "You're here on an investigation that's probably going to tie you up for the next six months and you're looking for a way to make it worth your while."

Krausse recoiled a bit. "It's legitimate. I don't know about you but me and a lot of other guys in this precinct could sure use the extra bread."

"Don't get me wrong, Paul."

Krausse shrugged it off. "Okay, listen, let me know how you make out with that list, will ya?" He turned back toward the agent.

Chris padded out to the front desk. Fingerprint powder and chalk outlines were everywhere, mingling with blood. He picked up the phone from a ledge under the desk and placed it on top. He called the next three names on the list, letting the phone ring ten times on each one. No one answered. The owner's agent came out from behind the partition, walked the length of the lobby to the front door and left. In a few seconds Krausse came out from behind the partition also.

"How you makin' out?" Krausse asked.

"One for five," Chris said. "I think you might be right about half these people being scattered around the world on their yachts."

Krausse nodded in frustration.

"Hey, did you happen to see any more brass in here after I left?" Chris asked.

"Nope. They all left right after you went upstairs."

Chris smiled to disguise the seriousness of his next question: "The P. C. didn't show up, huh?"

The detective seemed genuinely surprised. "You've got to be kidding. That cocksucker wouldn't get out of bed in the middle of the night to come here."

Chris laughed at Krausse's unknowingly apropos description of the commissioner.

"The fuckin' P. C.," Krausse laughed, turning and walking back from where he came. "That's funny."

Chris, pleased with his private joke, came out from behind the desk and walked to the rear exit door, pushing it open a bit, clicking the button on the side to unlock it. He closed it and stepped to the elevator, got on and rode to the second floor. He got off, crossed the hall to his right, to the door marked exit, and went through. The stairway was dark. He went down. On the first floor landing the door to the lobby was on his left, the door to the alley on his right. He opened the alley door and looked around. It was even darker out there. The street was about fifty feet away. No doubt that was the way Windsor had left. It was cold and damp and a wind blew suddenly giving him a chill, prompting him to go back inside.

Sandy called from the kitchen. "Chris, come on, everything's getting cold."

"I'll be right there," Chris said loud enough to be heard. He got up, retrieved a tan shirt from the closet

[103]

and slipped it on on the way out of the bedroom. A short hall led to the small but efficient kitchen. The mood was yellow and white. Stained-wood cabinets lined the right side, head high over all the major appliances, and accented the walls, papered with daisies. The woodwork shone of white enamel. A window trimmed with canary-yellow curtains centered the far wall and afforded a view of the backyard. None of the appliances were brand new, but all sparkled from daily polishing. A flower clock near the door read six twenty-five.

Sandy Chamber sat at the far end of the dinner table, flanked to the left by her six-year-old daughter, Mayam, and to the right by her eight-year-old son, Chris, Junior. She liked to have dinner between six and seven as often as she could so the family could eat together. It wasn't always possible, though, with Chris working eight in the morning to four in the afternoon one week, then midnight to eight the next, four in the afternoon to midnight the next, then back to eight to fours. A policeman's schedule meant inconvenience for the entire family. When he worked four to twelves they would usually eat dinner around two in the afternoon, and most of the time when he worked late tours she would feed the children early, then eat with Chris around ten.

After eight years of the crazy schedule she was used to it; but she still didn't like it. She kept hoping that one day Chris would be assigned to regular tours. Even if they were four to twelves, or midnights. It really didn't matter, as long as they were regular—every week. Getting used to one schedule like that would be easy and certainly a relief from adjusting to a new one every five days. The ultimate satisfaction would come if he were assigned straight days, Monday through Friday with weekends off. The way his present assignment worked, not only did his hours change constantly, but he was off on weekends only five times a year. With straight days they could live like a normal family, go visiting on Sundays, go to the beach on Saturdays, or whatever. They could socialize regularly with their old friends, their non-police officer friends. Because of a policeman's odd hours and days off, it was just impossible to keep in touch regularly with anyone who was not a policeman, anyone who worked conventional hours with weekends off.

Chris sat down at the dinner table facing his wife. "What's on the menu tonight?" he inquired.

Sandy smiled and reached to the center of the table, removing the cover of a casserole. Steam swirled out of the dish. "Spanish rice," she said.

"Good enough." He grabbed a serving spoon and helped himself.

Chris still loved his wife as much as the day they had married ten years before. She was good to him. They argued as much as any couple, but they always had enough sense to know when to stop, and a rift between them never lasted longer than a day. Usually, even if she felt she was right, Sandy made the first move to make up. Letting her hair fall to the shoulders, clad only in sheer nylon, knowing exactly what pleased her husband the most, she never failed to break the ice. Chris could hardly resist. Sandy had the most exciting body he had ever laid eyes on, and two births had hardly taken a toll. Firm breasts, thin at the waist and full hips and thighs was the perfect shape for a woman as far as Chris was concerned, and Sandy had that. Sandy had more. An unblemished face complemented soft, pouty lips and crystal eyes. She was to Chris the complete woman.

But most important to Chris, Sandy was trustworthy. Too many married women did he know who had cheated on their husbands.

Chris did not go to bed with other women very often, although his good looks could have afforded him a different pickup every night. He was not shy with women. On the contrary, he was very open, never hesitating to speak his mind, no matter who was listening. He played around sporadically, always taking every precaution to insure that it would never get back to his wife. He had a good woman, and he didn't want to lose her. He wasn't so sure anyhow that she would leave him even if she found out he had been to bed with another woman. Nevertheless, he didn't want to test her.

Sandy, only daughter in a middle-income family of five, was devoted to her husband. Even if she were not wildly in love with him, which she was, she would respect no other man as much. Chris was right for her. He was honest and fair and gave her what she wanted—love. Her experience with other men was very limited before she married, and was nil afterward. She had no inclination to go to bed with anyone else, although a few men had made the offer. She depended heavily on Chris and he responded with the necessary warmth and affection.

It seemed he always knew when to say the right thing. She did not suspect he cheated on her, but could understand it if he did, though she would never let him know that. She was a meticulous cleaner and a good cook. She took pride in her home, as modest as it was. And, realistically, she would be satisfied when they finally were able to fix it the way they wanted.

Sandy was happy. Chris was a good husband. She would rather he had chosen another profession, but she would never stand in his way. She knew full well how much he had wanted to be a police officer, and she shared his enthusiasm the day he was appointed, although she was prepared for a rocky road. She had had more foresight than he and had known that their lives would be affected seriously when he joined the Department, but she had confidence that they would be able to handle it. She had been right. While assigned to Bedford-Stuyvesant, Chris had come home some nights too tense to even converse without getting annoyed at the slightest thing or using foul language. He had not been happy there and it nearly destroyed their marriage. But since his transfer to the Two-One, life had been smoother and he was back to his old self. It upset her terribly when he told her he might be getting transferred back to Bedford-Stuyvesant. He was very vague as to why, and said it was not definite, but he wanted her to be prepared.

Chris never talked with his wife about corruption on the police force. She might not have understood how the system worked. She might not have understood that the peer-group pressure was on the man who did not participate. Whenever the subject of taking money had come up while assigned to the Eight-O, he had tactfully changed the subject.

Sandy felt that Chris might have been participating in corruption while he was in Bedford-Stuyvesant. There was just something there. Something undefinable that a husband cannot contain from his wife, that hinted he was committing a wrong in the eyes of society. One day he even talked of leaving the job for good. She guessed correctly that it was because he had accepted one bribe too many, although he never admitted it. He was not happy. Something was constantly bothering him, eating away at his insides, transforming him into a wretched personality. She watched from the sideline, studying him, until one day it dawned on her what the problem was. Chris was basically an honest individual. And he was sensitive. She could not fully appreciate or comprehend how he got caught up in taking money on the job, but she knew he did, if for no other reason than because he gave her every paycheck and never asked for money, yet he always had ten or fifteen dollars in his pocket. She knew it was that conflict with his true nature that caused him so much anguish. He never talked about it because he didn't want her to know. But because it affected her and the family, she had decided to approach him. She wanted to be certain she did not injure his pride. She had to be tactful and was trying to figure out the best way to bring it up, when Chris received his notice of transfer. From the first day in the Two-One, he was a different man. He was happy once again to be a police officer and it showed. His revitalization was contagious and for nearly two years they had been experiencing a very rewarding marriage. Whenever the subject of taking money came up after the transfer to the Two-One, Chris would simply say that he didn't think it was right, but that each man had to make his own decision and live with it.

Sandy especially appreciated Chris because he was a good father. He was affectionate, yet firm. He spent a lot of time with the children and often took them out of the house for a day just to give her a rest. He was considerate and she loved him for it.

There couldn't be a better mother for his children than Sandy as far as Chris was concerned. She worked very hard at raising them correctly and very rarely complained. They were always clean and dressed properly when they left the house. She had taken most of the burden of being a good father off him by being so attentive, yet she did not overdo it. She knew when to let him be the boss in front of the kids.

"Frank Roselli called this morning," Sandy said, scooping Spanish rice onto her daughter's plate, "but I didn't want to wake you."

"Did he say what he wanted?"

"No, not really. He said it wasn't important and that he'd call you later this week. He didn't say much more."

"I'll have to get back to him."

"He said to be sure to tell you he's saying the nine o'clock Mass this Sunday."

"Oh, yeah. That's in honor of my father. I wish it wasn't so early."

"He's got to say whatever Mass he's assigned. You can't expect him to go telling the bishop how to run things, can you?"

"Not yet, anyhow. He's not there long enough. But give him time, he'll figure something out."

"Chris!"

He laughed. "You know, sometimes I still can't get over Frank being a priest. It just seems so strange."

"I'm sure he's happy."

"Oh, I know he is. And I'm happy for him."

"He also congratulated you on your heroics. He said he didn't know you had it in you."

He smiled. "He still won't let me forget that time he beat the hell out of me 'cause I dated his girl. Wait'll I talk to him." He was laughing now. "For having nothing much to say, it sounds like he said an awful lot. Anything else?"

"No, that was about it."

They finished eating, and the kids ran into the living room to watch television while Sandy put on coffee and gathered up the dishes. Chris stared down at the table and got to thinking about his captain's threat to have him transferred if he didn't stop stepping on toes. It was simple enough: he was just to stop issuing summonses for Health Code and Administrative Code violations at the businesses that were paying the captain. They were paying for immunity, and they weren't getting it. But they weren't paying Chris—though they had offered and had been refused quickly. The offers were made to Chris only once, because he warned that on the next offer they would be arrested for bribery. He was determined to do his job and not to let anyone stand in his way; especially not a greedy superior officer who was supposed to help him instead of hinder him. He had had his fill of corruption in the Eight-O. It had almost caused him to turn in his gun and shield in disgust and had very nearly broken up his marriage. He would have nothing more to do with it. He just wanted to do his job, and he was convinced that he could do it without serious repercussions. Honesty had to begin somewhere. But Captain Varing made him wonder. Varing was as determined to honor the contracts he had set up with the merchants in the area, profiting handsomely in the process, as Chris was to enforce the law the way it was supposed to be enforced. Chris did not set out to break the captain's contracts; in fact, in the beginning he was not aware that contracts even existed. He simply issued summonses where violations existed in an attempt to have the violations corrected. When the merchants retorted that they were paying off the captain for protection against summonses, they expected the matter to be closed. But Chris felt that backing down was tantamount to accepting money to ignore the violations. In addition he would lose face in the community. He had no intention of fighting a one-man crusade against corruption. Were that the case he would have been turning in his fellow officers left and right, for he was privy to most of what went on. But he turned no one in. Corruption was too pervasive. More important, he understood the system, the tradition, that pressured men into venal activity. He did not condone it; he understood it. He, himself, had been a part of it and had escaped. He was content to stay clean alone. As far as he knew, he was the only one in the Two-One who did not take part in corruption of one form or another. He didn't want to step on anybody's toes, but since he had done so accidentally, he would not be bullied into retreat. He wondered, though, if he were making a serious mistake, for the captain might make good his threat to have him transferred back to Bedford-Stuyvesant. Back to the rats and roaches, filth and degradation, militancy and danger. What a travesty, he thought, that he should be punished for doing his job, that he should fall victim to the injustice of the Department which allowed avaricious tyrants such as Varing to wield an ax on those who refused to conform to his will. He thought of Captain Otto Varing and he grew very angry. He would not let Varing or anybody else push him around, especially when he was doing the right thing and they were not. Damn it, he thought, God damn it, he would go through with it.

Before realizing it, he had crashed his fist down on the table, rattling the cups of coffee his wife had just set down. She looked at him in puzzlement.

"Sorry," he said.

"What's the matter?" Sandy asked again.

Chris smiled. "Listen, I've got to leave early tonight. I won't be back before I go to work, so I won't see you till the morning."

Sandy nodded. It would not be the first time Chris had gone out early. And often he came home hours after his tour had ended. Most times he called and let her know he would not be home, but sometimes she just expected him, and he never showed up. She knew enough not to ask him why. As long as no one called with bad news. She realized the danger of his profession and feared for his safety. She never doubted for a moment that the time away from home was related to his work, and that was all she had to know. A stake-out; an investigation; an informant; whatever it was, she knew it was important if it meant Chris had to use his own time. He was committed, and they both knew it.

Chris finished his coffee and went back to the bedroom. From the closet he retrieved a black attaché case and placed it on the bed. Stepping to the highboy, he opened the middle drawer and rummaged about a few seconds until he came up with a small box. He brought it to the bed and opened it. Inside, amidst an entanglement of wires, was a Japanese-made tape recorder, about the size of a pack of cigarettes. He picked it up and examined it. Dipping again into the box, he withdrew a small cassette and slid it into place in the opening on the side of the recorder. He laid the device on the bed. Unlatching the attaché, he opened it and pressed his thumbs against each side. The bottom of the case sprung loose, revealing a hidden space beneath. He lifted out the false bottom and placed it on the sheet. Taking the tape recorder from the bed, he fit it into a strap fastened to the actual bottom of the case and snapped it tight. He jiggled the device to see if it was secure. Satisfied, he untangled one of the black wires in the box and plugged an end into the recorder. On the other end was a minuscule square microphone. He slid the button on the side of the mike to "on" and counted aloud. Sliding to "off," he pushed the "rewind" button on the recorder, then "stop," then "play." His voice was very clear. Again he pushed "stop." He ran the wire along the inside edge of the case, fitting it tightly into guide clips, bringing

[113]

the microphone to the top of the attaché. There he stuck his finger against the upper side and popped out a small square, obviously precut to the size of the microphone. He fit the mike snugly into the hole so the button extended to the outside of the case near the handle. It blended perfectly. Over it, on the inside, he snapped a strap attached firmly to the case. Taking the false bottom from the sheet, he laid it over the equipment and pushed it downward until it clicked into place. Not a thing protruded. To an unknowing eye, the case was empty. He closed it.

He changed clothes, picked up the attaché case and went out to the kitchen. Sandy was drying dinner dishes and at the same time talking into the telephone, nestled between her shoulder and cheek. Chris mouthed "I'm leaving" and she nodded acknowledgement. They kissed the air at each other simultaneously. Chris walked into the living room where the children were watching television.

"Give me a kiss goodbye," he said. The kids ran to him, kissed and hugged him and ran back to the sofa, anxious to rejoin the program on TV.

"Can you hold on a minute, Pat?" Sandy said into the phone. She put down the dish she had been drying, took the phone from her shoulder and laid it on the kitchen chair. "I'll see you in the morning," she said, walking to Chris, opening her arms. She slid them around his waist and pulled him close. He responded by putting his arms around her, still clutching the attaché case, and they kissed. Sandy's soft lips excited Chris and when she rubbed her lower body against him he felt for an instant like taking her to the bedroom to make passionate love. Sandy would have liked that, but she knew Chris wouldn't do it. Not right then, anyway. He was good to her, but many times she came second to his police work and from the strange way he had acted that night, she knew he would just pull away gently, kiss her on the nose and say he would see her in the morning. But she wanted him to know that he excited her, too, and that she was ready to go to bed and please him in any way she could—right then, if he so desired. She brushed herself against his pants and felt his manhood harden.

Chris pulled away gently, with knowing eyes gazing upon his wife. He leaned forward and kissed her softly on the nose. "See you in the morning," he said.

"I'll be waiting," she answered with a smile.

He smiled back and left.

Cruising his five-year-old Chevy in the slow lane of the expressway, Chris reconstructed the end of his conversation with Stuart Pierce. He remembered how Pierce had said he enjoyed the visit; and how lonely he got sometimes; and how he must have considered Chris pleasant, handsome and exciting. He recollected how Pierce had intentionally touched him by the door and his stomach tightened. The makeup and the smell of perfume were very vivid in his mind, and it sickened him.

Homosexuality disturbed Chris when he was close to it; close to it in the sense that it involved him.

Off the expressway, over the 59th Street bridge and into Manhattan, Stuart Pierce and homosexuality remained in Chris's head. He would love it if they could get together again soon, Pierce had said. At the time,

Chris had thought that highly improbable, but now he thought differently.

He pulled to the curb near the Corinthian. A ruddy-faced man, forty-five or so, alcoholic-thin, stood in a doorman's uniform out front. Looks like he's straight off the Bowery, Chris thought, approaching. The man looked at Chris, then turned away. Willie O'Brien would have opened the door, Chris thought, entering the lobby. Surprisingly, there was a semblance of order and normality and nothing was left to indicate that there had been a gun battle raging there early that morning. The cardinal velvet sofa had been replaced with a large circular settee of black kid leather. The mirror on the walls had not a crack. The carpet was without a stain or splinter of glass. Several people stood waiting at the elevators, two elderly couples registered at the front desk and a middle-aged woman in a black sequined gown sat impatiently on the leather couch.

Chris walked to the front desk and stood to the side, waiting for the elderly couples to finish up. The man behind the counter, late fifties, dark, thick-rimmed glasses, looked over, made no expression, and returned his attention to the people in front of him.

"Very good," the deskman said, retrieving two registration forms from the couples, "I'll have someone show you to your suites." He tapped a bell on the desk and before the ring had died completely a bellhop emerged from behind the mail partition. He, like the doorman, Chris thought, looked like a man who enjoyed his whiskey. "Ten thirty-six and ten thirty-eight," the man at the desk said, handing over two keys. The hop picked up two of the five pieces of luggage belonging to the elderly couples, explaining that he would return for the other three after he had shown them to their rooms, and led them off toward the elevators. Chris moved closer to the desk.

"Hiya, Chris," the clerk said.

Chris nodded.

"Damn, from what I heard, you're lucky to be alive. How do you feel?"

"I'm okay, Pete." Chris looked around. "It's unbelievable, though, how everything's been fixed up. Everything looks normal . . . like nothing happened."

"Yeah, they cleaned it up pretty good. They only finished about fifteen minutes ago."

Still amazed, shaking his head, Chris turned back to the desk.

A sudden veil of grief came over the clerk's face. He lowered his eyes. "Poor Willie."

Chris was silent. He knew Pete through Willie O'Brien; the two hotel employees had been good friends.

"Listen, Pete," Chris said, "can you do me a favor?"

"Sure, if it's legal," he chuckled, breaking the somber mood.

Chris smiled politely. "I'd like to check out a floor . . . the twenty-third floor." He didn't want to single out room 2320.

"No problem." The request was not a new one. Often the police asked for hotel records during an investigation. A veteran of many years in the business, the bespectacled clerk knew exactly what Chris wanted and bent down to open a file cabinet. He straightened up with a batch of index cards in his hand.

Chris took the cards. "Thanks, Pete." He shuffled

off to the side, thumbing through the packet. He plucked out the card for room 2320: "P. F. M. Incorporated. Representative—Stuart Pierce; Safe-deposit box—34; Annual rates, paid."

Nothing new. He really hadn't expected anything. A police nature was the only reason for poking around; other than wanting to be prepared. He moved back to the desk.

The clerk pushed his glasses from the tip of his nose. "Got something on somebody?" he said in a mock low voice.

Chris played along. "Maybe," he whispered. "Keep my visit quiet, Pete?"

Pete winked.

Pointing to the mail partition, Chris returned to his normal voice level. "Security man in the back?"

"Yep."

"I'd like to talk to him."

The clerk nodded, and Chris walked around the mail partition into the room marked "Employees Only." Aside from some of the safe-deposit boxes hanging off their hinges, irreparably bent, that room, too, showed little sign of the early morning robbery. A grey-haired bellhop sat at the table playing cards with a heavy-set man, acne-skinned and balding, wearing a suit a size too small. They both looked up at Chris, who flashed his shield and introduced himself. "I wonder if I can take a minute from your game?"

"Chris Chamber!" the man in the suit sputtered. "Was you the cop in the shootout last night?"

"Yes."

[118]

"Shit, you're gonna get a medal for that. No doubt about it."

Chris smiled at the fat man and changed the subject. "Are you on security?"

"Yep. I just finished my rounds. Why?"

"I was just wondering if you get much call to be on the twenty-third floor?" He was reluctant to be specific, not wanting his interest in room 2320 to go too far.

"Sure, every night I work. I gotta check every floor."

"How often do you work?"

"Four nights a week. Tonight's my first one back. Sure wish I'da been here last night, though." He was trying to bring the conversation back to the robbery.

Chris ignored the oblique reference. "Ever see anybody you recognized on the twenty-third floor?"

"Like who?"

"Anybody. Anybody at all that you might have said to yourself 'Hey, there goes so and so.' "

The fat man contemplated a while. "Not that I can think of. I seen a few movie stars in the lobby and I once seen the Vice President on the penthouse floor, but nobody on twenty-three."

Chris looked to the bellhop. "How about you? Get to twenty-three much?" The oldtimer shook his head. Chris looked disappointed. "Well, okay. Thanks a lot."

"Hey, who you looking for, anyhow?" the security man wanted to know.

"Nobody in particular. Will you do me a favor, though?" He turned toward the door. "Will you keep me in mind when you're on twenty-three and let me know if you see anybody important?" He turned back. "I'll be around again." The two men nodded and Chris left.

The clerk was busy with two women at the desk, so Chris walked past. He padded to the near wall on the right, picked up the house courtesy phone and dialed room 2320. It rang ten times before he hung up. He had not expected an answer. Crossing the lobby to the front door, he went out. A stiff breeze chilled the night air.

Back in his car, Chris took out his wallet and noted the home address on the business card Stuart Pierce had given him. He pulled away from the Corinthian, heading for Park Avenue, northbound. The streets of the Upper East Side, canyons amidst the skyscrapers, were relatively fast moving at night and after a short ten minutes he arrived at his 93rd Street destination, a modern, towering apartment building. He parked across the street. Checking the attaché case which lay beside him, he was satisfied it appeared empty. He got out of the car, locked it and headed for the fairly new, red-brick building. In the front lobby a uniformed security officer, chewing on an unlit stogie, sat reading the sports pages of the evening edition. Chris, without breaking stride, took out his shield, showed it to the guard and continued on to the elevators. He stepped into a waiting car and pressed eighteen. The elevator sped upward, floor lights blinking overhead, and with a metallic click came to a stop on eighteen. Before getting off, Chris pushed the microphone button near the handle of the attache case, activating the recorder inside. He walked left a few yards to apartment 18D, took a deep breath and rang the buzzer. Thinking of what he was about to do made him nervous, but he gathered himself. In an instant the door opened and Stuart Pierce appeared, maroon-velour, skin-tight jumpsuit with an oversized collar. His face was made up only half as much as at the hotel, but neatly applied mascara and rouge manifested his feminine demeanor. The smell of perfume was heavy.

"Why, Patrolman Chamber," he exclaimed. "What a happy, happy surprise."

Chris smiled. "Good evening, Mr. Pierce. I hope I'm not interrupting anything."

"Not at all, not at all. Please come in." Pierce stood aside, his open hand gesturing inside in a gallant manner. Chris entered.

The apartment was exquisite in its elaborateness. A dining area, magnificently adorned with a crystal chandelier, Italian Provincial table, buffet and armoire, opened into the opulence of the living room, fashioned in Renaissance. Deep-pile, shamrock-green shag spread throughout, lavishly complementing gold and black velvet walls. To the right, a fully equipped kitchen sparkled between marblelike floor and sculptured ceiling.

"Please, have a seat in the living room," Pierce said, closing the door. Chris sauntered to the green, crushed-velvet sofa and sat, setting the attaché case on the floor at his side.

"Would you like a drink?"

"Scotch and soda?"

"Certainly, certainly," Pierce bubbled on the way to the kitchen.

Chris looked around the room, awed by the tremendous wealth on exhibit, and after a few moments the homosexual reappeared.

Pierce handed his guest a tumbler. "Tell me, now," he said, sitting next to Chris on the sofa, "to what do I owe this visit from such a hero? I saw the newspapers. Very heroic, indeed."

Chris was uneasy. He was no stranger to danger and violence, but this was different. Never could he remember being the kind of nervous he was right then, sitting next to Stuart Pierce. Was it worth the sacrifice? he wondered.

"I'm here for two things," Chris stuttered, his queasiness evident, "some questions and . . ." His throat was dry. ". . . And you."

"Me!" Pierce exclaimed in a teasing voice of mock flattery. "Oh . . . you don't know how happy that makes me."

Chris felt sick. His heart wasn't in what he was about to say, but it was absolutely necessary if he were to get what he had come after. He stood and moved closer to Pierce, who looked up at him. He touched the homosexual gently on the cheek. Nausea gripped his stomach, but he forced himself to continue.

"Last night I felt very attracted to you," Chris said, sliding his fingers ever so softly along Pierce's cheek. "I know you were attracted to me, too." Pierce closed his eyes and savored the touch of the warm hand. "I thought about you all day and remembered how you said you were lonely. Well, I'm lonely, too, and I got to thinking that there's no sense in both of us suffering when we can get together and enjoy each other. You know what I mean?"

Pierce still had his eyes closed, responding to Chris's hand. "What's your first name?" he asked.

"Chris."

"Chris Chamber. That's nice. Well, Chris, I can't explain it, but I just knew you felt that way last night. I just knew it. And if you hadn't gotten in touch, I would have been crushed. But I must confess, I didn't expect you so soon." He paused. "Mmmm," he moaned, "your hands are so warm."

"I felt you were the kind of person who enjoyed a man with bulging muscles," Chris said. "Rippling muscles in his arms, a strong, hairy chest, a thin waist and powerful legs, bursting with muscles in the calf and in the thighs. Especially in the thighs; in the inner thighs; in the uppermost thighs." Uncomfortable, unwilling, Chris spoke clumsily. He was new at this game and it showed. "I know you're the kind of person who enjoys a real man. I know you can appreciate my yearning for someone like you who won't just take me for granted, who can give me satisfaction. I dreamt last night of sharing unknown pleasures with you. Of sharing my body with you. And in return, giving your body excitement and sensations it has never experienced."

Pierce cuddled Chris's caressing hand. "Oh, God!" His voice cracked in apprehension, his eyes still closed. "You're an answer to a prayer." His forehead beaded with perspiration, his heart pounded in expectation.

Chris pulled his hand away gently and sat down. "But first I have to ask you some questions. Let's get them out of the way." He rubbed cakey face powder from his palm.

Pierce was dumbfounded. "God almighty, you've got

[123]

to be kidding." He placed his hand on Chris's thigh. "Let the questions wait."

"No," said Chris in a firm voice, removing Pierce's hand. Not wanting to sound too harsh, in a soft tone he added: "It'll give us more time, Stuart."

"Oh, all right. But for goodness sakes, let's hurry up about it. I'm on the verge of an orgasm right now."

Chris took a small pad and a ballpoint pen from his shirt pocket. Everything up to this point would be erased on the tape, he thought, so the first thing to be done, since this was, in effect, the beginning, was to identify the voices. But he had to do so without making Pierce suspicious. "What's your real name?" he asked.

"Stuart Pierce. What the hell do you think?"

"I just want to be certain. Some people *do* change their names, you know."

"Hey, wait a minute. Why are you going to question me, anyhow? I thought that was the detective division's job."

"Oh, it is. But I've got to file a follow-up report on my initial investigation and I just want to be sure I've got all the right data." Pierce shrugged, seemingly convinced. "Some of this will sound basic, boring and repetitive, but please bear with it. Now, briefly, you are the representative of P. F. M. Incorporated, right?"

"Right."

"And you maintain a suite in the Corinthian Hotel on Fifth Avenue?"

"Right, room twenty-three twenty."

Chris scribbled on the pad sporadically to make Pierce think he was interested in notes for the report. With luck, the notion that this conversation was being recorded would never occur to him.

"And you rent a safe-deposit box at that hotel?"

"Number thirty-four."

"And last night in that box you had a gold, Baccardi watch and a diamond pinky ring, each valued at approximately fifteen hundred dollars."

"Right."

"What time did you get to your room last night?"

"About ten o'clock."

"And what time did you leave?"

"About eleven thirty this morning."

"Were you with anyone at the hotel, between 10 P.M. last night and 11:30 A.M. this morning?"

Pierce eyed Chris quickly. "What the hell does that matter?" He grew angry. "And what does the time I got to my room and left it have to do with the investigation?" It had nothing to do with the investigation. Chris was stretching. "My watch and ring were stolen out of a safe-deposit box on the ground floor. What difference does it make what I was doing in my room on the twenty-third floor, and who I was with at the time?"

"Please, Stuart, don't get upset," Chris said softly. "I assure you these questions are just routine. I don't know what difference it makes, seriously, but if I turn in a report without that information, my boss will have my head." He paused. "Come on now, take it easy."

Pierce swallowed it and nodded.

"Now, who were you with last night in your room at the Corinthian?" Chris asked again.

"I was alone."

Chris tightened his lips and shook his head. "You know, I thought you would level with me. I saw someone come out of your room last night. I think I know who it was, too, but I want you to tell me so I'll know for sure. Just for my own satisfaction. You know I wouldn't put it on the report or tell anyone else."

"I was alone, I'm telling you."

Chris shook his head again. "Boy oh boy. I really am disappointed in you." He had to be careful not to lead him on too much or the statement would be useless. "I said I saw who it was and that I won't tell anybody. Don't you trust me?" Pierce was silent. Chris stood up and unbuckled his pants, pretending to fix his shirt as the homosexual's eyes widened. He pulled down the zipper and lowered his trousers to the knees, exposing the bulge in his jockey shorts. He straightened his shirt in a cursory motion, making sure his host got a good look. Pierce's mouth opened as he fixed a stare on the outlined penis. His own began to throb. His throat was dry and perspiration again formed on his forehead. Chris adjusted his shirt properly and pulled up his pants. "You can trust me," he said, "you know that." He sat down and took Pierce by the hand. "Now why don't you tell me who was in your room last night." Pierce looked into his eyes. Chris guided Pierce's hand to his thigh. His stomach turned in disgust, but it would be worth it if the queer would only say the magic words. "Who was in your room last night?" he repeated.

It was too much for Pierce. "Oh, he's a bitch, anyway," he said.

"Who is?"

"You know damn well Harold Windsor was in my room last night. You couldn't have missed him in the hall."

Chris had difficulty hiding his enthusiasm. That was what he wanted to hear, and now he had it on tape. Now he held a card that sooner or later Captain Varing would have to reckon with.

Pierce stood, aware that he had said something that he shouldn't have. Even if Chamber had known, he should not have admitted it. He comforted himself, though, with the fact that he could just deny it if it should ever come up again. What difference did it make what he said now? He would deny everything later. Besides, once he took Chamber to the bedroom, the officer would be in no position to ever tell anybody anything.

Little did Pierce know that the tape recorder whirred noiselessly in the attaché case. And Chris was not about to let the subject drop. "So Harold Windsor was in your room last night, huh? Why?"

"Come on, Chamber, don't play games with me. Your police commissioner is a switch-hitter. He was there to fuck me. You knew that before you came here."

Chris couldn't have asked for better lines for the tape recorder if he had written them himself.

"How long has your relationship with Windsor been going on?"

Pierce shook his head. "That's enough questions and answers."

Chris would press the issue. He moved next to Pierce and touched his cheek gently again. Pierce relaxed.

[127]

"Come on, Stuart, you're making me think you don't trust me again."

"I can't tell you anything else," Pierce said, eyes closed.

"How long has Windsor been fucking you?" Pierce was silent. As a last resort Chris slid his hand slowly from the homosexual's cheek, down the front of his jumpsuit, and brought it to rest on his outer thigh. Softly, but firmly, he moved toward the inside. "Is he good?"

"No more questions. No more answers," Pierce said softly. "If you want to know more about your police commissioner you're going to have to ask him yourself."

It was enough. Police Commissioner Harold Windsor was a part-time homosexual and Chris had it on tape. But there was something Chris didn't know: that Pierce was not just another homosexual, that he was probably the king of the New York pimps who paid plenty for police protection.

"Well, if you're not going to answer my questions, Stuart, then I'm going to leave." He withdrew his hand and stepped away.

"You're kidding," Pierce said. He gestured toward his bulging groin. "My God, I'm ready to burst."

"Sorry, Stuart, but you're holding back on me and I don't like it." He retrieved his attaché case. "Besides, I've got to go to work."

Pierce saw through the charade. "You didn't come here for me. You came to find out what you could."

"There you go mistrusting me again. Oh, ye of little faith."

"You bitch."

[128]

"Listen, Stuart, if you ever want to get in touch with me, call me at the Twenty-first Precinct. But only if you feel like talking." He turned and walked toward the door.

"You son of a bitch." Pierce's voice was loud.

"And if you call and I'm not there, just leave a message." Without turning around, Chris opened the door, waved, and was gone.

"You son of a bitch," Pierce screamed. He sat down on the sofa steaming. He had been taken in and he didn't like it. He sat for a few minutes, putting his thoughts together. He wanted to strike back. Suddenly, something struck him and he smiled. He moved to the phone and dialed. A few seconds passed, then: "Commissioner Stephens, please," he said. There was a pause. "Oh, okay. Would you ask him to call Mr. Stuart Pierce when you hear from him, please." He hung up. He sat back on the sofa, gloating that he would be able to get even with Patrolman Chris Chamber.

On his way to the Two-One, Chris was nearly ecstatic over his success with Pierce. Stopping for a light, he reached across the front seat, opened the attaché case and popped out the false bottom. He pushed "rewind," the recorder whirred; then "stop," then "play." There were a few seconds of silence until a door opened, then Pierce's voice: "Why, Patrolman Chamber. What a happy, happy surprise." He listened to the tape as he drove and when he reached the stationhouse, he parked and waited until it had finished before he left the car. Everything had come out as clear as it could.

He entered the stationhouse with his case in hand and

was greeted by a uniformed patrolman, Marty Winthrop, who was on his way out. They stopped outside the captain's office.

Tall and thin, Winthrop talked in a deep voice. "Hi, Chris. Congratulations."

"Thanks, Marty."

"I hear they're writing it up for the medal of honor."

"You're kidding."

"Too bad Joe will be getting it posthumously. He deserved a better death."

Chris nodded as Winthrop went on about the details of the wake and funeral.

"Day after tomorrow. Nine o'clock at St. Cecelia of Avalon in Bethpage."

Chris nodded again. "Instructions posted, too, I guess."

"Yeah. You gotta do a late one tonight? You'd think you'd get a day off after getting shot at with a machine gun and a forty-five."

"Through rain and sleet and hail of bullets . . ."

"We can all do without excitement like last night."

"Amen."

Captain Varing, dressed in civilian clothes, came out of his office, heading home after a long day.

Winthrop saw him first. "Well, I've gotta be going, Chris. I really hope you get that medal of honor; you deserve it."

"Thanks, Marty. Take it easy."

Varing approached. "Chamber, I'm glad I saw you. I'd like to talk to you if you've got a little time."

"Sure." Chris was apprehensive.

"Doing a late tour?"

"Yes, sir."

"Good. You've got plenty of time." They walked into Varing's office, an austere room with a bare wooden desk, a swivel chair behind it, a straight-backed chair in front and on the wall to the right a blown-up print of the famous flag-raising at Iwo Jima. Chris wondered if Varing's Marine Corps had been like his own. Filthy with soot and ashes, the floor was also bare wood and echoed the footsteps.

"Sit down," Varing said and Chris complied. The captain took a seat behind the desk. "First thing first. Congratulations are in order."

"Thank you, sir."

"That was a fine piece of work. I understand the inspector has taken it upon himself to put you and Hummel in for the medal of honor."

"So I've heard."

"I don't think there is much chance that you won't get it. Especially with all the newspaper and television coverage."

"It's really the best honor the Department can bestow and I'd be proud as hell . . ."

"Well, we'll see what happens." Then he paused. "I don't mind telling you, though, Chamber, that the real reason I want to talk to you now is to see if you've reconsidered my request to ease up on the Administrative Code and Health Code summonses."

"I've given it a lot of thought, sir, and I've decided to issue summonses."

"I was pretty sure that's what you'd say." He leaned

[131]

back on his chair. "I've requested that you be transferred out of the Two-One."

Chris drew his lips tight in anger.

"I know you're a big hero and a very active man, probably the most active I've got right now, but you've got to understand that I cannot tolerate a prima donna, and you've got to learn how to obey orders."

"Orders to refrain from serving a summons on a merchant who's on the pad are not legitimate in my book, sir."

Varing pounded his fist on the desk. "You are in no position to judge what is legitimate and what is not, Patrolman Chamber. You seem to forget who the hell is the commanding officer in this precinct. I wear the bars, not you. I give the orders and you obey. It's as simple as that."

"With all due respect, sir," Chris said very calmly, "I'm only doing my job."

"Your job is to obey your commanding officer. You can take your heroics and stick them up your ass."

Chris was silent.

Varing paused a few seconds to regain his composure. "There's really no sense in my blowing up like this and I apologize. You *will* be transferred. You have my word."

Chris answered quickly. "I wouldn't bet on it, if I were you . . . SIR."

Varing's face turned a deep red and the veins bulged in his forehead. "Don't push me too far, Chamber. I'll have your fuckin' ass on a silver platter."

"Is that all, sir?"

"Get the fuck out of here."

Chris turned and exited the office.

The captain followed him to the door and slammed it behind him.

Chris was smiling.

CHAPTER 6

PIRUNDINI'S restaurant in the Bay Ridge section of Brooklyn enjoyed the reputation of serving first-class Italian meals. In an excellent location, a few short blocks from the Belt Parkway, the building, a modern façade of brown fiberglass imitation brick, was equipped with a thirty-five-car parking lot which filled and stayed filled during luncheon and dinner hours, always an indication of the capacity crowd within. Primarily a meeting place for local businessmen in the afternoon and residents in the evening, the restaurant was visited at one time or another by almost every connoisseur of good food living in or visiting the metropolitan area.

Inside, the piano bar, conveniently situated near the entrance, was jammed two-people-deep, while miniskirted waitresses shuttled cocktails to the tables. Red and white checkered tablecloths, melting candles in empty wine bottles and an abundance of healthy plants set the background in a simple but comfortable decor. A spicy aroma filled the air.

In a secluded corner in the rear, specially designated for VIPs, Police Commissioner Harold Windsor and First Deputy Commissioner Lawrence Stephens sat in a dimly lit booth, eating their lunch. Stephens had finished a double order of shrimp cocktail and was nursing a Scotch and soda, while Windsor waded through an oversized entree of veal parmigiana and spaghetti. Pirundini's was Stephens' suggestion because the first deputy was familiar with the restaurant and was assured of privacy for conversation.

Stephens was telling Windsor that he had been in touch by telephone with Stuart Pierce. ". . . And I called him back this morning."

"What did he have to say?" Windsor asked with a mouthful of veal.

"He was paid a visit last night by a Patrolman Chamber, who asked a lot of questions."

The commissioner stopped chewing and stared at Stephens with quizzical eyes. "Chamber? Chris Chamber?"

Stephens nodded. "The same."

"God damn it. I told you he recognized me in the hallway at the Corinthian."

"No doubt he did."

"What the hell was he doing up there anyhow? You'd think after a goddamn shootout, he'd want to take it easy."

[135]

"From what I gather after talking to the inspector who responded to the scene, that's exactly what he was trying to do. One of the men in the squad asked him to help check out box holders, so he agreed, figuring he could get lost for a couple of hours. Running into you in the hall was just a coincidence."

"Yeah, but dropping in on Pierce last night was no coincidence."

Stephens nodded assent.

Windsor cut a piece of meat and hurried it into his mouth. He was understandably very sensitive about his homosexual life and understandably concerned when threatened with public disclosure. "So he's on to me."

"Don't get excited. We can handle this."

"What the hell was he after at Pierce's?"

"I'm not sure. But it could have been very innocent. We can't let our imaginations run away."

"What reason did he give Pierce?"

"A follow-up investigation about the safe-deposit box."

"That's bullshit. The squad handles that. He's after something."

Stephens took a sip from his glass. "Maybe."

"What did Pierce have to say?"

"He said Chamber asked a lot of questions. He was mainly concerned with who was in the hotel room with him just before he got there."

"Did he tell him?"

"He said he didn't have to, Chamber said he saw you in the hall and wanted him to admit it. Pierce claims he refused."

Windsor chewed a little faster. "What do you think?"

[136]

"Pierce is hard to figure, but who can trust a fag?" It was out before Stephens realized what he had said.

Windsor let it pass.

"We should find out for sure what he said, shouldn't we?"

"I've got every intention of doing just that."

"What's with this Chamber? Think he's looking to get on the pad?"

"I doubt it. I doubt he even knows about it. His name has been popping up all over the fuckin' place lately and just yesterday I talked to his commanding officer, Otto Varing, about him. Chamber is square business. He's been knocking over the merchants in the Two-One and Varing doesn't like it. Seems Varing has cerain, shall I say, 'arrangements' with the businessmen and Chamber isn't honoring them, so he wants him shipped back to Bedford-Stuyvesant where he came from."

Windsor stopped chewing again. "Do you think he's after *me*?" His face was deadpan.

"I really don't know."

"Square business, huh. I wonder if he's ever had five big ones waved in front of his face . . ."

"I'm getting the full sheet on him now, but from what I've heard so far, he's not taking a nickel from anybody."

Windsor wasn't listening. ". . . Funny how the physical presence of money can make a man change his tune."

"But that's the point. He already has changed his tune."

The commissioner looked to his first deputy.

"He took when he was stationed in Bedford-Stuy-vesant. For some reason he doesn't take now."

[137]

"That doesn't make sense. It should be the other way around."

The deputy commissioner began thinking out loud. "He drinks only occasionally, he doesn't smoke, he keeps his private life to himself."

A waiter interrupted. "Everything all right, gentlemen?"

"Yes, thank you," Stephens said, snapping back to reality.

They ordered coffee.

A bus boy cleared the table.

Windsor felt he had good reason to be concerned over Patrolman Chamber. "Has he ever turned another member of the force in?"

Stephens took another sip of his Scotch. "Not that I know of. It entered my mind at first that he might be waging a one-man crusade against corruption, but I don't think so. It's his own show."

"We can't afford to take any chances."

"I know."

Windsor was shaken.

"Has he made any bribery collars on civilians?" the commissioner asked.

"Unofficially, no, but I won't know for sure till I get a full report on him."

"When will that be?"

"It should be on my desk right now."

"Give me a call later, will you, and let me know." There was a subservient quality in nearly everything the police commissioner said. It was better that Stephens ran the show and Windsor knew it. His next question, an

[138]

inevitable one, confirmed that. "What do you think we should do?"

Stephens was prepared. "We've got to see what he's up to without stirring his interest, just in case everything is as innocent as we'd like to think."

"How about bringing him in on the transfer to feel him out?"

The deputy nodded.

Windsor continued. "It's not that unusual that the first deputy commissioner should want to speak to someone before transferring him at his commanding officer's request, is it?"

Stephens was well aware that that was not standard operational procedure, but he wanted to talk to Chamber and he didn't really care how it looked. "I'll notify his command this afternoon. I'll make an appointment for tomorrow."

The waiter brought coffee and left.

Windsor was still very uneasy. "Be careful with this guy when you talk to him," he said, sipping from his coffee cup.

Stephens masked his condescension. "Don't worry, I'll take care of it."

"When you get his file, I'd like to take a look at it."

Stephens nodded acquiescence.

A few moments of silence and the coffee was finished.

Stephens picked up the conversation. "Until we find out for sure what his intentions are, I'm going to put him under twenty-four-hour surveillance."

"Good. You're using Wilson, I hope."

[139]

The deputy commissioner nodded. "Yeah, I'll get to him this afternoon."

"How about a wire on his phone?"

"I told you I'd take care of it, Commissioner."

"You'll let me know what's happening on a daily basis?"

Stephens motioned for the check, but the waiter approached and smiled.

"Compliments of Mr. Pirundini."

Stephens had expected the courtesy. "Please tell Mr. Pirundini we are very grateful." He handed the waiter a three-dollar tip.

"It could very well be we're letting our imaginations get the best of us," Stephens said, rising from the booth.

Windsor rose, too, with a look that at best could be described as sardonic. He was not so optimistic.

CHAPTER 7

CHRIS parked his car on Third Avenue and walked three blocks, attaché case in hand, turning right on to East 20th Street to see the New York City Police Academy, the tallest building on the street, rectangular, freshly steamed, white brick, rising high before him. In front, three grey-uniformed probationary patrolmen leaned against a car, catching a smoke between classes. Chris recalled his own probation eight years earlier. He passed the rookies and turned left into the recessed entrance of the Academy. Through glass doors, he flashed his shield to a uniformed patrolman, sauntered a few feet to the elevators, and pushed the down button. He got off at the basement and took his time down an azure tiled corridor until he reached a pair of swinging doors, which he entered. Beneath him, at the bottom of five asphalt stairs, a swimming pool stretched the length of an echo-filled cavern, every inch of the floor, walls and ceiling tiled with blue plasticlike squares. Four men were in the water, playing a game called "Dunk and Give," a wrestling free-for-all aimed at dunking opponents into submission, and their voices bounced around in the chasm.

Chris was no stranger to the Police Academy swimming pool, nor was he to ocean water. He had been trained years before as a Marine reconnaissance diver and had been at the top of his class. He never swam without recalling the four miles of open ocean it took to earn his flippers.

He liked to stay fit and so he was a regular visitor to the pool. Every chance he got, before four to twelves and after midnight to eights, he'd stop in to work out. And the pool was only five minutes from the Twenty-first Precinct.

Today in particular he needed a workout: to forget the Corinthian and Stuart Pierce. He descended the stairs and headed to the right for the instructor's office, specially equipped with a large picture window to afford a view of the pool at all times. Inside, standing with his back to the door, a man, clad only in a T-shirt and a bathing suit, hung clothing in a six-foot, metal locker, one of several around the room. A walnut desk, papers cluttered on top, sat in the corner by the window.

"Hi, Barney," said Chris.

The man turned and smiled. In his fifties, he was in extraordinary shape. His chest was extremely well-developed, a swimmer's chest.

"Chris," Barney said, happy to see him, "I was won-

[142]

dering when you were going to come in. Congratulations, son. You did a fine job." Obviously he was referring to the shootout.

They shook hands. Barney Monaghan meant a great deal to Chris. He respected him not only as a fine, dedicated police officer, but also as a man, and he was glad to be his friend. There was no question that Barney thought Chris's performance in the line of duty was heroic, but it was also expected.

"Thanks," Chris said simply, and they both characteristically left a lot unsaid.

"You here to work out?" Barney asked.

"If I can."

"Sure."

Barney looked out at the pool. "They'll be out of there by the time you change."

Chris glanced at the clock on the office wall, thanked Barney and walked through an unmarked door that led to the instructor's personal locker room.

Barney sat on his desk and stared in thought out the window. He was glad Chris had come, and wished he came more often. In his fourteen years as swimming instructor for the Police Academy Recruits Training School he had seen many good swimmers. He had coached metropolitan swimming champions, college stars, even former members of the United States Olympic Swimming Team, but no one he had seen could compare to Chris Chamber.

Barney saw a great deal of himself in Chris. He, too, had kept up with his swimming after becoming a police officer and he, too, had had a distant goal in mind that drove him to the pool, even when he didn't feel like making the trip. However, when he was a young patrolman he had had to travel to Brooklyn from his home in the Bronx to pursue his ambitions, for the indoor pool at the Saint George Hotel was the only one in the city at that time that was open at night and was not too crowded to allow a person to swim nonstop from one end to the other.

When Barney was younger he had been obsessed with the challenge of the English Channel. It had been on his mind constantly and had been the driving force behind his daily trek to the Saint George. Chris, however, had no desire to swim the English Channel, despite Barney's urging. His goal was to swim the shark-infested Molokai Channel in Hawaii. Separating the island of Oahu from Molokai, the twenty-seven-mile channel had been crossed successfully only once and Chris had been stationed briefly in Hawaii when the feat was accomplished. He had read the newspaper coverage with great interest, surprised that the trip had taken over sixteen hours. The swimmer had averaged one and a half knots at fifty-two strokes per minute and Chris believed he was capable of better than that. The trick, however, was to cross the shark-infested waters in one piece. But he was not as obsessed with swimming the Molokai Channel. Certainly not obsessed as Barney Monaghan had been about the English Channel. That particular swim was too played out for Chris because too many people had swum it. The Molokai, on the other hand, had been crossed only once, though attempted many times.

In a more practical vein Barney was also glad to see

Chris come to the pool for a workout as often as possible because he knew very well that the job of being a police officer was a very demanding one. Barney felt as Chris that swimming was the best exercise, and numerous times he had suggested a mandatory training program for police officers to keep them in shape. He was always put off and it incensed him that the Department would not make an attempt to keep its men in condition, especially those who neglected to help themselves. Barney never ceased to be amazed at the number of poor physical specimens working on the New York City Police Department. From the flabbiest oldtimer to the skinniest recruit, as police officers, their very lives might one day depend on their condition. Many of them, he felt, could be shaped up rather effortlessly with a regular swimming program, but neither the administrators nor the specimens themselves saw the value.

Chris didn't train as rigorously as Barney would have liked, but, even so, Barney was convinced that he could probably break the English Channel record. Barney himself had forgone an attempt on the English Channel when he was a young police officer only because the Department would not allow it. You just didn't do things like that in those days. He had been fit and fully prepared to tackle the challenge, but the police commissioner denied the request, emphasizing that it was too dangerous. He had contemplated leaving the Department because of it. Things certainly were drastically different on the job thirty years ago. Staring into the pool he thought back to when he was on uniformed patrol in midtown Manhattan. A police officer was respected then. He was the champion of the people and tolerated no backtalk from those who stood in his way. There were no gangs hanging out on street corners, at least when he was in the area. The teenagers knew that if he caught them standing around looking for trouble, he'd give them a good boot in the ass and send them on their way. And when they got home, if their parents found out that a police officer had reprimanded them, they, too, would have given them a good boot in the ass. Nowadays, though, he thought, if there were fifteen kids hanging out on a corner and you approached, not only didn't anybody move away, they called you names, spit at you, flicked cigarette butts at you. If you gave them a boot in the ass, you were likely to have a war on your hands. And if they went home and told their parents, right away it was: "Did he hit you? Are you hurt? Can we sue the city?" But, then, the police officers had been a lot closer to the community when he pounded a beat. With the advent of the radio car, radio motor patrol moved the cop on the street indoors and made him a stranger in a strange land.

Barney's thoughts were interrupted as Chris emerged from the locker room wearing a red, white and blue striped bathing suit.

"They left already, huh?" Chris said, looking out to the empty pool.

Barney looked through the window. "You know, I'm sitting here dreaming; I never noticed them leave. My mind just isn't in focus today."

Chris chuckled. "Today?" They both had a laugh.

Barney walked out to the pool and Chris followed.

"When you taking your vacation this summer?" Barney asked.

"One week in July and two in August. Why?"

"Just wondering. How'd you like an all-expenses-paid trip to an exotic land? Plane, hotel, meals, tips, everything paid for."

"What sweepstakes do I have to win?"

"No sweepstakes. You just have to swim the Channel."

"You never give up with that, do you?" Chris said with a smile, although he was annoyed that Barney brought it up so often.

"I have confidence in you, that's why. I know you can break the mark."

"I need much more training than I'm ready to sacrifice time for, Barney, and, besides, if I'm going to swim any channel I'm going to be greeted at the end of the trip by a beautiful Polynesian girl in a grass skirt."

"That can be arranged."

"You know what I mean."

Barney shrugged in disappointment.

"What's this free trip to an exotic land?" Chris asked.

"England."

"England! You call that exotic?"

"Well, I just didn't want to say England and get turned down right away."

Chris shook his head. "I've gotta hand it to you, Barney, you're a persevering gentleman. What have you finagled?"

"Great Britain Overseas Airways will put up the money in return for the promotion value. They'd play it up big and drum up all sorts of publicity. You'd be an overnight star."

"How the hell did you get a deal like that out of them?"

"Oh, a friend of a friend. You know."

"Yeah, I know."

"Includes your wife and children. Not a penny out of your pocket."

"Man, this must've been a real good friend of a friend."

Barney laughed. "It includes my wife and kids, too." Chris stared poker-faced for an instant, then burst into laughter. They both held their stomachs in pain for a minute, unable to catch their breath, until finally they regained their composure.

Barney wiped a tear from his cheek. "Damn it," he said, "another good deal down the drain."

"Even if I agreed, which I won't," Chris said, "you'd still have the Department to contend with."

"I know, I know. But they're bending. They're not half as reluctant now as they were when I brought it up last year."

"They'll never give in."

"No, they will. You'll see. There's too much potential promotion to let something like this go by for too long. It wouldn't surprise me if they come looking for you pretty soon, asking you to do it as a favor to the department."

"Then I'd surely turn it down." He was just kidding and Barney knew it.

"I wish they'da let me try it when I was in shape," Barney said.

"So do I. Then you wouldn't be asking me every time you see me."

"I just hate to see talent like yours go to waste, that's all, Chris. I don't mean to bug you."

"I know, Barney. I'm just breaking your balls. You don't bug me."

Barney smiled.

Chris walked to the edge and dove into the water. He would swim at least three miles, sixty-six laps, before getting out. Some days he would swim two or three times that amount, depending on how he felt and how much time he had before work. This morning he had plenty of time and planned on pushing himself.

With every complete stroke Barney was visible for an instant on the side of pool. As Chris swam, he thought. He had great confidence in Barney and was tempted to tell him about the police commissioner, but hesitated because his friend was a police officer. As much as he trusted Barney, he had convinced himself that the fewer people who knew the better, the fewer police officers who knew, the more advantageous his position, should he ever have to play his hand. Besides, how could Barney help? It was just better all around, Chris thought, if he didn't know anything. In that way, also, he wouldn't have the responsibility of having to make certain he didn't slip in a conversation or mention it to anyone else. Chris could only confide his newfound information to a non-police officer and the best bet was his priest friend Frank Roselli.

He cut through the water, concentrating on form when he could, sometimes pretending that he was back in high school at a big meet. Stroke, stroke, complete

[149]

stroke and follow through. Kick, kick, knees straight, kick. Turn, head down, knees tucked, twist, spring. But his concentration wasn't as it should have been. After seven miles he felt he had had enough. He pulled himself from the pool and walked to the office. Barney had long given up watching and was sitting at the desk catching up on some paper work.

Barney looked at his watch. "That was a good workout."

"I feel great," Chris said.

"You looked pretty good out there, too. You're really disciplining yourself lately. I think that might have been one of your most important problems."

"I felt distracted today, Barney."

"I could tell."

Chris nodded. "I'm going to change. How about some lunch at Bill's . . . on me."

"Thanks but I've got a lot of work here. I'd better pass."

Chris went to the locker room to shower and change and was in the office again in fifteen minutes. Barney was on the phone, so he waved, exiting through the swinging doors. He made his way through the hall, up the elevator and out of the building, again flashing his shield to the man at the door. He started off toward Second Avenue. Rounding the corner he could see Bill's restaurant in the middle of the block. It was his habit to stop in Bill's for a bite to eat after every swimming session. He reached the restaurant and stepped inside.

Along each wall, paneled with cheap, sticky-looking wood, a row of photographs hung eye-level. To the left, behind the cashier, were a half-dozen shots of the incumbent mayor with Bill Lombardi, the owner, a short five-five, olive-skinned, dark eyes, a neatly trimmed grey moustache and straight grey hair combed back, overhanging his collar. To the right hung eight or nine more with Bill and various city and police officials. In the rear, the dingy restaurant widened a bit, then narrowed again into a greasy, stain-filled kitchen, visible through the door that swung open as two waiters shuffled back and forth. The walls back there were also lined with photos. Under the photographs black vinyl booths showed foam padding through numerous rips and slashes. The lighting at the booths along the walls was poor and the bare slatted floor was a quarter inch thick with grime. There was a strong smell of garlic.

Bill's was a police officer hangout and despite the overall dismal atmosphere and inexpensive look about the place, the food was excellent.

From the rear, Bill, in a dark blue suit and white tie, recognized Chris and approached to seat him in the lunchtime crowd. The only empty booth was in the right-side rear.

From the waiter he ordered a meatball hero and resisted the temptation to have a beer. Before he could begin to think about the coming afternoon's activities, his attention was directed to the front door. Entering was a well-tanned brunette, a clinging-nylon blue dress outlining every curve. Sleek, statuesque legs rose into well-rounded hips, a thin waist and firm, voluptuous breasts. She wore no bra. Her hair fell past the shoulders. As she approached, Chris could see that her eyes were a soft blue, her lips pink. She wore little or no makeup.

He was entranced. He was self-conscious about staring at her, but that she appeared a bit upset only made him more curious. Opening a small brown change purse in her left hand, she removed a coin. She walked straight at Chris, then turned to the phone on the wall near his booth. Placing the open purse on the service counter beneath the telephone, she removed the receiver and started her right hand toward the slit. The dime dropped to the floor. As she bent to retrieve it, her curvy buttocks came to rest on her heels and the skirt slid up to the top of her thighs. Her knees were pointed toward Chris. He didn't want to be obvious, but he couldn't resist looking as she groped around the dimly lit floor, her dress hitching higher and higher. Her legs spread for an instant and Chris saw the white panties deep within the darkness of her thighs. His loins told him that he wanted her before his mind did. He had never been so excited by a woman before in such a casual, social setting. She was undoubtedly one of the most electrifyingly attractive women he had ever seen.

She couldn't find the coin and stood up. Stepping to the phone, she took another dime from her purse and dialed. It was impossible for Chris not to hear the conversation.

"Hi, Mike," she said. "I had an accident. I'm okay, but the car's a mess." There was a pause. Her face indicated her increased disappointment. "God, Mike, it wasn't my fault. I'm sorry about the car." Another pause. She appeared on the verge of tears. "I thought you'd be more concerned about *me*." She listened for a moment. Then softly, "Okay, goodbye." She held the phone from her ear for a few seconds before hanging up.

The waiter brought lunch, but Chris never took his eyes off the woman as she stood by the phone, obviously shaken. Moving her hand to her brow, she knocked the open change purse from the service counter to the floor, numerous coins and keys spilling and rolling. Chris seized the opportunity and jumped up. He rushed to her side as she bent once again to collect her things. His heart pounded as her skirt pulled high, revealing her copper legs to the naked thigh. He picked up a few coins and two keys without saying a word, and she accepted his help in silence. When he had gathered all he could see, he held out his hand to hers.

"I think that's it," he said.

She looked at what he had given her and nodded. "My car keys. They're all that really count. Thank you." They stood.

Chris sensed her anxiety. "Listen," he said, "I couldn't help but hear your conversation and I'd like to help if I can."

"That's very kind, but I'm okay. Thanks, anyhow."

"You really should sit down and relax a few minutes. There's always the danger of shock after an accident." He smiled and enjoyed the knowledge that he had said the right thing.

She smiled, and her eyes caught the dim light of the restaurant nicely. "You sound like you've been in a lot of accidents."

[153]

"I've never been *in* one, but I've been *at* hundreds."
She tilted her head in puzzlement. "I'm a police officer,"
Chris said.

She nodded understandingly. "Oh, I see."

"Why don't you just sit down for a little while," he
said, motioning to his booth. "You'll feel a lot better."
He was taken with her innocent look. She had a girlish
way about her, yet her mature, alluring body was that
of a woman.

She studied him boldly for a moment. "What's your
name?" she asked.

"Chris Chamber."

"I'm Sabra Garrett." She walked over to the booth.

Chris breathed deeply. Her presence quickened his
pulse. "Sabra," he said as they sat. "Very nice. I've
never heard that name before."

She nodded and smiled. Obviously she had heard
that statement many times before, and Chris silently
cursed himself for saying what an ordinary man might.

"Have you eaten yet?" Chris asked. "How about
some lunch?"

"No, thank you. Go ahead and finish."

"How about something to drink?"

She hesitated.

"Come on. It'll make *me* feel better."

"Okay. After that experience I need something. A
whiskey sour would be nice."

"Good." He smiled, motioned for the waiter and
ordered.

He took a bite of his sandwich. "Why don't you have
half," he said.

[154]

She was amused. "I'm really not hungry. But the drink will be fine, thanks."

He took another bite, feeling awkward eating alone. Even so, he was glad to see her relax a bit and at ease in his presence.

"How bad's the car?"

"I can't drive it. The right front wheel is nearly off. I had to leave it at the collision shop that towed me."

Chris realized it might not be such a good idea to talk about the accident. "Where you from?"

"New Jersey . . . West Caldwell."

They talked. Chris told her a little about being a police officer and it apparently intrigued her. For her turn she told him she was married. He had guessed as much. The man she had called obviously was her husband.

Once again Chris caught himself staring, but he couldn't help it. Every once in a while as he ate he could feel her looking at him, and he enjoyed that.

When he had finished the sandwich, she had finished all but a sip of her drink.

"Well, I'd better get going," she said. "Thanks a lot for the drink . . . and the advice about shock. I do feel better." She smiled and got up to slide from the booth.

Chris didn't want it to end there. If she left he'd never see her again and the thought was devastating, all the more so because he had never been affected by a woman quite the way he had been affected by Sabra. In his mind's eye, he saw them in bed together, her warmth against his. His brain raced to delay the emptiness he would feel when they parted. "Can I give you

[155]

a lift somewhere?" he asked, standing.

"Well, I was going to take a cab to the Port Authority."

"Good, I'm going that way." It hardly mattered that he really wasn't, and it didn't matter where she said she was headed, because he would have said he was going that way.

She was pleased that he offered. "Great. I'd appreciate it." The waiter approached with the bill. Chris tipped him, walked over to pay the cashier, and then held the door for Sabra.

"I knew it," she said, walking out of the restaurant.

"Knew what?"

"Chivalry is not dead." Her tone was teasing.

Chris grinned.

"The knight helping the damsel in distress," she added.

"It's the boy scout in the policeman."

They talked as they strolled slowly to the car, each probing, anxious to know the other. Chris was mesmerized by her beauty and could sense her interest in him. When they reached the car he unlocked the passenger side door and opened it.

"You know," she said, "there was no doubt in my mind that you'd open the door for me."

"How so?"

"It's what any good knight would do . . . Sir Chamber." She giggled.

Chris responded with a mock gesture of gallantry, a sweeping motion to the front seat.

Sabra's face grew serious as she got in. "You're one

[156]

of a rare breed, Chris. It's not hard for a woman to like a man like you."

Chris once more was distracted by the snug-fitting dress as it moved up to reveal long, slender legs and a soft whiteness deep between well-toned thighs. He felt self-conscious, almost silly as his body responded with a throbbing erection. He closed the door and encircled the car to the driver's side, as Sabra leaned across the seat and opened the latch. As he got in he thought he should never feel silly about such a reaction to this woman.

"A bit of female chivalry, eh?" he said, getting in.

"The girl scout in the damsel in distress." They smiled at each other.

On the way uptown, they chatted idly, Chris trying very hard not to be too obvious about his attraction to her sensuously muscled legs. He fantasized as he drove. She would sit closer. He would place his hand on the soft, warm skin of her thigh and stroke gently upward to her sex. He would have her body close to his. He would excite her and feel her writhe to his touch.

But all too quickly, they had arrived at the Port Authority Building on Eighth Avenue. Again Chris felt empty at the thought of parting. But it was time.

"You know," he said, "you made my whole day." He was determined to see her again.

"I enjoyed being with you, Chris."

He hesitated, searching for the right words to propose another meeting. "What would you say if I asked you for your telephone number?"

She was slow in responding. "I'd say no." She said it quietly.

Chris was crushed and showed it. Did she regret it, he wondered.

"Unless, of course," she added, "you agreed to call only between nine and five on weekdays." She was smiling now. What an extraordinary woman. He didn't mind the teasing.

Chris smiled, too. "Agreed." He opened the glove compartment, pulled out a small pad with a pen clipped on and handed it to her.

She wrote the number. "If anyone but me ever answers," she said, "just pretend you have the wrong number."

Chris nodded.

Their eyes locked for a few seconds. "I'll call," he said.

Sabra's smile told him that she would be waiting. She got out of the car without saying a word.

CHAPTER 8

THE white and green panel truck, shining clean in the late-morning sun, glided slowly along tree-lined Cedar Street, pulling to a stop on the corner in front of number twenty-one. The burly, raven-haired driver got out of the vehicle, stepped to the rear door and opened it. He took from the floor a belt laden with a hand drill, pliers and screwdrivers and slung it around his hips. Also from the floor he removed a black, rectangular tool box. He closed the door to the van and strode slowly, deliberately, to the house. He rang the bell. A few seconds passed before the door swung open and Sandy Chamber appeared.

She saw the truck and belt. "Oh, hi. Come on in." She opened the door wider and stepped to the side as the man entered. "It's been dead all morning," she ex-

[159]

plained, closing the door and leading the way to the kitchen. "There's no dial tone, no sound at all. I had to call from a neighbor's."

In the kitchen the repairman set down the tool box, picked up the receiver of the white wall phone and listened. There was nothing. He stuck a screwdriver into the bottom of the plastic casing and popped it off. Checking the extension cord connection, he was satisfied it was not the trouble. "Sometimes these wires have a way of pulling loose," he said. "But these look okay." He probed another area of the exposed mechanism with his screwdriver.

Sandy stood watching with mild interest. Although she knew nothing about telephones or electronics, she enjoyed watching people who did. The doorbell interrupted and she excused herself. Quietly taking the opportunity to work unobserved, the telephone man picked up the receiver and unscrewed the mouthpiece. Turning the end upside down, he shook it. A round metallic unit, the voice amplifier, fell into his hand. He quickly slipped it into his left pants pocket. From the right pocket he retrieved another voice amplifier, seemingly identical to the one he had removed. He placed it, screwed the mouthpiece in place and returned the receiver to the hook.

Sandy meanwhile had opened the front door to a husky young man with glasses and a turned-up nose. In his left hand he held a brown briefcase, in his right a pamphlet.

"Good morning," he said. "I'm here with the message of God. 'I am the way, the truth and the light,' God said, 'and he who follows me . . .'"

[160]

Sandy interrupted. "I'm awfully sorry, but I don't have time right now."

"You don't have time for God?"

"No, for you. I *am* terribly sorry, but if you come back some other time I'll be glad to hear what you've got to say."

She closed the door and walked back to the kitchen.

"How're you making out?" she asked the repairman.

"I'm going to have to check the pole. Everything in here seems fine. I won't be long."

He walked out the rear door to the backyard.

Sandy watched from the window as he climbed the pole, fitted with alternately spaced spikes, and buckled a safety strap into place. He removed the cover of the terminal box and plucked a screwdriver from his belt. What Sandy could not see was that the two wires to her line were not only disconnected from their terminals, but also tied back intentionally on the side of the box. The repairman untied the pair of wires and connected them properly. He unhooked the safety strap and climbed down the pole. Sandy met him at the rear door.

"I think I got it," he said.

"What was the trouble?"

"The lines were disconnected in the terminal box. Could have been a cat or a squirrel walking on the wires. They're not that difficult to pull loose." He moved to the wall phone and picked up the receiver. "Yeah, that was it." He held the phone out for Sandy to listen.

She put her ear next to the receiver and nodded. "Sounds normal."

He dialed a number and hung up. In an instant the phone rang. He picked it up, listened, then hung up again. He replaced the plastic casing on the wall set, gathered his tools, picked up his box and headed for the front. "You shouldn't have any more trouble with it," he said, opening the door, "but if you do, don't hesitate to give us another call."

She thanked him and tipped him a dollar.

"Thanks," he said, and was off to the truck. He stowed his gear in the back door, got in and drove off. Seconds after he pulled away Chris Chamber arrived and parked in the vacated spot.

The telephone van cruised the length of Cedar Street, turned left for two blocks, then right a half block, stopping in front of a store with windows clouded by unwiped glass wax. The driver got out and entered.

Inside, sitting at a brown metal desk in the center of the room, a slender, well-groomed man, mid-forties, red, just-cut hair, freckles, sporting a plaid suit and matching tie, talked on the telephone. To his right, on a wooden folding chair, sat the "messenger from God" who had rung the Chamber doorbell. Aside from a card table with two chairs in the rear of the room and three folding chairs nearby, the store was empty. The floors were bare wood, swept, but grimy, and the walls were peeling a pale green paint.

"Sorry to ask you, Jack," the man at the desk said into the phone, as he watched the repairman entering, "but we've just been assigned a special job and I'm going to need you." He listened for a few seconds, still glancing at the repairman, then returned to the conversation. "You can take your other week after the job; as soon as it's over." He listened again. "Okay, then,

I'll see you Monday morning. My apologies to the wife. The last thing I like to do is interfere with a man's vacation, especially if he's got plans, but I've got no choice." A pause. "Thanks again. So long." He hung up and turned to the repairman. "How'd you make out?"

"No problems. Everything's set up."

"Was he home?"

"He pulled up just as I took off."

"Good, good. Then he didn't see you."

The repairman shook his head.

"Good. Now I can use you on surveillance."

"Bob, get the equipment set up and let's see what we've got."

"Ten four."

Lieutenant Jerome Wilson was fond of well-tailored but vibrant suits, especially the plaid one he was wearing, and took pride in his wardrobe. A twenty-one-year veteran of the police department, for the past three years he had commanded the Saturation Unit, a special task force of twelve men and two women, highly trained and trustworthy, who handled only top-secret assignments. The unit was unique. Its very existence was top secret, known only to the police commissioner and his first deputy. Members were hand picked by Wilson. Only men and women on the waiting list to become police officers were considered: that is, those who had passed all the written and physical examinations and were waiting to be sworn in. There were no exceptions. No applications were considered, and those who were selected, seemingly at random, were chosen after careful screening. The true nature of the unit was not revealed to a pros-

[163]

pect until it was certain he qualified and he was willing to join. Prior to his appointment to the Department, each candidate was called to a clandestine personal interview where he was unknowingly accepted or rejected by Wilson. If rejected, he was told the interview was a marketing device to measure the effectiveness of the Department's advertising campaign. If accepted, he was told to inform all friends and family, except his spouse, that he had changed his mind and had decided not to become a police officer, that he had taken a job elsewhere. No one, except his spouse, was to know he was a member of the Department and even she was not to know his particular function. He received the same salary and training every other police recruit received, except his training was administered privately at the Police Academy in the early morning hours. In addition, he received an abundance of specialized training in areas such as electronic surveillance, wiretapping, undercover techniques, advanced judo, makeup and disguises, automatic-weapons use, breaking and entering techniques, and so on, and attended refresher courses in each area periodically. Each man was issued a gun and a shield, but rarely had occasion to use either in his assignments, which primarily consisted of nefarious surveillance details designed to keep a person or place under continuous observation. On some assignments he was to know a person's every move—where he was, who he was with, what he was doing and why, where he was headed and how. He made no arrests. In fact, he was told to avoid them at all times, regardless of the crime. At one time or another each man was unknowingly tested for his trustworthiness. All subordinates in the unit were responsible to only Lieutenant Wilson and he in turn was responsible to only Police Commissioner Windsor and First Deputy Commissioner Stephens, the latter his regular contact.

Upon promotion to his present rank, Lieutenant Wilson, a member of the Plainclothes Division for the last four of his seven years as a patrolman and all of his eleven years as a sergeant, was hand-picked by First Deputy Commissioner Stephens to command the special task force. His record was outstanding and his loyalty to superiors unquestionable. He was well-mannered and highly disciplined and demanded the same of his men. His charges trusted and respected him implicitly.

Lieutenant Wilson had designated to himself the responsibility of securing all court orders necessary for legal break-ins, searches and wiretaps, and the men of the unit assumed they were operating most times within the boundaries of the law and of the Department's rules and regulations. They assumed incorrectly. Because of the absolute secret nature of the unit's work, where even courts were not to know its assignments, Wilson most often merely feigned the acquisition of required documents. He made it a point to direct searches and wiretaps personally, and since the searchers were always conducted when the premises were vacant and the subjects of wiretaps were never aware that they were under surveillance, there was never a need to explain why a court order had not been secured. However, on rare occasions when proper legal documents would have to be produced eventually, the lieutenant subscribed to the law and obtained the required papers. Thus, the unit operated un-challenged.

The private stock of the police commissioner and first deputy had at their disposal sophisticated equipment of the highest order and disguises of every nature with which to carry out their work.

The current "saturation" had been dictated personally to Wilson by Deputy Stephens and the subject was Patrolman Christopher Chamber. The lieutenant was to make a daily verbal report, outlining the subject's activity, and a weekly written report, detailing his every move.

Wilson's first action had been to establish a headquarters as close to Chamber's home as possible, thus the vacant storefront. To facilitate the surveillance, the next step had been to get a "bug" into the house to monitor all telephone conversations and whatever private conversations were capable of being picked up. Under ideal conditions, that is, with the television, radio or stereo playing at average volume level and the participants in the conversation speaking at normal voice level, the estimated effective range of the transmitting device that had been inserted into the telephone mouthpiece was fifty yards in all directions. According to the layout of the Chamber home, that probably meant simply the kitchen and the living room. Naturally, the closer the conversation to the wall phone, the more effective the device in picking it up distinctly.

The telephone repairman, actually Patrolman Robert Mandich, an ex-installer and repairman with the New York Telephone Company, qualified as the special force's wiretapping and "bug" expert par excellence. The messenger from God, Patrolman Lester "Smokey" Riggins, was the newest member of the saturation unit and a former semi-pro running back. On the table in the rear of the store the pair had set up receiving equipment and a tape recorder and were listening to Chris and Sandy Chamber conversing in their kitchen. They called Lieutenant Wilson over.

"Getting anything?" the lieutenant asked.

"Yes, sir," said Mandich, "clear as a bell."

"They're in the kitchen," Riggins added.

The three men listened for a moment to a small speaker sitting on the table in front of them as muffled sounds of cups and saucers clicking suggested the couple was sitting down to coffee. The tape rolls of the recorder turned slowly.

"How's Barney doing?" Sandy asked.

"He's okay," Chris said matter of factly. "He's still after me to swim the Channel."

"You'd think he'd get tired of asking."

"Not Barney. He's got a new wrinkle now, too. He's arranged with some airline for an all-expenses-paid trip to England for me, you and the kids, and even *his* family, if I consent to swim the Channel."

Sandy was surprisingly reserved. "You turned him down? Or you said you'd think about it?"

"Both. I said I'd sleep on it, but I was pretty sure the answer would still be no."

There was a pause for a few seconds and the lieutenant and two patrolmen heard nothing. Then Chris cleared his throat. "He said you'd be awfully disappointed if

[167]

I turned it down." Another pause. "Are you?"

"Hey, hon, if you want to take me and the kids on a vacation, that's fine. I wouldn't care if it was to Hoboken, New Jersey. But I certainly wouldn't want you to feel pressured into taking us if it meant you had to do something you really didn't want to do . . . know what I mean?"

"I think so."

"Not that I could ever apply enough pressure to force you to do anything anyhow. Except maybe in the bedroom and lately I'm not even so sure about that."

The eavesdroppers could not see Chris smile. "You've got me tied around your little finger in there and you know it."

"Sometimes. And then other times I could swear you're not even paying attention, like . . . like you're daydreaming, or thinking of something else. Maybe you're fantasizing that you're making love to another woman."

"It's your imagination. Besides, even if that were true, it would still be better than going out and actually making it with somebody else, wouldn't it?"

The Chamber phone rang.

Chris answered.

It was Bob Dressen, an alcoholic police officer permanently assigned to switchboard duty.

"What's up?" Chris asked.

"I've got a notification for you. Instead of a late tour tonight, you're to do an eight to four tomorrow and report at 10 A.M. to the first deputy commissioner's office."

"What the hell is that for?"

[168]

"Beats me. I just got it from Caramella."

"He didn't say anything about it?"

"Nope."

"Is he there now?"

"Yeah, but I don't have a line for you. You'll have to call him direct."

"Okay, Bob, thanks a lot. I'll be talking to you."

"Okay, Chris."

They hung up. In a second Chris picked up the receiver and dialed. Lieutenant Wilson and the patrolmen listening in directed their attention to a foot-long panel fitted atop the receiving equipment on the table before them. The panel was broken down into ten black squares and as Chris completed dialing the first number, an orange light danced in the first black square. Suddenly a digit appeared. It was a number five. Chris dialed the second number and, after a short dance, an orange two appeared in the next black squre. When Chris had completed dialing, the telephone number was lit up in orange on the panel. It was the telephone number of the Twenty-first Precinct roll call office.

The other end rang once and was answered. "Roll call, Caramella," came a deep voice.

"Al, Chris Chamber."

"Oh, hi, Chris. I guess you got the notification."

"Just now. What the hell is up?"

"I don't really know. I got a call . . . direct from his office about a half an hour ago. They didn't say why and I didn't ask."

"Uniform or civvies?"

"Civilian clothes. Didn't Dressen tell you?"

[169]

"No."

"Jesus, he can't get anything straight. You got the right time? 10 A.M.?"

"Right."

"I don't know what to tell you, Chris. Could be nothing."

"You don't just get called to the first dep's office for nothing."

"Well, you'll find out soon enough, tomorrow."

"What's the P.B.A. number, Al? Maybe I'll give them a call."

"Hold on a minute and I'll get it." In a few seconds he was back. "Okay, it's 873-5531."

"Five . . . five . . . three . . . one . . . right. Thanks a lot, Al. I'll be talking to you."

"Good luck."

They hung up. Again Chris picked up the receiver and dialed a number. The orange lights danced on the screen in front of Lieutenant Wilson and his men, and when Chris had finished dialing, the telephone number of the Patrolmen's Benevolent Association was lit up in the black squares. The other end rang eight times, nine times, ten times and Chris hung up.

"What's the matter, honey?" Sandy asked.

"Nothing yet," Chris said, "except I can't get anybody at the P.B.A. office. Everytime I call them it's either busy all day, or no one answers."

"What are you calling the P.B.A. for?"

"I've got to report to the first deputy commissioner's office tomorrow and I just want to make sure I'm prepared. I know pretty much what they're going to tell me

[170]

at the P.B.A., anyhow, but I just want to make sure."

The speaker on the table of the saturation unit's makeshift headquarters was silent for a moment. Then . . .

"I'm going to lie down, hon," Chris called to his wife, who had apparently left the kitchen. "I don't have to go in tonight, I'm doing a day tour tomorrow instead, so we can eat about six, okay?"

"Okay," came Sandy's voice, farther away, yet distinct.

"Call me if I'm not up."

Lieutenant Wilson and his men relaxed a bit, as silence fell upon the speaker.

"We should have that luck with all our jobs," the lieutenant said. "It's picking everything up beautifully." He stepped to his desk. "Let me know if his wife gets into any juicy conversations on the phone." Riggins and Mandich smiled.

Cedar Street was quiet as the early afternoon sun slowly shifted the shadows. A slight breeze rustled the fallen leaves and gently swayed the branches. Three doors away from number twenty-one, the mailman methodically made his way down the block, stopping for a deposit at every house. He was a new man on that route, not unusual because there had not been a man steadily assigned to it for well over a year. But this man, although his outward appearance gave no indication to the contrary, was not an ordinary mailman, for under his jacket he carried a .38-caliber Smith and Wesson revolver . . . Patrolman Michael Schaeffer, shield number 24707, Saturation Unit.

Diagonally across the street from 21 Cedar Street,

a blond youth, not more than eighteen, rang the bell to the corner house. A few moments passed and an elderly woman, with thinning grey hair, stocky, flowered house dress and black, laced shoes, opened the front door.

"Yes?" she said, with a hint of an accent.

"I called about the room."

"Oh, yes. Come in." The accent was middle European.

The woman moved aside to let the youth enter. She closed the door and led him up the stairs.

"You don't play loud the stereo, I hope," she said.

"I don't own a stereo."

"Good, good. We like it very quiet."

They reached the second floor, walked the length of the hall and started up another flight of stairs.

"You're a student?"

"Yes. At Hofstra University in Hempstead."

"Ah, yes, yes. I know Hofstra. I hear . . . good school."

"It's a very good school."

"So you'll study most times, no?"

He nodded.

They reached the third floor and turned to the door at the right. The woman opened it and stepped in, motioning for the youth to follow. "This is it," she said. "It's clean."

The boy looked around and seemed satisfied. He moved to the window in the far corner and looked out. Across the street, in full view, was 21 Cedar. "I'll take it," he said.

The new tenant looked younger than he was—Patrolman Robert Melville (twenty-three years old), shield number 5027—and that's precisely why he had been selected for the Saturation Unit.

To the rear of the Chamber house in the middle of Mooring Avenue, which crossed Cedar, a blue and yellow gas company van was double-parked. Two men got out. A strapping black man, a short-sleeved shirt pulled taut against his muscled body, unhooked the ladder affixed to the top of the vehicle. A tall, comparatively thin white man, a short handlebar moustache prominently coating his upper lip, removed the manhole cover in the center of the roadway. While the Negro lowered the ladder into the hole, the man with the moustache set up four yellow wood stanchions, blinking amber lights imbedded. Each man took a yellow hard hat from the truck's front seat and descended into the opening . . . Patrolman Leroy Stanton, shield number 33044, and Patrolman Augustus Harrison, shield number 17665, Saturation Unit.

Four blocks away from the Chamber home, in the basement office of St. Peter the Fisherman Grammar School, a young redhead, primly attired in an orchid, knee-length jumper and white dacron blouse, sat talking to the nun in charge of advanced adult religious instruction.

". . . And I'd like to attend," said the redhead.

"We'll be glad to have you, Margaret. Classes started last week, but I'm sure you haven't missed so much that you couldn't catch up. Father Gilligan is the instructor."

Policewoman Margaret Richardson, shield number 442, Saturation Unit, was pleased. It was her assignment to get friendly with Mrs. Sandy Chamber, also a member of the religious instruction class.

In the Twenty-first Precinct stationhouse, Patrolman Bob Dressen ripped a dozen sheets from the teletype machine and filed them numerically in a half-filled, removable-hardcover book on the left-hand side of the desk officer. On one of the pages he circled a notation that a new cleaner, Julio Hernandez, tax registry number 185382, was to report for duty to the Two-One the following morning at 7 A.M., filling a month-old vacancy. He brought the message to the desk sergeant's attention. The sergeant scribbled a note for the next tour's desk officer, advising him of the civilian assignment, and hung it on a hook in front of him. With each stationhouse in the city being assigned two or three cleaners—civilian employees of the Police Department, with a very high turnover—one new assignment did not amount to much. However, the new cleaner at the Two-One was not the run-of-the-mill civil servant . . . Patrolman Julio Hernandez, shield number 36060, Saturation Unit. It was his job to keep on top of all activities in the Two-One, with special attention to any involving Patrolman Chamber. In his position as cleaner, he was free to roam the entire stationhouse and was likely to strike up friendly relations with the police officers to facilitate his assignment. And, as a cleaner, when his assignment was completed and he was officially transferred out of the Two-One, hardly would he be missed.

In the rear of a metallic-green van parked in the middle of Cedar Street, two men sat with an unobstructed view of number twenty-one. With the front seat cordoned

[174]

off with curtains and the rear window made of one-way glass, chance of detection was remote. On the floor between them buzzed a walkie-talkie . . . Patrolmen William Sommers and Anthony Provenzale, shield numbers 6236 and 24401, respectively, Saturation Unit. Their assignment was to keep the subject in sight at all times, reporting his whereabouts to temporary headquarters every hour on the half-hour. The van had been designated "Adam." Around the corner on Mooring Avenue, a few short yards from the ersatz manhole operation, sat designation "Boy," a dark-brown Plymouth station wagon with two other members of the special task force.

After midnight, on the first early morning of surveillance, Patrolmen Sommers and Provenzale quietly exited the van and walked toward the old Chevy parked directly in front of 21 Cedar. Surveying both sides of the street carefully, nonchalantly, they stopped abreast of the car and glanced toward the house across the avenue. Patrolman Melville flashed a light from the top floor, indicating the cross streets were clear. Abruptly, Provenzale slid beneath the auto, while Sommers moved to the side window, forcing a curved metal instrument between the glass and the rubber of the post. The instrument was a homemade tool especially designed for this purpose. In an instant he had hooked the u-shaped end over the latch. He pulled up. Click. The door was unlocked. Removing a minuscule metal cylinder from his pocket, he opened the door and laid down on the floor inside. He reached under the dash amidst the wires and partitions. Meanwhile, underneath the vehicle, Provenzale wriggled face up in the gutter. Eye level with the

[175]

bell housing, rubbing a spot clean, he removed a tiny metallic disc from his shirt pocket and clicked it against the iron casing. He squirmed from beneath the car and brushed himself off as Sommers locked and closed the door. They hurried back to the van.

The bugging was complete: Sommers' cylinder, in fact, a tiny monitoring device intended to pick up any and all conversations inside the auto, and Provenzale's disc, a magnetized transmitting unit capable of pinpointing the exact location of the vehicle within a radius of three miles.

Though some of the unit's members might not be able to provide any useful information in the future, their deployment had been necessary to achieve Lieutenant Wilson's end. There were few moves Chris Chamber could make without the ubiquitous eyes and ears of the special force upon him and those moves were confined to certain areas inside his home. And even they were frighteningly few.

CHAPTER 9

CHRIS lay awake in his bed as dawn crept into the room through shaded windows. He dwelled on his appointment later in the morning. Why did the first deputy commissioner want to see him? Maybe he wanted to commend him on his performance at the Corinthian. No. He would have been notified to that effect and instructed to report in uniform. Besides, although it was rare, if it had been decided that he was to be commended by the upper echelon of the Department, policy dictated that it would be done publicly and ceremoniously by the police commissioner, not the first deputy. Maybe there was an investigation under way into some wrongdoings in the Two-One. In that case he had nothing to worry about. Though witness to most, if not all, of the corruption in the Twenty-first Precinct, he himself did not participate.

[177]

What if he was asked to rat? Often he had thought of the unwritten code of silence that prevented a police officer from ever revealing the true nature of any corrupt practices, that steered a police officer's first loyalty to his fellow officers instead of to the public, and more than once he had had the urge to break it, to tell of the rampant corruption on the force, to clean up once and for all the system and the tradition, to make the position of police officer a truly respected position. But he had dismissed the notion every time. It was against his nature to do something like that, to rat. Too many people and the wrong people at that might have been hurt in the aftermath. He held no grudges; there was no need to rat to get even with anyone. Things weren't too bad in the Two-One. When he had made his decision to go straight, to refuse all graft, to defy the system, he had expected worse. Though ostracized to a certain extent, at least he wasn't considered a lunatic as were most police officers who refused money and favors. One man he had worked with in the Eight-O had always been referred to as "the psycho." Granted, he had summonsed his own brother once, which was incredible on the face of it, and he had gotten out of a buddy's car one day on the way to court to summons a car parked by a fire hydrant, but he was not a psycho or a lunatic. He simply took the job too seriously; much too seriously to ever participate in corruption. But even *he* dared not break the code of silence. So, maybe there was an investigation of some sort and maybe the first deputy commissioner thought Chris would rat on the other men. But if there was an investigation, why hadn't anyone else been called down, or scheduled for an appointment as was normal procedure?

He swung his legs out of bed and sat up, rubbing the back of a stiff neck. With little enthusiasm he retrieved his attaché case from the floor near the highboy and laid it open on the bed. He took out his swimming trunks and towel, a clipboard with sector runs on it, an extra set of handcuffs, a few loose sheets of scrap paper and a batch of various departmental forms held together with a rubber band. He pushed out on the sides of the case and the false bottom popped loose. Removing it, he pressed the microphone out of the hole near the handle, unhooked the wire from the guides along the side of the case and unsnapped the tiny tape recorder from its holder. He removed the cartridge, tucking it away in the middle drawer of the highboy, replacing it with a fresh one taken from the same place. Laying the recorder on the bed, he went to the closet and returned with his girdle-holster—an elastic band, six inches wide, with two pockets sewn on the inside, one holding his off-duty revolver. He slid the small Japanese recorder snugly into the other pocket and stretched the band around his hips, the gun coming to rest comfortably on his left side, the recorder in the small of his back. Bringing the black microphone wire around the top of the girdle, tucking it in neatly, he taped the mike itself to the center of his chest.

It was not the first time he had fitted himself with the minuscule tape recorder. He had worn it during the course of several investigations by the civilian complaint review board and by the division inspector's office. The

[179]

primary purpose behind wearing it was convenience, that always he would be certain of what had been said during an interview—or, better termed, an interrogation —but also there was an element of protection in case at some point he was alleged to have said something incriminating when actually he had not. Never had he had to produce a tape to prove the latter, but he was glad to have taken the precaution just the same. Never had he told anyone he sometimes used the recorder. Friends were hard enough to come by.

He dressed in a grey-blue suit and went to the kitchen. Sandy was sitting at the table, reading the morning paper.

"Good morning, hon," she said. "Want some breakfast?"

"Just a glass of juice." As Sandy fetched the juice from the refrigerator, he glanced at the sports headlines.

"You were up early," she said, pouring some orange-pineapple.

"I couldn't sleep."

"Worried about the appointment?"

"Not so much worried as I am puzzled. I just can't figure it." He gulped the juice.

"Well, it's probably nothing."

Chris shrugged. He kissed her on the lips and left. He couldn't stop thinking about the impending appointment. So intense was his concentration, he arrived at the Two-One hardly aware he had been in two traffic jams, let alone suspecting he had been followed by Adam and Boy of the Saturation Unit. He parked the car and entered the stationhouse.

[180]

The sergeant on the desk eyed the suit. "Whatever it is you're selling, we don't want any," he said with a deadpan face. The expression evolved quickly into frivolity and he laughed.

"Hi, sarge," Chris said.

"Where the hell're you goin'?" He gave him the onceover. Very rarely did a uniformed officer come to work in a suit.

"First dep's."

"For what?"

Chris shrugged.

"He probably wants to tell you what a fine job you did the other night."

Chris nodded politely. He had already eliminated that possibility. "Maybe. Could be anything." He continued on past the desk to the clerical office. There was no one there. Picking up the phone, he dialed the Patrolmen's Benevolent Association. It rang twice.

"P.B.A., Edwards," came a voice.

Chris was actually surprised to get an answer at such an early hour. "Good morning. This is Patrolman Chamber from the Two-One. Who am I speaking to, please?"

"Patrolman Edwards," the man said, "Brooklyn North Trustee."

Instantly Chris recognized the name and voice. Edwards had represented him at a civilian review board hearing five years earlier and had fallen asleep right in the middle of the proceedings. He had been drunk. As vivid as the incident was to Chris, he doubted Edwards would recall it at all or recognize his name.

"Patrolman Edwards, maybe you can help me," Chris

[181]

said. "I've been notified to report to the first dep's office at ten o'clock this morning and I'd like to know if I should have any P.B.A. or legal representation with me."

"Well, what are you being called down for? Do you know?"

"No, not at all."

"Well, it could be anything. As long as you haven't actually been accused of anything, I can't see why you'd need somebody with you."

Chris had anticipated that answer and accepted it. "Okay, I just wanted to check with you to be sure. You know."

"Sure, you did the right thing. If you *are* accused of anything, either formally or informally, you get right back to us and we'll get somebody over to you right away. But right now, like I say, it could be anything."

"Okay, thanks. I'm glad I got you in. Every time I call I usually either get a busy or no one answers. Tell you the truth I didn't really expect anyone to be around this early, but I figured I'd take a chance."

"Usually we don't come in till nine thirty or so. I just stopped in to pick up some papers. I have a hearing this morning at C.C.R.B." Chris wondered for an instant if he were going to be able to stay awake for that one. "I was just walking out the door when you called."

"Okay, I won't hold you. Thanks a lot."

"Anytime."

Chris hung up, shaking his head. Again the P.B.A. had proven itself useless. He looked at his watch. It was 8:01, and he heard the sergeant telling everyone to fall in next door. He slipped into the muster room and stood behind the ranks as the roll was called. In a few minutes all were ordered to take their posts. Sauntering out of the stationhouse, he strolled slowly to the subway station five blocks away. The air was crisp, the sun warm, and Chris momentarily felt better. There was plenty of time. He took the local and twenty-five minutes later exited the City Hall station. He was early. Coffee and a Danish wasted twenty minutes. He bought a newspaper and settled down for a while on a bench in a nearby park, trying to relax, trying to prepare himself for the unexpected. When it was time, he headed for his appointment.

The new Police Headquarters building was only a few short blocks from City Hall. Resembling a giant, honeycombed cube, the fifteen-story, fireproof-bombproof structure had reputedly cost over fifty-eight million dollars to construct. Chris crossed the plaza in front of it and entered through a glass door, flashing his shield to a posted security officer. Headquarters had been moved only recently and this was his first visit to the new location. The pleasant combination of glass walls and columns from end to end impressed him. He approached the circular information desk in the center of the main lobby and asked a freckle-faced policewoman for the office of the first deputy commissioner. Fifth floor, he was told. Purposely missing a crowded elevator, he made the ride alone on the next one and switched on the tape recorder before getting off.

The office of the first deputy commissioner faced the elevator. He took a deep breath and pushed open the

[183]

door, trying not to think about the equipment he was wearing; things would run a lot smoother if he could. He wondered if his knowing the conversation was being recorded was an advantage or a disadvantage, so he tried not to think about it. If he was too nervous, he might tip his hand and if the first deputy found him out, he'd no doubt be fired. Going through the door, he put the equipment out of mind.

The anteroom of the office was small and rather cramped, to the right a black leather couch sided by a square, magazine-laden table, to the left a clothes rack and two chairs. On the other side of a windowed, grey metal partition sat a plump secretary, upturned nose, dyed-black hair and glasses. Above the window was a harbor scene painting, predominantly blue.

Chris stepped forward, stooping, and the secretary slid open the glass. Muffled voices emanated from the deputy's office behind her.

"Can I help you?" she asked.

"Patrolman Chamber . . . I've got a ten o'clock appointment."

"Okay, just have a seat. The commissioner is with someone right now." The voices were loud and they continued.

Chris thought of the recorder and a lot of wasted tape, then dismissed the thought as the shouting stopped and the door to the inside office opened abruptly. A uniformed inspector, his face quite red, eagles glimmering on the shoulders, hurried up to the interim door in the grey partition, and quickly passed Chris.

"Just a minute, officer," the secretary said. "I think he'll see you now." She went into the deputy's office.

Chris nodded and straightened. He inspected the painting above him for a few seconds. The door to the partition opened and the secretary said: "You can come in, officer."

"Thanks." He stepped past her to the commissioner's office, and heard the door close behind him. Stephens was sitting at his desk, writing, his horseshoed-white head down in concentration. Chris paced slowly to the desk.

"Sit down," Stephens said without looking up, an unmistakable hint of command in his voice.

Chris complied. He could see the furrow in the commissioner's brow, and his mind was inundated with the countless rumors he had heard about this man. The word was he had fought his way up through the ranks, unequivocally favoring the old-school methods of a police officer. He had a fierce reputation as a thick-headed Irishman, set in his ways, intolerant of the slightest sign of insubordination. His appearance gave no hint to the contrary. Reputedly, he was also cold-blooded and ruthless. Chris could believe that as he saw Stephens for the first time.

A bit uneasy, Chris scanned the titles in the massive bookcases behind the first deputy, then glimpsed out the window at the Brooklyn Bridge.

Stephens put the pen down and leaned back in his chair, his face stern, staring at Chris. "I'll get right to the point," he said in an authoritative tone. "I've received a request from your commanding officer to have you transferred out of the Two-One."

[185]

So that's what this was all about, Chris thought. But why here?

The commissioner continued. "Why, Patrolman Chamber?"

Chris was reluctant to reveal the reason. It would imply Captain Varing was on the take. "I'm not sure," he said, hedging.

"Any guesses?"

Chris hesitated. He didn't want to indict anyone. But there were certain times when the truth had to be brought out and this was one of them. "You might say I'm conscientious about certain violations in the precinct, sir, and I've been knocking them over with summonses."

"So."

"Well, most of the people I summons appear to be friends of one of my superior officers."

"What do you mean *friends*?" He leaned forward and narrowed his eyes. "Are you implying that Captain Varing is involved in something dishonest?"

"Sir, I give him more combined activity than anyone in the precinct. He can't want to get rid of me because I don't work hard enough." Again he hesitated at revealing the true nature of the friction between him and Varing, but he continued after a pause. "He's had me in his office a couple of times and has told me to lay off a few people. I refused." At all times Chris spoke with an air of politeness and respect.

Stephens spoke curtly. He rested his elbows on the desk and squinted as he spoke. "That's a strong accusation you're making, Officer. Can you back it up?" Stephens knew perfectly well that Varing was up to his neck in protection payoffs, but he wanted to get an indication of just how much of a troublemaker this Patrolman Chamber really was. Already he had seen that if pressed Chamber was willing to bring up in conversation the captain's selling protection.

Chris was not afraid to speak up. "I'm only answering your questions and telling you how it is, sir. You asked me why I guessed the captain wanted me transferred and I told you. I don't want to make any official allegations against him. I just don't want to get dumped for being a good cop."

Stephens had his answer and was relieved. Chamber for his part didn't want to make waves if he didn't have to. The deputy shuffled some papers on the desk until he came to what he was looking for. "If you're so active and so conscientious," he said, holding two sheets, "how come you want to go on the tit at the Police Academy pool?"

Chris eyed the transfer requests he had forwarded some time before and his mind raced to come up with an intelligent answer. "I feel there's an important job to be done there, too, sir. I'd be as conscientious at the Police Academy pool as I would anywhere else."

Stephens paused. Enough of the diversionary conversation; he decided to get to the real reason he had called Chamber to his office. Standing up, he turned his back to the patrolman and looked out at the Brooklyn Bridge. "It has come to my attention that you have been doing some investigating on your own."

Chris was aware immediately of what Stephens was referring to and wondered how he had found out. "I do a lot of investigating on my own time, sir."

"Well, maybe you shouldn't."

"No one in the department has ever complained before about getting something for nothing. What exactly are you referring to, sir?"

The deputy turned away from the window and again squinted his eyes in grim determination. "I'm referring to Stuart Pierce."

Chris glowed inside. He thought of the recorder strapped to his chest.

Stephens went on. "I read the report on the Corinthian Hotel job and your action was quite commendable. But why did you approach Pierce on your own after having interviewed him at the hotel? He called this office and complained about your attitude and conduct. He said you were asking some very personal questions. Just what were you after?"

From that moment Chris knew he had made the right decision not to tell anyone about Windsor. Did Stephens know the police commissioner was a homosexual? Where exactly did the first deputy stand? He was anxious to know. He dodged the question tactfully. "It was just a routine follow-up investigation, sir."

Stephens grew angry. "That's not your job, officer. You're a uniformed patrolman, not a detective."

"Yes, sir."

The commissioner resumed. "Mr. Pierce says you indicated to him that you saw someone coming out of his room at the Corinthian, someone of importance. Just who was that someone? And what difference would it make if he was with Pierce?" He paused. "I don't understand the nature of your private investigation, your routine follow-up investigation, Chamber."

"He must be mistaken, sir. I didn't see anyone."

Stephens knew differently, but accepted the answer. He really had no choice at this juncture. As long as Chamber would not press the issue, neither would he. Stalemate.

"Okay, Chamber," the deputy said, sitting. "Return to your command. But stay away from Pierce. This office will not tolerate harassment. And leave the investigating to the squad." Stephens looked down at his papers, the signal to Chamber that the interview had ended.

"Yes, sir." Chris rose and started for the door. He wasn't satisfied with the way the talk had turned out. It occurred to him that it was time to see exactly how strong a hand he was holding. He turned to the commissioner and mustered a resolute tone. "Sir, I'd like you to know that I'd be mighty displeased if I were transferred to a bad or inconvenient precinct, like Captain Varing has strongly suggested might happen. Know what I mean? I've done no wrong. I've been quiet thus far about what I've found out, but . . ." He let the sentence die.

Stephens returned the serve without hesitation. "Get the idea out of your head that you saw the police commissioner at the Corinthian, Chamber. If it'll make you feel any better, he was with me that night. I don't know what Pierce told you, but I'm sure you're smart enough to know you can't believe everything you hear."

So he does know about Windsor. Why else would he cover up? Chris wondered if he could be on to some-

[189]

thing bigger than he had first suspected. Now Stephens had committed himself by lying about being with Windsor and he had it on tape. Right then he had a confirmation of what he really knew all along: the first deputy was not to be trusted. If there was anything more to this than his imagination, Stephens was surely involved.

Chris spoke softly, but firmly. Stephens had to know that he was capable of playing a card if he had to. "I'm smart enough to know that everything I hear is not always true. I might even be mistaken about everything I think I've seen. But I'm also smart enough to know that there's a time to keep things to myself and a time to spread them around."

Stephens gave an icy stare. He was being challenged and he didn't like it.

"So about the transfer, sir," Chris said politely.

The commissioner welled with anger, but controlled himself. This young patrolman was an adversary to be reckoned with. There was a lot at stake, and there was time to plan and do it right. "We'll see," he said calmly.

Chris nodded and left the office, aware that he was holding some very high cards.

CHAPTER 10

THE coffin, draped in an American flag, lay on a six-
wheel cart at the foot of the altar. Vased lilies were
everywhere. Stained-glass windows dulled the morning
sun and burning incense added to the gloom. Every pew
in the tiny church was crammed, men and women all in
black, uniformed police officers spilling into the street,
black mourning tape across their badges. In the first
row on the left side sat the mayor and the police commissioner. An organ bellowed somber tones, appropri-
ate to the mood of a funeral. The priest, white vestments
to celebrate the Mass of the Resurrection, a reminder
that only the body dies, the soul lives forever, moved
from center altar to the elaborately carved pulpit on his
right. He blessed himself and addressed the crowd.

Chris, a pallbearer, sat on the aisle in the third row, listening to the eulogy. He had been to the funerals of three police officers in the past and, basically, all the eulogies had been the same—extolling the virtues of the deceased, praising all the men of the Police Department for doing such an outstanding job, lashing out at the rampant violence and permissiveness evident in society. Naturally, all members of the force grieved for a fellow officer killed in the line of duty, even if they had not known him. The true danger of the job was starkly obvious on those occasions and commanded respect. But this funeral was different to Chris. Not only had Joe Hummel been a member of the Two-One; Chris had been with him at death. He winced as he saw once again in his mind's eye the look of surprise on Hummel's face the instant the slug from the forty-five hit, and he also thought of the ambush years before in a distant corner of the world. At the other funerals Chris had grieved knowing that it was one of his own kind who had been killed, that one day it might very well be himself in the box. But at this funeral Chris grieved because he had known Joe Hummel. The others had been fellow policemen—but just names. Hummel had been a personality—flawed, but real.

The Mass passed quickly for Chris and before he knew it the priest had cued the pallbearers. Chris rose and approached the corner of the flag-covered coffin. The organ droned until the six men were in place, three on each side, then sounded a low-toned dirge, signaling the procession to begin. He glanced across the aisle at Joe Hummel's wife, sobbing, behind a veil. Behind her, an old

[192]

woman, wrinkled face, white hair veiled in black, cried softly. Chris guessed it was Hummel's mother. Beads of perspiration formed on most brows. The smell of incense was stifling. And the organ played on in the deep, whining key. Why did they play that sad music? Chris wondered. Why did they have to make things more tragic than they were already?

Slowly, the six uniformed officers rolled the coffin down the aisle as the family, friends, the mayor and police commissioner, and other policemen fell into line behind. Onlookers jammed the vestibule, but parted in the middle, clearing a path. Arched in the gothic style, typical of such churches, the huge oaken doors opened inward in slow-motion, admitting a bright sun. Police officers, silent, motionless, in brilliant array, white gloves, shiny peaks and shoes, lined the steps of the church. The pallbearers gripped the handles of the coffin firmly and hoisted it to their shoulders. It seemed lighter now to Chris than when they had brought it in.

One pace at a time, bringing both feet together, hesitating before stepping out again, the honor guard carried the coffin to the hearse. As the back door to the limousine swung open, the air filled with a lonely bugle sounding taps and every one of a thousand police officers snapped a salute. Chris didn't have to turn around to know that Joe Hummel's wife was despondent with tears, that his mother and sister walked with assistance. He suppressed the tears welling in his own eyes. The void was unmistakable and wouldn't be filled. He had learned that, too, in Vietnam, and it took him years to realize that he was fortunate to have learned it as a young man.

[193]

How distressing the solemn ritual of funeral was, he thought, lowering the end of the coffin from his shoulder, sliding it into the hearse. He stared at the box and to himself said, *Goodbye, Joe.*

CHAPTER 11

FATHER Roselli held the Host in front of him and recited the Offertory Prayer. "On the night he was be-
trayed, he took bread and gave you thanks and praise.
He broke the bread, gave it to his disciples, and said:
'Take this, all of you, and eat it: this is my body which
will be given up for you.'" He raised the eucharistic
wafer high above his head, staring at it in adoration as
the altar boy rattled a hand-set of bells. He lowered
the Host, laid it on the golden paten, genuflected and
grasped the wine-filled chalice. "When supper was
ended, he took the cup. Again he gave you thanks and
praise, gave the cup to his disciples, and said: 'Take
this, all of you, and drink from it: this is the cup of
my blood, the blood of the new and everlasting covenant.
It will be shed for you and for all men so that sins may

be forgiven. Do this in memory of me.' " He raised the chalice on high and again the bells rang out. The small group of worshipers in the church bowed their heads in reverence.

Francis Anthony Roselli. His father, founder and president of a large department store, had assumed his son would one day fill his shoes. His mother, publicity director for a large publishing company, on the other hand, had always pictured him an attorney. Raised in the Bay Ridge section of Brooklyn, young Frank had spent his grammar school years at exclusive Lafayette Preparatory, a private institution, close to home, but stuffy with rich kids and snobby instructors. He had been more down-to-earth than most in the school and never liked the atmosphere, mainly because there was no sports program there. Even at grammar-school age it was evident that he would be athletic. Understandably, after much persuasion, his parents allowed him at fourteen to transfer to Saint Francis High School. Academically sound, but not the caliber of Lafayette, Saint Francis had won the Catholic Football League championship three years running and that was most important to Frank. He played football and baseball for four years, leading his teams as quarterback and shortstop to league titles in both his junior and senior terms. He received full scholarship offers from three colleges for football and two for baseball.

It was at Saint Francis that Frank met Chris Chamber. By chance, they lived only a few blocks apart and accompanied each other to school every day on the subway. Chris, too, liked football and was a strapping fullback. The two boys became best friends after a while, and were nearly inseparable in everything they did. Frank was a bit more gregarious and often took the initiative in making new acquaintances, but Chris was liked as much by the entire student body of the school. There was hardly a party given by a student at Saint Francis to which both were not invited.

However, Frank was also a bit more aggressive and quick-tempered, and possessed a latent mean streak. The pair had sided together in several fist fights, and one of those fights had a revolutionary, and in a real sense, revelationary effect on Frank's life.

". . . And the Yankees went on to win in the eleventh inning," eighteen-year-old Frank Roselli said as he and Chris walked home from the subway after school one day. Summer was nearly upon them, and in two short weeks they would be graduated from Saint Francis. The early afternoon sun had encouraged them to loosen their ties and carry their sports jackets. Each had an arm laden with books. Teeming with kids, the street they walked was lined with high-stoop, three-family brownstones, attached on both sides and fronted with wrought iron fences. They talked baseball as they walked.

Suddenly there was a roar of engines from behind, and the pair turned to see two motorcycles racing up the street. On one rode Jake Termotta, leader of a troublesome group called the Wild Bunch; on the other, his cousin, Bill, a hanger-on. Jake was Frank's age but rather slim by comparison, with a full mop of black, unkempt hair and a bushy goatee. Blue sunglasses shaded his eyes, and a sleeveless denim jacket matched his jeans. Frank suspected trouble. Jake's sister, a plain sixteen-year-old with a crush, had been hounding him constantly, but he had not been interested. The night before, he had told her to leave him alone. Knowing she might have reported it with some exaggeration to Jake, Frank half expected a confrontation. The bikes roared past and pulled to the curb near the corner. The riders dismounted, obstructing the sidewalk. Bill, his face scarred with acne, was dressed similarly to Jake. Chris and Frank approached, and the hostility was evident. Jake opened it. "You try to screw my sister?"

"You've got to be kidding," Frank said, with a mock laugh. Chris stood ready for trouble.

"She says you did."

Frank's mean streak was triggered. He put down his jacket and books. "Well, then she's not only ugly, she's a liar."

Jake threw a quick right, which Frank easily blocked before he crashed a fist to Jake's face, sending him reeling, his head slamming hard against an iron fence. He slumped to the sidewalk, his mouth bleeding. The fight was over. But Frank's rage fed on itself. He swung his foot blindly at Jake's face, and the heel of Frank's shoe smashed the blue sunglasses. Jake screamed, clutching at his eye. The crushed sunglasses fell to the ground. Disbelieving what he had done, Frank watched in shock as Bill bent down to his cousin and pulled his hand from his face, to expose a sight that would haunt Frank every day of his life.

[198]

His father pulled some strings and avoided prosecution—the right of self-defense in his son's favor—but the damage was irreparable, Jake lost his eye and Frank would never be the same. He became a recluse. When finally he did leave his home, it was to church, and he went every day. At first it was to beg forgiveness for having blinded Jake, a reality he could not live with. But he soon realized he had to live with it as all men must live with their mistakes. He learned that suffering was man's lot. Not long after, he announced his intention of becoming a priest. Reluctantly, his parents helped to register him in Saint Anthony's Novitiate in Long Island.

The gathering in the church recited aloud the Lord's Prayer. The small attendance was not uncommon for a weekday morning. Gothic buttresses separated arched, stained-glass windows and every pew glistened with wax. White chrysanthemums adorned the altar from end to end. Draped in green and gold vestments, 28-year-old Father Roselli faced the gathering with his hands spread apart, palms down before him. A shock of dark, wavy hair had been freshly trimmed.

The prayer completed, the priest glanced upward. "Deliver us, Lord, from every evil, and grant us peace in our day. In your mercy keep us free from sin and protect us from all anxiety as we wait in joyful hope for the coming of our Savior, Jesus Christ."

In the rear of the church, Chris read aloud from a blue booklet, joining the people in response. "For the kingdom, the power and the glory are yours, now and forever."

He picked up his head and watched his friend with admiration. Funny how things work out, he thought. Frank seemed right as a priest. So many years before, the priesthood had seemed such an unlikely calling.

The outstanding sports tradition had attracted Chris, also, to Saint Francis. He hit it off well with Frank right from the start and was glad to have him his best friend. He enjoyed visiting in the most extravagant house he had ever seen and was always treated cordially by Mr. and Mrs. Roselli. Coming from a lower-middle-class family—his father a truck driver, his mother a housewife—Chris was impressed by the movement and style of the wealthy.

But Frank's family wealth had little to do with this friendship. Frank was basically good-natured and shared Chris's interests: sports and girls, and they scored together with both.

It was because Frank enjoyed sports and girls so much that Chris at first found it hard to accept that his friend had chosen the priesthood; he respected the vocation, but somehow didn't think Frank would fit. He tried everything he could think of after the incident with Jake Termotta to snap Frank out of his despair. Nothing worked. When Frank entered the novitiate Chris was sure it wouldn't last, but that was not the case. Frank barely kept in touch and when Chris joined the Police Department, he too found little time to write. Two years passed in which neither communicated. Then, one night the Chamber telephone rang and Chris answered to hear Frank's voice.

[200]

They exchanged hellos.

"I'm in the Bronx. I've just been assigned to Saint Ignatius Loyola on Whitebridge Avenue."

"You ordained yet?"

Frank explained that he was serving an apprenticeship.

"Man, it's good to hear your voice. How about getting together?"

"That's really why I called."

Chris sat in the back of the church, watching his friend lay communion wafers on the tongues of the faithful, remembering how he had recognized Frank's voice immediately that night four years before. It struck Chris that he sounded more like the Frank Roselli of old, confident and full of energy. It was good to renew the friendship. After ordination Frank had been assigned to Saint Edward's in Queens, where he had stayed for four years before transferring to his present parish, Our Lady by the Sea in Brooklyn. Chris trusted no one more. They never discussed Jake, though both knew it would always be there.

Chris walked up the side aisle and entered the first pew as Frank began to end the Mass. He had not called Frank to tell him he was coming.

"May almighty God bless you . . ." The priest waved his hand in the sign of the cross. ". . . The Father, and the Son, and the Holy Spirit."

"Amen."

"The Mass is ended, go in peace."

"Thanks be to God."

Picking up his chalice to leave the altar, he spotted Chris in the first row. Chris winked and the priest smiled as he crossed to the sacristy. Chris blessed himself, walked to the side exit and waited in the vestibule. In a few moments Frank emerged.

They greeted each other warmly.

"What brings you by?"

"Just wanted to ask a favor."

"Sure. What can I do?"

"Well, first let me fill you in with a little background." Chris explained as clearly and as concisely as he could the events of the past few weeks, starting with Captain Varing's warnings, through to the meeting with First Deputy Commissioner Stephens. As they talked, they made their way out of the church, across a courtyard and into the rear entrance of the rectory. At all times they talked as friends. Frank's being a priest never prevented a candid conversation. When Chris had finished the story, they were sitting down to a cup of instant coffee in the rectory kitchen.

"What do you suspect?" Frank asked.

"I'm really not sure yet, Frank, but I'm on to something. I don't even know if it's worth the trouble to pursue, but at least as of now I've got some leverage in case they decide on shipping me back to Bedford-Stuyvesant."

"Is that what you fear most—being shipped back to Bedford-Stuyvesant?"

Chris thought before he answered. "Frank, I want to be a good cop. To be that, I have to keep my self-respect. I can't let myself be victimized by a system that is at best hypocritical. It's true that I'd hate to be sent back to that hell-hole, not only because it is a hell-hole, but because the wrong side would have won if Varing has his way."

"What can I do to help?"

"I'd like you to hold the tapes for me if you could. I've made copies that I'll keep home, but I'd feel better if you safeguarded the originals. In case this thing gets sticky, and it's likely to, they'll be worth a lot to me and I'd like to know they're in good hands. I won't be able to carry them around with me all day." He paused. "Can you just keep them in here somewhere? No one will ever know where they are but me."

"No problem. I'll hold them as long as you want me to."

Chris reached into his pocket for keys. "I've got them in the trunk of my car."

"Where you parked?"

"Right out front."

They got up from the table and chatted idly to the front door. Chris went out to retrieve the tapes. Not for an instant did it occur to him that he was being watched by the driver of the brown station wagon parked across the street and the two men in the green van on the next block. However, neither were the members of the Saturation Unit aware that Chris had taped any conversations and, consequently, were not suspicious of the paper bag he took from his trunk and brought to the priest waiting at the rectory door. The team did make a note of the seemingly innocent transaction, and watched as the priest and cop shook hands. When Chris pulled away from the curb for home, they followed at a discreet distance.

CHAPTER 12

"I WANT him out of the house," the woman shouted. "If you don't take him out, you'll be responsible when you find him dead in the morning." Tears rolled down her flabby cheeks. Under five feet and bleached blonde, the woman buried her head in her arms, sobbing on the kitchen table.

"She's crazy," her pajama-clad husband insisted. Balding, with a narrow face, he shrugged his shoulders helplessly. "I don't know what to do with her; she's crazy."

The woman jumped up from the table and rushed toward him. "You bastard," she screamed, as Chris stepped in front of her. "You shameless, lying, no-good bastard." Chris's partner for the night, Matt Sistrunk, a tall, well-built patrolman, stood in front of the husband. The woman went on. "You go fucking everything in the neighborhood with a skirt and when I catch you, *I'm* crazy."

"Settle down," Chris said as she strained to get past. He had to exert himself to contain the powerful female. "Settle down," he repeated in a firmer tone. He guided her back to the table. "Now what's going on? Start from the beginning."

"She's crazy, I'm telling you," her husband muttered.

"You be quiet," Sistrunk said. "You'll have your turn to speak. Her first." The husband nodded in compliance.

Chris was relieved to see Sistrunk knew how to handle himself. It was the first time they had worked together. "Now, what happened?" he asked the wife again.

The kitchen was resplendent with green-tiled walls and linoleumed floors. The refrigerator had been freshly sprayed with white enamel; the stove had not had that benefit. Everything sparkled, however, and there was an uncanny sense of cleanliness present.

She looked at Chris and wiped her eyes. "He's been cheating on me. I've suspected it for months . . . out late, perfume smell on his shirts, long, dark hairs on his suits, and little things, other little thing that just made me know . . . so I hired a private investigating agency and they followed him. I just got the report tonight . . ." She buried her head again in her arms. Her husband started to say something, but Sistrunk silenced him with a gesture.

"Are you legally married?" Chris asked. It was a natural first question, since most of the family disputes

[205]

he had handled in Bedford-Stuyvesant for six years had been between common-laws. It hardly made any difference what the woman's answer was, because, common-law or not, Chris never made a practice of expelling any man from his home. If it was a legal marriage, he could say simply that the law prevented him from forcing either party out of the house. In the case of a common-law marriage, technically, the partner who held the rent receipts—and it was usually the woman—was entitled to the apartment. But a police officer who attempted to eject a husband soon found out that no matter how angry the woman appeared and how adamant she was to have him removed, she would refuse to press charges if an arrest was made and would turn to her husband's side if force was necessary. Chris was very much aware of that pattern.

The woman's response was condescending. "Of course we're legally married," she said.

"Don't be offended," Sistrunk said. "We've got to ask."

The husband spoke up quickly. "You mean to tell me that you had me followed?" He raised his voice. "You fat piece of shit, I oughta throw you out the goddamn window."

"Don't you yell at me," she screamed.

Chris interrupted, calling attention to the late hour, but the woman wouldn't stop. "Screw the neighbors. It's too goddamn bad they can't get to sleep. I'm not going to get any sleep either. I want him out. I want him out of the house."

"Now we're back where we started," Sistrunk said.

Chris took the husband aside and led him out of the kitchen. "Listen," he said, "you got a place to stay for the night? If I were you I wouldn't sleep here. She's so mad, there's no telling what she might do." The husband listened as Chris continued. "Let her sleep on it for tonight. If you want to come back tomorrow and try again, you'll probably stand a better chance. But right now she's not going to listen to any excuses. Besides, it'll give you a while to put your head together and figure out what you really want to say. Know what I mean?"

The man nodded. "I think you're right. Let me get some things together and I'll spend the night at my sister's." He headed for the bedroom as Chris turned back toward the kitchen.

"Okay, lady, he's leaving," Chris said.

"You're goddamn right he's leaving," she said. "I know my rights."

Chris wouldn't press the issue. They waited in silence until the man reappeared, dressed for the street.

Chris and Sistrunk followed him from the apartment and heard the door slam behind them. Down two flights and they were back on the street.

"Can you give me a lift?" asked the man as they left the old building. "I've got to go crosstown."

"Sorry," Sistrunk said, "we've got another job waiting for us." Too many people thought all cops had to do with their time was drive people around the city. The man nodded and walked away.

Chris entered the recorder side of the radio car and Sistrunk sat behind the wheel. "Well, there's another satisfied customer," Sistrunk said.

[207]

"I don't know how satisfied he is," Chris said, "but he's sure a lot safer out of the house with that bleached meatball. She reminds me of a tackle for the Cleveland Browns."

"I don't mean he's the satisfied customer. I'm talking about the person who called. At least now he'll be able to get some sleep."

Chris laughed, happy to get by another family dispute without too much trouble. He couldn't help thinking that sometimes stepping between a brawling couple was as dangerous as entering a bank in the middle of a stick-up. If only the average citizen knew what it was really like to be a cop. If only the public could appreciate how a police officer was called upon to mediate family disputes nearly every day and how difficult a task it was. And that was only one role a policeman played in the community. If only more people realized that a police officer was not just an enforcer of the law, but a part-time doctor, electrician, plumber, coroner, and more. If only they could know how many crucial split-second decisions a man with a shield had to make every day; decisions that could mean a life. If only more people understood that cops were human, too, and subject to the same emotions and frustrations as the rest of society. The job was so all-encompassing. Often a police officer was the only personal contact a citizen would ever have with his government. When did anyone ever bump into the mayor on the streetcorner at midnight? At least Chris was better off with an average of one family dispute a night in midtown Manhattan, rather than five or six a night in Bedford-Stuyvesant, where usually both parties were drunk and it inevitably ended in violence. It was a thankless job for the most part, Chris thought, yet...

He picked up the radio-phone from the dash to report that the family dispute had been reconciled.

He replaced the phone as they pulled away from the curb.

"How about the paper?" Sistrunk suggested.

Chris looked at his watch. Twenty minutes to go. "Sounds good," he said. "It's pretty quiet."

Sistrunk cruised to the corner and made a left. Midway in the block he pulled over and hopped out, darting into an all-night stationery. In a few seconds he was out with two newspapers under his arm. He threw them on the seat, plopped down and pulled back on to the avenue. "Where do you want to sit?" he asked.

"You're driving," Chris said, picking up a paper, turning to the sports section.

Then the radio interrupted. "Two-One David, ten-two, kay."

Chris picked up the phone. "Two-One, David, ten-four."

"Ten-four."

"Why the hell would they want us in the house at this time?" Sistrunk said.

They drove to the stationhouse in response to the signal 10-2 and swung to the curb right in front. Chris got out to see why they were wanted. Approaching the entrance, he noticed a man's figure in the shadow by the door. Another two steps and he recognized him. It was Stuart Pierce.

[209]

His face was swollen, his eyes puffed terribly, his lips bleeding. Leaning against the brick, head tilted back, hair matted with blood, he held his eyes closed.

Pierce opened his eyes as far as they could go. "I want to talk," he mumbled, recognizing Chris.

Chris had to hear no more. This might be the break he needed. "Wait here," he said, stepping past him into the stationhouse. A trainee sat behind the switchboard and no one behind the desk. The lieutenant was probably in the back room having coffee. "Two-One David," Chris said. "You gave us a ten-two." He had never seen the trainee before.

"Chamber?"

Chris nodded.

"There was a guy here looking for you . . . all beat up."

"Oh, okay. Is that what you wanted?"

"That's all."

Chris stepped swiftly out of the stationhouse to the radio car. He opened the back door and took his attaché case from the seat. Slamming the back shut, he swung open the front.

"What's up?" asked Sistrunk.

"Just a message for me," Chris said, gathering his clipboard, flashlight and newspaper, placing them in his case. "Listen, something's come up. I'd like to get in early, so I'll be dressed by the end of the tour. Can you cover for me for ten minutes or so?"

"Sure."

"Thanks."

[210]

He closed the front door and strode to Pierce. "Listen, I'm parked around the block. Meet me on the corner." He pointed. "I'll be down in ten minutes."

Pierce nodded and stumbled away. Chris entered the stationhouse and was relieved to see that still no one was behind the desk. He climbed the stairs to the locker room and changed. Before coming down again, he popped the false bottom from his case, checking the recorder to be certain it worked properly. He waited on the second floor until he heard the midnight platoon turning out and walked out the door right behind them. Pierce was on the corner leaning against a building. Chris led him to his car and drove a few blocks. He parked in front of a supermarket, shut tight for the night.

"Okay, Stuart," Chris said, pulling his attaché from the rear seat to the front, quietly flicking the recorder button, "what happened?"

Pierce moaned with pain. Crumpled against the door, he curled into a fetal position. "They beat me, those bastards. They beat me till I passed out. I woke and asked them to please stop, but they beat me again." He was crying now.

"Who beat you? And why?"

"They beat me," he sobbed.

Chris tightened his lips, then spoke softly. "Listen, Stuart, if you don't tell me what happened I won't be able to help. Try to pull yourself together." He paused. "Who beat you?"

"I don't know who they were." He turned to face Chris. A space on the top, right side of his mouth marked obviously where at least two teeth had been broken.

[211]

"Three men . . . big . . . muscles . . . they rang the bell. When I opened the door they came crashing in."

"What did they want?"

"They kept asking me if I had been shooting my mouth off. If I had told anybody about the setup."

"The setup?"

"The protection setup . . . with Stephens."

Chris's ears perked up. "First Deputy Commissioner Stephens?"

Pierce nodded. A nod was no good for the tape recorder.

"Tell me, Stuart, right from the beginning . . . about the protection, about the payoffs, about Stephens, about the whole thing."

"Okay," Pierce whimpered, laying his hand on Chris's. "Right from the beginning."

Chris did not pull his hand away. He knew Pierce was seriously hurt and trusted Chris to help. Chris was not sickened by him now. As raw as his face was, beaten and bruised, bleeding, it was not as disgusting to Chris as the made-up face. He could accept the distorted features of a man after he had been severely pummeled and could sympathize with anyone who had taken such a beating. He was accustomed to seeing it frequently; in Bedford-Stuyvesant, hardly a weekend had gone by without a case where someone had been shot or stabbed or had had his ear severed by a broken bottle in a brawl. A fleeting picture of Frank Roselli and Jake Termotta flashed across his mind.

"I've got a stable of girls and guys," Pierce spoke slowly, his pain obvious, "and most of my clients are

the elite of New York City: judges, doctors, stock ty-
coons, people in City Hall, brass in the Police Department, all top shelf, successful people who look to in-
dulge in an occasional night of sex with the best-looking
men and women in town. Your Commissioner Stephens
has been getting paid plenty to keep from breaking up a
good thing. Windsor's a switch-hitter, and he's been balling me for months."

Chris understood now the grave importance of what
he had stumbled upon and why Stephens had called him
down to his office in such a whirlwind. He had wanted
to know how much he knew, and what he was going to
do with it.

"Stuart, I need specific details." He comforted Pierce's
hand with a pat. "Times and places of payoffs, times you
saw Windsor, names of the people you've been supplying with women and men: specific references."

"Okay." Pierce was resolute.

"Do you have records?"

Pierce shook his head. Chris guessed that this was a
lie. Most likely, Pierce did have records, but he wasn't
sure if he should give them up. Assuming he had such
records, Chris was fairly certain that Pierce would let
him see them later. He decided against pressing that
point. He took out his handkerchief and wiped some
blood from the lips of the beaten homosexual. Pierce
was grateful.

"I want to hear everything," Chris said. "Even if you
think it's unimportant, tell me anyway. Let me decide
what's important and what's not."

Pierce recounted all he knew, recalling names, dates,

[213]

places, times with an uncanny knack for detail and precision. Chris was astounded at some of the people who had availed themselves of the pimp's services: the mayor's brother was queer; a renowned television news commentator was also gay; a world-famous female rock singer had wanted both young boys and pretty girls for bed partners; a very famous author, who flaunted his homosexuality, had been a regular customer; a first-string professional football player, married to a beautiful sex kitten, had requested a girl of grammar-school age for fellatio every visit to New York; a blond actress noted for her roles in children's films, with a reputation as an all-American girl, regularly asked for a black, muscle-bound stud to take care of her; and a good percentage of the cream of the crop in the business world, the legal and medical professions, the political field, and the enormous cluster of the very wealthy living in New York had at one time or another bought a one-night, conventional, heterosexual affair. It wasn't until an hour after he had started that Pierce stopped talking. Chris, for his part, was flabbergasted.

One block away, in the metallic-green van, Patrolmen Bob Mandich and Smokey Riggins listened to every word emanating from the hidden "bug" in Chamber's car. They recorded the conversation, unaware that Chamber was doing the same.

When Pierce had finished, Chris started the car and headed for the homosexual's apartment. "What do you want me to do?" Chris asked.

Pierce answered quickly, "Turn them in."

"To whom? Who the hell do you tell that the police

commissioner is queer and he and his first deputy are on the pad? Who?"

Pierce sighed. "You've got to do something."

Chris was quiet for a moment, collecting his thoughts, not really knowing what course to take. He pulled in front of Pierce's building and turned to look at the brutally beaten figure beside him. "Sit tight till I get back to you. As soon as I figure out what to do, I'll let you know."

Pierce lowered his head in consent.

"Can you make it upstairs all right?"

"I'll be okay." Pierce got out slowly and closed the door. He bent into the window. "Thanks." Chris smiled and said nothing.

The pimp walked toward his building as Chris pulled away from the curb. It would be a thirty-minute drive to Brooklyn and Our Lady by the Sea.

CHAPTER 13

TO the two men who listened so intently, Chris Chamber's voice was very clear. "What do you want me to do?"

"Turn them in."

"To whom? Who the hell do you tell that the police commissioner is queer and he and his first deputy are on the pad? Who?"

"You've got to do something."

There was a pause.

"Sit tight till I get back to you. As soon as I figure out what to do, I'll let you know."

Deputy Commissioner Stephens pushed the "stop" button on the tape recorder. Turning from his desk, he gazed out the window at the smog-shrouded Brooklyn Bridge. It was the third time he had played the tape since receiving it from Lieutenant Wilson. Harold Windsor stirred uneasily in his chair by the desk. He, too, had listened to the tape.

"Now what?" Windsor asked with a quiver in his voice. He was obviously upset, straightening the crease in his pants, toying idly with the bottom button of his jacket.

Stephens was silent, staring at the bridge, not really seeing it. He knew what had to be done and already had set the wheels in motion. He was appallingly calm for a man who contemplated murder. "We've got to get rid of him," he said without emotion.

"Chamber?" Windsor asked incredulously.

"No. There's too much action when a member of the force gets killed. There'd be too many waves that even *I* couldn't quell. Chances are it would hurt us instead of helping." He turned from the window. "But nobody would miss Pierce very long."

Windsor was shaken—Stuart was his lover. But Stephens was probably right. The quickest and easiest escape from potential trouble was to eliminate the only person who could actually corroborate Chamber's story if he decided to tell it. A man of such a passive nature, the commissioner was surprised at his own voice when he heard himself ask: "How?"

"It'll cost us, but they're reliable." Stephens said.

The fact that Stephens knew whom to go to to set up a murder contract and his implication that he might have dealt with these people before weakened Windsor's stomach. The police commissioner saw Stephens as if for the first time.

Stephens was relieved that Windsor was agreeable.

[217]

Not that he would have changed his plan if the commissioner had resisted, but success to a great degree depended on agreement of all involved. Stephens was convinced that Pierce's elimination was the right move and it was all the better that Windsor in his weak-kneed, self-pitying way concurred. Both men knew that the commissioner had little choice but to concur.

Windsor put Pierce out of his mind. "What about Chamber?"

"It's time to talk to him again . . . soon . . . before he does something foolish."

"He knows too much. What if he tells somebody?"

Stephens had a confident air. "Who? You heard him yourself; who's he going to tell? And even if he does find someone who'll listen, it's his word against ours. With Pierce out of the way there's not much that can be proven. I think our friend Chamber is smart enough to know people will certainly believe the police commissioner before they will a patrolman."

Windsor was not as confident. "Just the same," he said, "it wouldn't hurt to keep him happy."

Stephens mulled over the suggestion. "You might be right. If he got what he wanted—which isn't very much —he might just forget what he's heard."

Windsor got up and moved nervously toward the door. "I'll leave it in your hands, Larry. Whatever you decide is okay with me."

As if he had any alternative, Stephens thought.

"Keep me posted, please," Windsor added. The first deputy nodded and the commissioner left.

Stephens shook his head and turned back to the window

[218]

and stared at the bridge. After a few minutes he sat down and swirled the chair around to the desk. Taking a blank piece of paper from the top drawer, he printed SUICIDE in block letters, folded it and placed it in his side pocket. Also from the top drawer he removed a bulky white business envelope that he placed in his inside jacket pocket. He left the office for the parking compound.

Traffic moved slowly across the bridge into Brooklyn. Stephens followed a series of expressways ultimately leading to the Bath Beach section. He exited on 86th Street and rode for ten minutes, stopping at a red light on nearly every corner. Numerous gas stations and fast-food sites lined the road. The side streets were quiet and residential, with row after row of attached two-families, mostly red and white brick, a small stoop out front. At 18th Avenue an elevated train structure hid the daylight considerably, and the character of the neighborhood changed. On the sidewalks now were familiar sights to Stephens: fruit and vegetable stands, clothes racks in front of dress shops, lawn furniture in front of hardware stores, cardboard boxes filled with dishes, cups and water glasses in front of variety stores. Almost every business spilled its wares onto the sidewalk in front, a minor violation of law, since technically it hindered pedestrian traffic. Stephens knew most of the owners by their first names; he had been assigned to that precinct, the Six-Two, for a while as a lieutenant and had extorted money from nearly every one of them.

On 24th Avenue, under the el, he parked his car near a bicycle shop. He got out, looking around nonchalantly. The streets bristled with midday shoppers searching for bargains in the flea-market atmosphere. Satisfied there was no one taking special note of his presence, he entered the shop. An array of bicycles, racers and non-racers, big and small, high seats and low seats, assorted frames, handlebars, accessories and colors, lined both sides of the store. The wooden floor, noticeably buckled in spots, was covered with sawdust. In the rear, on the left-hand side, a man with grey, soiled work clothes pumped air into the front wheel of a new yellow racer. Stephens approached and the man looked up. They smiled at each other as the first deputy continued past to a door farther back. He opened it and stepped in. A stove and refrigerator nestled side by side to the left. They were clean, but old, very old. Even older was a sink sitting on cast-iron legs, an open space beneath. To the right stood a cheap, white-metal china closet, half-filled with dishes and cups. The room was painted in a pale, semigloss green.

A broad-shouldered man in his late 30's wearing a white shirt, light green V-neck sweater and black corduroy jacket, sat at a table reading an Italian newspaper. Half-full in front of him lay a small cup of espresso. He looked up from the paper, his dark brown eyes and black curly hair contrasting with an olive complexion. His nose was misshapen, broken in the past.

Stephens knew him only as Antonio, though certainly that was not his real name. They had dealt together before, most recently on the beating of Stuart Pierce. Antonio came high, but he was good at his trade. Though arrested and charged with murder on two different occasions in the past, he had not been convicted.

The men greeted each other; an empty formality without the use of names. Because of the nature of his business, Antonio trusted no one. "When I heard you had called I was surprised."

Stephens' face was without expression. "I like the way you do business."

"So I have been told." Dispersing with any more foreplay, he came right to the point. "When would you like the bicycle delivered?"

"As soon as possible." Stephens was anxious to part ways. The least amount of time together, the better for both.

Antonio nodded and stretched his hand across the table. Stephens removed the envelope from within his jacket and placed it in the open palm. The price was twenty thousand dollars. He took the piece of paper from his side pocket and showed it to the Italian. Again Antonio nodded. Stephens ripped the paper several times and placed the pieces back in his pocket.

"I'm sure you'll be satisfied."

Stephens was biting and blunt. "I better be." Nothing else needed to be said.

Having bought the death of Stuart Pierce, Stephens returned to his car.

CHAPTER 14

CHRIS lapped the pool in the plasticlike cavern of the Police Academy. Kicking away from the far end, he looked up at the office. Barney was working busily at his desk, head down in concentration. Chris glanced at the clock on the wall. It was two-thirty. He reached the near end, pulled himself out and walked to his towel, hanging on a wall hook nearby. Wiping his face left-handed, he stuck the index finger and thumb of his right hand into the inside pocket of his bathing suit and pulled out some coins. He dried himself, made his way to the side exit, pushed open the swinging door and stepped to a wall phone in the tiny, asphalt hallway connecting the pool to the main locker-rooms. Slinging the towel around his neck, he dropped a dime into the slot and dialed the operator. He told her the number, deposited an additional sixty-five cents and listened as the phone on the other end rang. Once. Twice. Then, an answer. He recognized Sabra's voice immediately.

"Oh, hi, Chris. I didn't think you would really call." She sounded genuinely surprised. "I was kind of hoping you would."

"That sounds encouraging. I was wondering if we could get together."

"I've been looking forward to it."

Chris was seeing her in his mind's eye, as if that were enough. "This afternoon."

"You couldn't have picked a better time."

"How does an early dinner sound?"

"Fine."

"Any problems being out of the house?"

"None. I can take care of it."

She gave him directions to a movie theatre in West Caldwell, New Jersey, where she would be waiting in front. Chris repeated them: "Forty-six to West Caldwell, Bloomfield to Passaic. Four o'clock."

He hung up, smiling, and banged his right fist into an open hand. But there was still his scheduled tour of four to twelve. After a few seconds he picked up the phone again, deposited a dime and called to ask for an "emergency day" off. "Something personal came up" would be enough to do it.

Desk officers frowned on granting emergency days off right before the tour, but as long as there were enough men to cover, there was no real problem. Chris had plenty of accumulated time on the books, and he hadn't made a practice of asking for emergency days at the

[223]

last minute. More important, Lieutenant Kilkenny was the desk officer.

Chris got the time off.

He had yet another phone call to make and deposited his last dime. He dialed and listened till there was an answer.

"Hello." It was Sandy.

"Hi, hon."

"Oh, hi. I didn't expect to hear your voice. What's the matter?"

"Nothing. I just wanted to tell you I'm going straight to work. I'll hang out here in the pool for another half-hour or so and then go in." He wasn't accustomed to lying to his wife and he wondered if it showed.

"Okay, hon." She was not the least bit suspicious. "I'll see you tonight."

He hung up and felt a quick pang of guilt. He loved his wife and enjoyed her, yet there were times—though they were rare—when he preferred the company of another woman. He took comfort in the realization that he didn't lie to himself. Life was moments and this was one.

He walked back through the swinging door to the pool area and up the stairs to the office. Barney was still at his desk. He wore a white T-shirt with "N.Y.P.D." emblazoned in red on the front. Chris waved and went through the private locker-room door to shower and dress. In about fifteen minutes he was back out in the office, attaché case in hand, to say goodbye. He left the building hurriedly, wasting no time getting to his car. He didn't want to be late and it wouldn't be long before the rush hour traffic began to build rapidly.

Chris was dressed in a chestnut sports jacket over a sun-yellow shirt, brown slacks and shoes. It occurred to him that his step had more of a spring than usual, and the reason was obvious. He arrived at his car and started up, pulling away without giving the engine a chance to warm. It sputtered for three blocks on the way to the highway. He had been right about the traffic. It was flowing nicely, but it would not be long before it turned heavy. He breezed along on the way to the George Washington Bridge and his thoughts were on Sabra. He didn't know her yet, but Jesus she was sexy in such a pure, natural, and elemental way. She would be exciting in flannel pajamas. Her girlish face and swollen breasts; her shapely waist and hips; and her legs: long and lean, tanned and silken, leading up to golden, tight-skinned thighs. The white rise between her thighs flashed to his mind. He would never forget. Before he realized it, he was over the bridge and into New Jersey. Following behind unobserved, the green van and brown station-wagon of the Saturation Unit alternated positions, so that Chamber would not get suspicious at continually seeing the same vehicle in his rear-view mirror. But their caution was needless, for Chris, perhaps for the first time in his life, never once looked in the rear-view mirror.

Chris followed the signs to Route 46 and soon was cruising past oil refineries, pharmaceutical plants and man-made lakes. Funny, he thought, that was all he ever noticed when driving through New Jersey. The whole state seemed to be covered with unending highways, oil refineries, manufacturing plants and man-made lakes.

[225]

It beat the hell out of him why its nickname was the "Garden State."

His mind flashed to his wife. She was sexy, too, but not in the same way as Sabra. Sabra had worn a clinging, thigh-high dress and had bent and stooped, exposing herself innocently. Sandy was different. She was more reserved. She didn't own a thigh-high dress. She didn't have to. Her eyes sometimes would betray suggestive thoughts. Or her pouty lips. And her body was as provocatively endowed as Sabra's. Chris smiled, thinking that she, too, would be exciting in flannel pajamas.

The sign was upon him: "West Caldwell—Bloomfield Avenue." He exited, following a semicircular roadway that brought him to the main thoroughfare of the town. Staying between thirty and thirty-five, on the right-hand side of the wide, four-laned road, he moved along Bloomfield Avenue, glancing at the signs on every corner. Each side street was lined heavily with burly trees and look-alike one-family houses, unattached, shingled, peaked roofs, well-sodded lawns encircled with wooden fencing. On every other corner, it seemed, there was a drugstore, and no three blocks passed without a gas station on either side of the road. Before long he reached the downtown area, similar to all downtown areas across America, complete with park and benches, domed city hall, bus depot and hamburger franchise. Instinctively, he slowed down, scanning ahead. Two blocks away was a theatre marquee. He continued on. From half a block the street sign was clear: Passaic. This was it. But Sabra was not in sight. Aside from an old, stooping woman walking her dog, the streets were void of pedestrians.

Then he saw her. Sabra, engrossed in the showcased pictures and posters describing the current attraction, strolled from within the cutaway lobby of the movie theatre. Chris had a side view and her breasts appeared even larger than he remembered. She was wearing a white blouse, ruffled on the cuffs and collar, and a kelly-green, knee-length skirt. When she turned toward him, he saw that the skirt was a wraparound, only half-buttoned down the front, and a slit revealed her copper-toned, sinuous legs to mid-thigh. His pulse quickened. Her hair hung loosely past the shoulders and caught the sunlight. As he pulled up, he saw that the ruffled blouse sank deeply between rounded, half-exposed breasts. She was devastating, and he felt good as she approached the car.

"You look happy," she said, leaning in the open window.

"I am happy," Chris said. "You look great."

"Stimulating, am I?"

Chris smiled. "That's a good word." He raised the gear lever to "park," jumped out and circled the car to open the door for her. She got in and Chris was quick to notice she was wearing light green panties as her legs parted toward him. She saw him looking and smiled. His heart began to pound and he was sure his face was reddening. So much beauty so close was difficult to bear without touching. He slammed the door shut, circled the car again and got in.

"Where to?" he asked.

"Dinner?"

"Sure. If it's not too early for you."

[227]

Sabra shook her head. She suggested a French restaurant, Rousseau's, in Montclair and gave him directions.

"Just stay on Bloomfield . . . about five miles."

He lowered the lever to "drive" and accelerated into the left lane. They chatted as they drove for about ten minutes until Chris spotted the restaurant on the right-hand side of the road. An unlit neon sign hung over the entrance of a square, red-brick building surrounded by a huge, yellow-lined parking lot. It was near empty.

"From the looks of this lot," Chris said, pulling into a space in front, "I don't think we'll have any trouble getting a table."

Unobserved across the street, the brown station wagon of the Saturation Unit pulled to a stop.

"It's good we came early," Sabra said. "This restaurant is very popular."

When he opened her door, he again enjoyed a good view of her legs as she emerged. He closed the door and they strolled toward the building. Through the front door they were transported into an atmosphere of Mediterranean wood, gold-linen tablecloths, and pleasant lighting. Most tables were empty. They were met by a black-suited maitre d', who led them to the rear and seated them in a secluded corner.

Over a four-course dinner, with cocktails first, then wine, the conversation drifted from music to religion, to fashion, to television, books they had read, politics and each other. They talked about likes and dislikes, habits, fantasies, work and play.

He liked her. Her personality was as stimulating as her body, and she was intelligent.

[228]

But the conversation was not so distracting that he didn't glance often to the cleavage bared by the plunging neckline of her blouse. She had been loose and relaxed when they entered and after two martinis and the wine was even more so. Time passed quickly. Appetites satiated and most of the usual conversational topics covered, Chris called for the check. He tipped and they leisurely made their way back to the car.

"Well, what now?" Chris said, opening the door, throwing his jacket across the back seat.

Sabra was staring at him. She reached out to caress his hand. "I feel like being close to you, Chris. I want to do what you want to do." He could see desire in her eyes. She sat on the seat and purposely lingered as she swayed her legs inside, her knees separating slightly. Chris closed the door and walked around the front. He could feel her eyes on him all the way. He got in and started the engine. He looked over and gulped her beauty. She was still staring. Without a word he swung out of the parking lot and cruised along Bloomfield Avenue. On the way to the restaurant, he remembered, he had passed a Holiday Inn and he headed straight for it. The green van followed.

In minutes they were standing before the door to room 415. Chris opened it and stepped in, gently pulling Sabra behind him. She was quick to respond and as Chris closed the door she reached for the light switch, but he caught her hand and drew her close. With the face of a young girl and the body of a woman, she looked at him, innocent, yet knowing. Releasing her hand, he slipped his arms around her and pulled her

[229]

body closer. Now the glimpses of legs and breasts and bulging panties flashed in his mind and triggered the natural physical reaction. She pressed her hips against his and felt him swell, inch by inch, rising quickly. He grew and hardened, and she pressed against him more tightly. He moved his mouth to hers, slowly and deliberately. Their lips touched, and his penis grew more rigid. She slid her arms behind him, clawing deeply into his back, and leaned her full-sized breasts forward to his chest. They tightened their embrace until their bodies could come no closer. He slipped out his tongue, gliding it smoothly along her top lip, lingering at the corner, slowly sliding it back along the bottom. She opened her mouth wide to accept it. He thrust it deep, recklessly, reaching for the throat. She was wild with lustful thoughts. Their bodies rubbed and moved, and the present became all. They were about to take each other where neither had ever been, and they shivered in expectation. She slid her hands up his back and onto his neck, playing, then moved to his ears, pinching, inserting her fingers inside quickly. Simultaneously she swiveled her body, and her thighs passed back and forth over his now enormous instrument of pleasure. Chris broke the kiss and moved along her cheek, brushing her hair aside, breathing heavily. He opened his mouth and covered her ear, jutting his tongue in and out slowly. His tongue was warm and alive. Finally he held it inside as chills flashed across her flesh, and her mind blurred in lust. She slid her right hand down his back and brought it forward. Easing the pressure of her hips for an instant, she slipped her hand to the bulge in his pants.

[230]

He moaned in joy as her fingers covered the lump and caressed it. She held it for a few seconds, then moved to the zipper, pulling it down at a calculated pace. He throbbed in anticipation. She slipped her hand inside around the shaft and stroked it gently and deliberately. He lunged forward at the hips, his brain scintillating with uncontrollable sparks of passion, his thoughts clouded with desire. Instinctively, she stepped back. He ripped at the buttons of his shirt. In seconds it was off. He unlaced his shoes and shoveled them and his socks to the side.

Sabra smiled and pulled the ruffled white blouse over her head in one swift motion. Her breasts were hard and erect, the pink tips protruding invitingly. She looked at Chris, his muscles firm, as if she wanted to please, to devour him entirely. One by one she opened the buttons of her skirt. It dropped to the floor. Chris looked at her standing before him clad only in green bikini panties. She stepped to the bed, smiling lustfully, and lay teasing him, her soft eyes gleaming. He approached, gazing at her naked body, hungry to have her. Lying down, he touched his bare chest to her hot, hardened breasts. He kissed her fleetingly on the chin, continuing quickly downward, brushing his lips along the skin to the top of her breasts. He slipped a nipple into his mouth. She opened his belt and unhooked his pants, hitching them around his hips. He pulled them and his shorts to the knees and swiftly wriggled them off. He slipped his hand inside her panties, exploring the treasure he had dreamed of. She writhed and wriggled as Chris fingered her pubic hair, then slipped his finger to the fold of flesh below. He stroked the slit until it was moist and inserted his finger deeply. She squirmed uncontrollably, licking his face, his ears, his neck. Her panties now off, he mounted her. She was panting feverishly, running her fingers along the nape of his neck, down his back, pawing, digging, scratching. He pressed his erection against her sex and with little friction he was inside. She groaned in ecstacy as she felt the stiff organ enter gloriously. She arched her back and accepted the full length of the staff. Chris strained at the loins forward into the chasm of divine pleasure. This could only be a dream. She writhed beneath him, contracting and expanding pubic muscles, squeezing the shaft of pleasure with each withdrawal. His mind built with frenzy as he rocked in fluid motion. Sabra followed as though she were in perpetual motion. He moved faster and faster, and he imagined her nerve endings tingling wildly until she would burst. She arched her back. "Oh, God . . . please," she moaned, ". . . please . . . plea . . ." Suddenly, joyously, Chris exploded inside her, filling the cavity with warmth and satisfaction. She tensed her body to accept the flow as Chris lay united and locked atop her. Their bodies quivered and their hearts raced.

CHAPTER 15

OUTSIDE the office of Lawrence Stephens, Chris switched
on the tape recorder, buttoned his shirt and took a deep
breath. He entered. Having been ordered there again,
his scheduled tour of 4 P.M. to midnight had been moved
to an 8 A.M. to 4 P.M. Past the black leather couch
and small magazine table, he approached the sliding-
glass window. The secretary, her thick-rimmed glasses
balanced at the tip of her upturned nose, sat reading the
morning paper. She noticed Chris and slid the window
open.

He cleared his throat and announced himself.

"Yes, he's expecting you. Just a second, please." She
buzzed the intercom. "Patrolman Chamber's here, sir."

"Send him in."

The secretary opened the door of the grey partition

and led Chris to the inner office. She smiled, closing the door behind him. Stephens was an imposing figure at his desk, clear of any papers. Only the bottom of the Brooklyn Bridge was visible through the window behind him, the top enveloped in an eerie fog.

"Sit down," Stephens commanded and Chris complied, moving to the chair facing the desk.

Stephens relaxed his brows and leaned back comfortably. He studied Chamber with penetrating eyes, his hands clasped in front of him, a shrewd tactician about to make a move. And it was indeed Stephens' move. Chris looked past the deputy commissioner to see the fog looming ominously in the background. "How would you like to be assigned to the Police Academy pool?" Stephens asked, the command quality of his voice conspicuously absent.

Chris was not expecting this. The Police Academy pool was the assignment he wanted more than any other in the department. But he had dismissed it because he hardly thought there was a chance. Wait a minute now, he thought. Stephens had played only one card. There would be others. There had to be conditions and most likely the reciprocation was high. He would proceed cautiously. "I'd like that assignment very much," he said.

Stephens smiled. "I was sure you'd be pleased. Of course, there is one thing you must offer in return."

Here it comes, Chris thought.

"You are to forget that conversation you had with Stuart Pierce the other night and you are not to concern yourself with any wild thoughts about me and the commissioner from now on."

[234]

How did he know about that conversation, Chris wondered . . . unless . . . unless he was being watched. Yes, of course, he was being watched. Pierce wouldn't have told Stephens about the conversation. He had come looking for help. Wait. Perhaps Pierce was the one being watched. No matter. He would know for sure before long. So the first deputy and his boss were worried and wanted to pacify him before it got out of hand. It was extremely satisfying to Chris, holding a flush to the commissioner's straight. And they didn't even know about the tapes. Or did they? Surely Stephens would ask for them as a part of the deal.

"Is that all?" Chris asked. "Keep quiet and forget what I know?"

"That's all. It's really not much in return for the pool assignment."

Chris chuckled to himself. They didn't know about the tapes—or the one he was recording at the moment. His brain raced. Why settle for the Police Academy pool? They're probably prepared to offer a lot more. And if they weren't now, they would be when they found he had recorded every conversation. Depending on how worried they were, he could no doubt demand and receive whatever he wanted. But, why be greedy? The job at the pool was the easiest in the department. The one he wanted. And something he enjoyed doing. Imagine, getting paid for recreation.

"That's very tempting," Chris said, stalling for time to think it over.

"Frankly, Chamber," Stephens said, "the commissioner and I are aware of everything Pierce told you, and there is no proof for any of it. Admittedly, you have

[235]

been presented with a cloudy picture, surrounded by coincidental circumstances that could very easily lead you to believe that what he said was true. But it's not, and rather than leave the possibility open that some of those untruths reach the wrong people, perhaps resulting in an embarrassing effort to clear ourselves, we want to quell it in the beginning. We're well aware that you have a good head on your shoulders and thought to offer you this transfer as a sort of reward for not jumping the gun thus far, and to discourage you from starting any ugly rumors in the future."

The weasellike approach was unbecoming. Yet the offer was a good one. What would it mean? Disappointing Pierce who had asked for help? But who the hell was Pierce to him, anyway? A goddamn pimp-homosexual who got himself in a bind and ran for the first cover he saw. And the public? Not exposing the corruption in the department could certainly be construed as a betrayal to the public. But that didn't wash. The public had been betraying themselves all these years, anyhow. It was the public who prompted most of the corruption: the motorist with the ten dollars to avoid a summons, the supermarket manager with the five bucks to walk with him to the bank, the bar owner with the ten for the sector to overlook a catalogue of violations. The public had had many chances to clean up the corruption themselves, but were unwilling to take the necessary steps. Why should Chris Chamber do the dirty work and let the freeloaders of society reap the benefits? And why get involved any further? Stephens offered a good solution.

"I'll cooperate, commissioner. I'd like to be assigned to the Police Academy."

"Good." Stephens was noticeably relieved. So much for Chamber. All that remained was Pierce. He leaned forward, resting his elbows on the desk. "It'll take a little while for the transfer. We don't want to be too conspicuous."

"I understand."

Returning to formality, Stephens opened his top drawer and took out some paperwork. "Okay, Chamber, you can go." Chris rose and crossed the office to the door. He smiled at the secretary as he passed through the outer office and strode to the hall, then made his way out of the building and down the street to his car. He got in, started up and pulled away, acutely aware that he might be followed, now conscious that every move he made, every word he said might possibly be under surveillance. It would be easy enough to find out. He crossed the bridge into Brooklyn, glancing at his rearview mirror every minute or so, noting what cars were behind. He was familiar with the methods and procedures employed when following someone—alternating cars, alternating positions, driving behind the subject most times, but in front of him when possible to divert suspicion—so he was careful to note all cars around him at all times. He presumed correctly that if he were being followed there would be at least two cars involved. He entered the expressway off the bridge and before he exited, had narrowed the field down to five cars and a van. When he got off the expressway he purposely took the long route to Our Lady by the Sea, turning as often as possible, not to lose his tail, rather to make clear who they were, and when he arrived, the station wagon and the van of the Saturation Unit were still with him. At least now he knew for sure he was being watched and by whom.

He had decided to stop by the church to tell Frank Roselli to be careful whenever they conversed and to pass on to the priest the most current tape. He was assuming that those who were watching now had been watching his other visits and were not aware of the reason behind them. At the rectory he was told by the receptionist that Father Roselli was out for the day, so he left a message that he had been there and would return.

Stuart Pierce peeked through the peep hole. His eyes were swollen and he couldn't see well, but in the hall outside his apartment he could make out a grey-uniformed workman, dark complexion.

"Who is it, please?" Pierce asked through the door.

"Kermit Exterminators," the man answered. A blue patch with white lettering on his chest verified the company.

"You have the wrong apartment. I didn't call you."

"Every apartment is being sprayed. The owner has retained us. You were supposed to have been notified."

Pierce opened the door. His face was still badly bruised and scraped. "Nobody notified me, but as long as I don't have to pay . . ."

"It's paid for." The workman was holding a black tool-box with brass latches and corner supports.

"Then come in," Pierce said, motioning.

The man entered and as Pierce started to close the door behind him a giant of a man in dark clothing pushed his way into the apartment. The uniformed exterminator dropped his toolbox and turned on Pierce, grabbing his left arm as the other man grabbed his right. Without easing his hold, the giant kicked the door shut. The uniformed workman pressed his hand tightly over Pierce's mouth, as the homosexual widened his eyes in terror.

"Don't make a sound," the workman ordered quietly, his eyes narrowed, hinting at what he might do. Pierce jerked his head side to side nervously and the workman removed his hand.

"Just don't hit me. Please don't hit me," Pierce whimpered, the recent beating vivid in his mind and body. The duo led him to the dining room and shoved him down into a chair at the table, beneath the glittering chandelier. As Pierce cried quietly, the workman retrieved his toolbox, sitting it on the polished table. He removed two pairs of clear rubber gloves and tossed a pair to his accomplice. They both put them on.

"Do you own a typewriter?" the exterminator wanted to know.

Pierce, for an instant, was relieved in assuming their intentions were merely larcenous, that they had not been sent there to beat him. "Yes, I do," he stuttered. "In the closet." He pointed to a narrow door separating the paneled walls of the dining room from the black and gold velvet of the living room. The man in grey uniform strode swiftly to the door, opened it, surveyed the closet and picked up the black-encased typewriter from the floor. He carried it to the table, laying it down across from the homosexual. Removing the case, he plucked a piece of paper from the holder within and rolled it into position in the machine. Pierce sat in utter puzzlement, not daring to question his tormentors. The workman typed at moderate speed for a few minutes, removed the paper and encircled the table. Covering what he just had typed with a blank sheet, he laid the paper in front of Pierce.

"Sign it," he commanded.

Pierce looked up into determined, icy eyes. He was reluctant to sign something he could not see. "What is it?" His voice was barely audible.

The giant spoke up. "Don't ask no questions. Just sign it."

Pierce shook his head nervously. "I can't sign it if you don't show me what . . ." He bit his lip in horror as the man in grey pulled a revolver from the open tool-box on the table. He cocked the hammer and held it perilously close to the black-and-blue, perspiring forehead of the homosexual.

"Sign it now," the exterminator demanded, "or I'll splatter your brains on the floor."

Pierce cried. "I'll sign." The dark-jacketed giant handed him a pen. Without seeing what had been typed on the page, he complied.

Expressionless, the gunman looked up to the chandelier, then to his muscular partner. "Give me a hand," he said, grabbing one end of the table. His accomplice grabbed the other and they moved it out of the way.

Pierce could not contain his bewilderment. "I don't understand. What are you doing?" he whimpered.

"Shut up," said the gunman, and the homosexual closed his eyes in obedience.

The uniformed assistant again glanced up at the chandelier, moved one of the dining room chairs underneath and stepped to the toolbox on the table. Pierce opened his eyes to see him remove a thick-woven rope. In an instant he saw that one end of the rope had been fashioned into a noose. Pierce looked in terror to the chair beneath the chandelier, then back to the emotionless, dark-eyed man moving toward him. He was gripped with a nauseating feeling of helplessness. "Oh my God, no. Please, no," he sobbed. Suddenly, he burst toward the front door, his mind racing with escape. The giant collared him, quickly clamping a hand over his mouth. Pierce struggled for all he was worth, laboring for freedom, knowing his life was in the balance, kicking, swinging, punching, but he was no match for the brute force that held him. Pinned to the floor on his back, he watched in horror, squirming intermittently with spasms of energy trying to free himself, as the grey-clad workman, standing on the chair, first tied the rope securely to the chandelier, then tried it with his own weight. The chandelier held, and the noose swayed below. On signal, the muscle-bound executioner rose slowly from the floor, still silencing the homosexual with one hand and clutching him tightly at the collar with the other. One last-ditch effort by Pierce: he mustered all his might and lashed out at the giant who held him, but his struggle was useless as the uniformed hood rushed to aid his accomplice. They forced him to stand on the chair, lifting him bodily, and slipped the noose around his neck. The exterminator pushed the knot to the nape. Feeling the rope, Pierce froze in fright and stopped struggling. The giant gripped the homosexual's arms. Quickly the uniformed executioner pulled the chair from underneath Pierce and grabbed his kicking legs. The crystals of the chandelier rattled noisily. It was an agonizing death, for the neck was not snapped.

As the weight of his body pulled the noose tight, Pierce squealed, tugging, straining to free his hands that he might relieve the pressure. His body quivered, his eyes widened, his swollen tongue shot from the mouth. A wretched stench flowed from involuntarily loosed bowels. He gasped for air but could not inhale. His face turned a deep purple, his eyes bulged from the sockets. The rope drew tighter and tighter, strangulating, cutting the skin around the neck. Bile spewed from his lips. It did not take long. His strength sapped from exertion, his brain unable to get air, Pierce died.

The contract called for the pair to stay until the end. Methodically they gathered their equipment and deposited the signed suicide note on the floor beneath the dangling body.

CHAPTER 16

THE room was sunless, drawn blinds and drapes. A cricket chirped sporadically outside the door. Chris sat up in bed and stared across at the mirror, studying himself as a dark reflection. Even under the covers, Sabra's naked voluptuous form was discernible and breathtaking. He shifted his eyes to her, arms beneath the pillow, lying still beside him. The sheet stopped at her waist and her breasts hung heavily toward him. Her hair was tousled, yet somehow seemed acceptable. Her lips were pink and tempting.

Again they had shared a night of ecstacy, unbounded by the slightest inhibition. During their lovemaking Chris had been guided into acts he had never known before; sexual acts that rendered his mind insane with pleasure beyond comparison. Without a doubt, Sabra was one of the best lovers he had ever experienced. She was able to excite a man with charms and skills few women possessed. Chris had climaxed six times during the night and never before had he been treated to such a thrilling sensation at the point of orgasm.

He drew the covers back and, naked, padded along the carpet to the bathroom. He closed the door before turning on the light, not wanting to disturb his sleeping lover. As he showered, he savored the previous evening, retracing it from the time he picked her up to the instant he took her in his arms and kissed her. He tingled thinking about how he had explored every inch of her body, how warm it was, how exciting her treasures. He ached at the loins at how eager she had been to reciprocate for every thrill received.

His thoughts turned to his wife. He had lied to Sandy, telling her he had made an arrest at the end of the tour, which made sleeping over at the precinct more convenient than going home. She had accepted it as truth, unquestioned. It had happened many times before. He felt some pangs of guilt, not only for betraying her trust, but also for spending money on Sabra without hesitation. It had been a long time since he had taken his wife to dinner or a late supper as he had done with his lover last night. So much of the romance that had existed in the early years of their marriage had vanished, replaced with routine: the natural order of things between man and wife.

He stepped from the shower, dried himself off and, flicking off the light, reentered the bedroom. He groped around for his clothes, spread about on the floor where he had thrown them, and when he had dressed he cursorily combed his hair in the mirror and went out. The sun was rising, dissipating the chill of the early morning. He should have taken his jacket, he thought. Sabra's car, windows frosted, covered with dew, was right in front. Chris surveyed Bloomfield Avenue and smiled at its desolation. Somewhere, he thought, there were three or four angry, frustrated men, sipping their coffee, wondering where the hell he was. He had done it all very well. Last evening he had slipped his tail with little difficulty. He had suspected that a transmitting device might have been affixed to his car, so he parked it in his garage and searched it thoroughly, concentrating on the underbelly. When he found the magnetic device clinging to the bell housing, he simply removed it and placed it in the glove compartment. It still would transmit, and his watchers would think nothing awry. He drove to work with it there. However, when he started out from the precinct after work en route to meeting Sabra in New Jersey, he waited for an opportune time and turned into a side street, accelerated swiftly, turned again at the corner, and again at the next, until he was certain his followers were not in sight. Quickly he removed the transmitting device from the glove compartment and, in an easy fluid motion, leaned out the door, stuck it behind the bumper of a taxicab stopped at a red light beside him. The cabdriver turned left and he to the right. He smiled grimly and would have paid twenty bucks to see the faces on the men whose job it was to keep him in sight after they realized they had been duped. When he arrived at the movie theatre where he was to meet Sabra, he was sure he had not been

[245]

followed. Even so, there was the possibility of a "bug" designed to pick up conversation in the car, so to play it safe he parked and they traveled in Sabra's car. She suggested they go to her house, her husband being away on business for three days, but Chris, uncomfortable with that arrangement, insisted on the motel.

Hands in pockets, wishing he'd worn a jacket, Chris sauntered into the office. The manager greeted him with a smile and offered a cup of coffee. Chris thanked him but declined. He bought a newspaper and started back for the room. As was his habit, he turned to the sports section first, his way of easing into the news of the day. The front-page news, like bad coffee, was too bitter to start with: wars, murders, rapes, fires; too many ugly wounds in society. He reached Sabra's car and leaned against it, digesting the paper, giving the woman with whom he was falling in love more time to sleep. He turned to the front and perused the familiar items quickly, working his way to the editorial page in the center. But he stopped suddenly to read the story on page 16. "Police Find Hanging Suicide." Stuart Pierce was identified as the victim in the first sentence. He read on with growing awareness of his own rage and fear. How coincidental and convenient the homosexual's death was for the police commissioner and his unscrupulous first deputy. Chris couldn't buy the story. He closed the paper with a slap and stared blankly, concentrating, trying to place things in perspective. He was certain Pierce had not committed suicide; he had been murdered. He had been executed to make the story of corruption on the highest level of the Police Department uncorroborated, thus unable to be proven. At least Stephens and Windsor probably thought that an allegation against them could not be proven now. But they didn't know about the tapes and the tapes were corroboration enough. If they ever did find out about them, obviously they would stop at nothing to get them. They would even murder. Chris had no proof that Pierce had been eliminated by Stephens and Windsor, but *he* was convinced and that was enough. Too many times had his instincts been right. For his own well-being, to be prepared for an attempt on his life, he had to assume these instincts were correct again. It was very clear now that he could not cooperate with murderers.

He pushed away from the car and stepped to the door, unlocking it with the key from his pocket. The lights were on and showed the mars on the cheap furniture that had not been noticeable in the dark. Sabra, clad in a form-fitting, black negligee, brushed her hair at the mirror. Her shape was highlighted by the sheer undergarment, firm buttocks pulled tight as she leaned forward. Her image in the mirror set Chris's heart pounding as he watched her breasts move with each stroke, her finely textured hair falling to the bare shoulder. The neckline of the negligee sloped across the nipples and sank deeply to the navel. She smiled at him in the mirror and for an instant he didn't think of Stephens or Windsor or Pierce or any of his problems. She engrossed him totally and made him forget. He walked toward her and once again he throbbed below, thinking of the way she had explored every inch of his body with her tongue.

He was falling fast for this woman and was convinced it was not infatuation.

He slipped his hands under her arms, fondling her breasts as he kissed her softly on the neck. Moaning, she writhed lustfully to his touch. She turned and unbuttoned his shirt, running her fingers through the hair of his chest, then embraced him, pressing her body tightly against his, burying her head in his brawn. She darted her burning tongue between her lips and slid it across his chest. The warmth of the moist organ shot wild sensations through his body and down his spine.

"I could do this twenty-four hours a day," he whispered, slipping his hands to the center of her buttocks, pulling her tighter against the lower part of his body, "but right now I've got something very important to take care of." He knew how easily they might wind up staying for a few more hours and he needed time alone to think things out.

"Whatever you say," she breathed heavily. She pulled away slowly, intentionally brushing his penis as she turned for the bathroom. "I'll be ready in a few minutes." She stepped inside.

"I'll warm up the car."

"Boy, you really are in a hurry."

"Not really. But if I don't do something right now I'm liable to rush in there, throw you to the floor and rape you."

She chuckled. "I'd like that."

He shook his head in amazement. What an impact this woman had on his life. But a time for her would have to come later. "Where's the key?"

Her voice was mocking. "Wham, bam, thank you ma'am."

Chris laughed. "Yeah, about six times." She laughed, too.

"C'mon, where's the key for your car?"

"In the change compartment of my wallet. My pocket-book's on the side of the bed."

Chris stooped to pick up her brown suede bag. He flipped the top over and dug for the wallet, brown suede also, with Indian designs, amidst makeup, loose papers, jewelry, barrettes and rubber bands. He pulled it out and unfolded it. Opposite the change compartment was a clear plastic folder with a charge card inside. Suddenly Sabra moved quickly through the doorway.

"Wait a minute. I'll get it," she said quickly.

Chris looked up. The way she appeared so suddenly made it obvious there was something inside she didn't want him to see, something she had forgotten was there until that instant. He looked down again into the change compartment. There was the car key and nothing else, not even loose change. She strode toward him, reaching her hand out for the wallet.

"I'll get it," she repeated.

Chris's eye caught the charge card again and his mouth dropped. The embossing on the plastic plate was very clear: "P.F.M. Inc." He looked at her in disbelief.

She stopped dead. She had been found out and it showed in her face. Her voice now had a different edge. "Don't get excited," she said.

Chris shook his head. He could not believe it. He didn't want to believe it. "You, too?"

"Chris, please," she said approaching once more. She slipped her hand inside his shirt.

Sex was not important for him now. Her naked body shimmering behind the flimsy material would not help her. He took a firm hold of her arm and pulled it from his body, his mind racing to comprehend. She was a plant. A goddamn plant to gain confidence. A call girl. And she almost had him.

"Who put you up to this?" he demanded to know.

She was silent. He grabbed her arms and shook her. "Who?"

Mascara tears rolled down her cheeks. "Stephens," she whimpered.

Chris knew even before she said it. Stephens. That maniacal bastard.

"But your house . . . the phone . . ." He shook his head again. "You're real. He couldn't have gone to the trouble of setting you up over here. He didn't have time."

"No."

"Then, what? I don't understand."

"I'm real. I live here."

"And you're married?"

"I'm married."

Chris was overwhelmed. This beautiful woman he had fallen for, a tramp? It hurt and it hurt badly. But it hurt more to know that he had allowed himself to be set up.

She went on. Her lips were dry and she was trembling.

[250]

"I've worked with Stuart for the last year. Every trick he sets me up with is top shelf and pays the money I'm looking for. Stuart takes care of me. He respects me as a person, not just a body. I'm a businesswoman." Her logic was sickening. Chris was gripped in the stomach by nausea as she spoke of Pierce with affection.

"How did Stephens come into this?"

"Stuart introduced us. I turned a trick for him one night and he liked me. I've seen him regularly since then." Chris's stare demanded more. "He called me last week and offered me good money for this job. It was too good to turn down."

"How much?"

She looked up. "A thousand when I bagged you, two hundred a night after that and . . ." She hesitated.

"And what?"

She stared downward. "And another thousand for pictures."

It dawned quickly. Stephens wanted something on him to counteract his knowledge, without even knowing about the tapes. If he had pictures of Chris in a compromising position with Sabra . . .

Chris stared deeply into the eyes of the woman he held. "And your husband?"

"He knows nothing."

Chris ached with his new-found knowledge. For an instant he was blinded with fury and overwhelmed with an impulse to hit her. But he couldn't. He had nearly fallen in love with her.

"You're a businesswoman, you say. You're a whore." He threw her to the floor, then took the newspaper from the bed and smashed it in her face. "Here! Read it, you little tramp. Read about your dear Stuart." Sobbing, she turned the paper right side up and read the gruesome details of the story. Chris continued. "Don't believe the suicide, Sabra. He was killed. Executed. Because he knew too much and was willing to spill his guts. You might find yourself in the same position." She turned to look at him, but he was too busy thinking of other things to concern himself with an explanation. "Get dressed and let's get the hell out of here."

The rectory door swung open and the elderly receptionist smiled at the two visitors. The morning sun was bright behind them. "Can I help you?" she asked, squinting.

The receptionist was unaccustomed to entertaining the type of men who now faced her. Both were big and dressed in ill-fitting suits. Both faces were cruel, with lazy eyes set deep. One had a bent nose and long black sideburns. He was younger than his partner, who was close to forty, with thin, neatly combed hair parted to the left and narrow lips over a square chin.

"Father Roselli, please." The younger man was the spokesman.

"Surely," the woman said, stepping aside as they entered, "he's just finished the eight o'clock Mass." She closed the door and, hobbling on arthritic legs, joined the pair in the vestibule. Dim lights reflected off polished wooden walls and linoleum floors, waxed to a high sheen. Doors were everywhere: to the left, an open doorway to the waiting room; next to it, and around the foyer, closed, windowed doors to darkened offices; to the immediate right, a door with no window, apparently leading to the rest of the building.

"Wait in here, please," said the receptionist, gesturing toward the waiting room. The two complied as she disappeared through the windowless door. The unmistakable aroma of bacon filled the air.

The waiting room was simple, a small table scattered with religious pamphlets and magazines, dark wooden benches stretching the length of each wall. Sheer white curtains offset quarter-paneled windows, two facing the sun, one the shade of the side street. They sat for a few minutes without speaking. The door across the foyer opened again and Father Roselli stepped through in a priestly black, floor-length robe. He entered the waiting room with a smile. His face was awake and vigorous. "Can I help?" he asked.

"We'd like to talk to you privately, father."

"Okay, why don't we move into an office." The priest led the pair to a door at the rear of the foyer, opened it and switched on the light. The same type curtains as were in the waiting room adorned a window facing the churchyard. A small wooden desk, green blotter covering the top, sat to the right with three straight-back wooden chairs in front. Father Roselli moved behind the desk and motioned for the two men to have a seat. The door was closed.

The spokesman leaned forward in his chair. "I'll get right to the point, Father. We want the tapes."

The priest flushed. Who were these men? How did they know he had them? His mind darted to the telephone

[253]

conversation with Sandy Chamber the night before . . .

"No, he's not home, Frank," Sandy had said. "He's working a four to twelve. Anything important?"

"Not really. He was here earlier and I missed him. He probably wanted to give me another tape." It was a slip. Chris might not have told his wife what was going on. Her reaction confirmed just that.

"What tape?"

"Oh . . . he gave me some tapes to hold for him; I'm not sure what's on them. You better talk to him before . . ." He wanted to bow out gracefully, and she let him.

"I'll tell him you called when he comes in."

It hadn't occurred to him at the time, but obviously Chris's phone was tapped. He vaulted back to the situation at hand.

"Exactly who are you gentlemen?" he asked.

"We're friends of Chris Chamber's," the spokesman said. The other remained mute.

"And what tapes are you referring to?"

"The tapes Chris gave you. He asked us to pick them up."

"I don't understand. Chris never gave me any tapes."

The faces grew hard and intent. "All right, father, no games. We know you've got them and we want them." He unloosened his tie. "If we have to, we'll rip this place apart."

Father Roselli rose and started toward the door. "Sorry, gentlemen, I can't help you." But his way was blocked.

"You ain't goin' nowhere, unless it's to get the tapes."

The other spoke for the first time. "And we're going with you." He grabbed the priest by the collar.

Roselli wanted to hit him. The image of Jake Termotta lying against the fence flashed to his mind. The gory sight of entangled nerves and blood vessels in the open socket was very vivid. He was as fit as ever, but. . . . He fixed an icy stare at the man gripping his collar. "Get your hand off me."

"Don't hide behind the cloth, pal. It don't work in my book."

"I'm not hiding behind the cloth," he said, his voice a bit apprehensive. "I'd just like you to take your hand off me."

"You gonna get the tapes, father, or do we bust up the place . . . you included?"

The priest wasn't listening. He had not moved his eyes from the man who clutched him tightly. He raised his voice. "For the last time, get out of my way."

"Oh, a fuckin' tough guy," the thug said, tightening his grip. Without warning he smashed his fist to the priest's jaw, sending him reeling to the wall.

Coming in the front door of the rectory, a burly Irish priest in black pants and shirt, stiff white square at the collar, heard the commotion from the rear office and looked up in time to see Father Roselli get hit. He rushed to the trouble quickly.

The blow was all Roselli needed. As his assailant moved in for another punch, the priest ripped a right to his face, sending him sprawling to the door. The Irish priest entered and was immediately set upon by the other, but the burly giant clergyman raised his knee swiftly to

[255]

the groin of his attacker and decked him with a round-house. Roselli charged his would-be assailant and hit him again full and hard in the face. The blow knocked him into the hall where he hit first the far wall, then the floor. Clearly overpowered, both men hustled to the foyer and out the door. The priests let them go.

"I'm almost afraid to ask what happened," the burly priest admitted, handing Father Roselli a handkerchief.

Roselli, smiling, wiped the blood from his chin. "God damn," he said aloud. The long wait was finally over. He knew now for sure that God had chosen him. "C'mon," he said, walking into the hall, "let's discuss it over bacon and eggs."

CHAPTER 17

FIRST Deputy Commissioner Stephens entered his outer office from the hall and was greeted at the door of the grey partition by his plump secretary. He had not been in his office the entire day, having been awakened at dawn to the news that a patrolman had been shot in the Bronx and having accompanied the police commissioner to the scene, to the hospital for a visit with the wounded man, to an impromptu press conference and lastly to a late, two-hour lunch.

His secretary had her coat in hand. "I was on my way home," she said. Stephens looked to the clock on the wall. It was 4:15. She stepped to her desk, picked up a few telephone message sheets and handed them to him. "Other than a few calls, nothing much happened."

Shuffling through the messages, he lingered on one,

but showed no concern in front of his secretary. "You really didn't have to stick around," he told her, referring to the fact that her day was finished at four o'clock.

"No problem."

"Thanks, Helen, I'll see you in the morning."
She left.

The first deputy entered his office, and closed the door behind him. He went straight for the phone on the desk and dialed hurriedly. Sitting, waiting for the ring, he swiveled to a rare view of Brooklyn on a clear afternoon, then swung back to his desk, resting both elbows atop.

"Hello!" The deep voice was familiar.

"Antonio?" Stephens asked.

"Ah, my friend, I have disappointing news."

Stephens knew what he was going to say.

"We were unable to pick up the bicycle as you requested. Too difficult a location to get to, my friend, if you know what I mean. I told you when you made the request we might not be able to satisfy you on this one. My men made an effort, but were unsuccessful. I can't send anyone back again. Not back there."

It had not been too difficult to figure out what tapes Father Roselli had referred to in his conversation with Sandy Chamber. Stephens' immediate step had been to employ his Italian henchmen from Bath Beach to retrieve them.

"That's truly disappointing news," Stephens sighed.

"What can I tell you, Steve."

The deputy commissioner was piqued at Antonio's lack of concern, but, then, it was not his problem. If the tapes could not be wrenched from the priest, Chamber had to be killed. It was that simple. Stephens wondered if Chamber had figured that out. Surely he would. Without him or Stuart Pierce, those tapes were worthless in a court of law. But as long as Chamber was alive to testify to their validity, Stephens was in jeopardy. And Lawrence Stephens was not a man to be held in such jeopardy. Although Chamber had not made a move up to this point, nor had he indicated he would make any move in the future, he couldn't be allowed such an edge. The elimination of Chamber. There was no other way out, and it had to be done immediately, before the patrolman's logic told him that he was a marked man.

"Are you still there?" Antonio asked.

"Yes, I'm here." He thought to order the execution right then, but hesitated. Chamber was not an easy mark. If he was not killed on the first attempt, it would be all over. He would surely divulge his secret to an outside agency—most likely the press. And that would be the end for Stephens, Windsor and many, many men in the Department. No, Stephens could not chance failure at this time, and Antonio had shown he was capable of failure. Chamber had to be killed, but the first deputy would have to do it himself. It was an awesome decision that Stephens made in a few seconds of silence as he held the telephone to his ear.

"I'll get back to you," Stephens said into the phone, breaking the silence. "Until then, don't contact me." They hung up.

Stephens had known for a long while that there might come a time when he would have to kill to survive. That time had arrived, and he girded himself for it. Another man's life was nothing when it meant his own survival. It would not be the first murder he had had a hand in, and the stakes were so high that there was no alternative. It would be easy. Chamber would never expect it from the first deputy commissioner. It was the only way. Stephens would tell no one. Not even Windsor. Especially not Windsor. The fewer that knew, the better.

But how to pull it off? Chamber was not Stuart Pierce. He would be armed. The first deputy swung his chair around facing the window and stared out at the bridge.

Chris Chamber picked up the radio-phone from the dashboard, held it to his ear and pressed the button on the handle. "Two-One David to Central, kay."

"Go ahead, David," came the reply.

"Second Avenue and Seventy-first Street, disorderly man, one drunk sent on his way, kay."

"Ten-four, David."

"Ten-four."

He reached toward the dash to replace the phone, but Central Radio came again.

"Two-One David, ten-one, kay."

"Ten-four."

His partner for the night, Charlie Waters, pulled the car to the curb on the next corner in compliance with the signal ten-one: call the stationhouse. "Here's a box," he said, pointing to the pale-green police callbox on the lamppost. Chris got out of the car, opened the green door and removed the phone from its hook. Automatically he was connected with the Twenty-first Precinct switchboard.

"Two-one," came the voice. It was Bob Dressen.

"Two-one David on a ten-one. Chris Chamber, Bob."

"Oh, yeah, Chris. You got a call from a Frank Roselli."

Oh, no! he thought. He had been alarmed when Frank told him of the circumstances surrounding the two men after the tapes. What had happened now? He felt terrible for having involved his friend.

"He said it was very important and that he'd call back at nine." Chris looked at his watch. It was eight forty-five. "He said you wouldn't be able to reach him, so, if you could, to try to be around when he calls back."

Chris was worried. It wasn't like Frank to call on the run like that. Something must have happened. Damn it. God damn it. "Okay, Bob, I'll come in."

"Ten-four."

Chris put the phone on the hook, closed the box, returned to his partner and told him to head for the station-house. When they arrived he went inside.

The lieutenant was not at the desk. Dressen, just finishing the last swig of a can of beer, manned the switchboard. It was the same story every time Lieutenant Felcum and Dressen worked together, Chris thought. They both liked to booze it up and spent the night downing six-pack after six-pack. By the end of the tour they'd be flying. If the public only knew. Felcum was no doubt in the back room having a beer with the clerical man, so Chris told Dressen to switch the call to the muster room where he could have privacy. Dressen nodded, popping the top off another beer. Chris walked away shaking his head. No sooner had he sat down in the

[261]

muster room than the phone rang. He looked out at the switchboard and Dressen was signalling that that was the expected call. He picked up the receiver.

"Frank?"

"No, Chamber, I only said Frank Roselli because I knew you'd respond and I'd rather not have anyone know it's me. Listen to my voice. Do you know who this is?"

Chris was taken aback. He recognized the voice of Lawrence Stephens instantly. "What do you want?"

"I want to meet with you. I think we've got some very important business to discuss."

The events of the last days rushed through Chris's mind. He knew a confrontation was inevitable.

"Just me and you. On an equal plane, if you know what I mean. No gimmicks, no gadgets, no tapes."

"When?" asked Chris.

"Tonight."

"I'm on till midnight."

"When you finish."

"All right by me."

"Good. I'll meet you on the Sixth Avenue 23rd Street Independent station—Brooklyn bound—north end of the platform at . . ."

Chris interrupted. "On the subway? Can't we be a little more civilized?"

Meeting on the subway was calculated. Stephens had good reason for that arrangement and he had expected Chamber to question it. "You forget you're being followed. There's nothing I can do about the tail. The P.C. ordered that surveillance and I can't lift it." The surveillance by the Saturation Unit was a perfect support for his defense should he ever be suspected or accused of murdering Chamber. Would he kill him, the logic demanded, knowing full well Chris was being followed twenty-four hours a day?

"You'll have to lose them," Stephens said. "You've done it before, I don't think you'll have too much trouble doing it again. It'll make it easier if you're not in your car when you try."

"Okay, what time?"

"One o'clock. 23rd Street station—Brooklyn bound —north end of the platform."

Stephens hung up.

Chris put the phone down slowly and reflected on the meeting and its implications. What would he gain by going? Stephens was backed into a corner and Chris wasn't exactly sure what to do about it. Maybe the meeting would help. What could Stephens be up to? A trapped animal attacks. Or perhaps he wanted to reopen negotiations now that he knew about the tapes. But what would he offer?

CHAPTER 18

DEPUTY Commissioner Stephens leaned against the up-
right iron girder, a fluorescent bulb flickering nearby.
The subway station was damp and unpleasant; a stench
of stale urine and vomit hung in the air. Benches and
vending machines crowded the debris-littered platform.
The tracks clicked, a signal that a train was approaching, prompting him to look out into the darkness. The
musty air about him rustled slightly. Suddenly, deep in
the black, bright lights flashed into view, moving closer
rapidly. The tracks clicked again and the rustling air
turned to stiff breeze. With each passing second a faint,
deep humming grew louder and louder, the lights intensi-
fied. In a moment the train, windows rattling, covered
with graffiti and grime, roared into the station, and with
piercing metal-on-metal screech of the wheels came to

a halt. Stephens saw only five passengers in the seven cars and was relieved. The chances were excellent that the car he boarded with Chamber would be empty. The doors rolled open. Two passengers got off at the other end of the platform and quickly ascended the stairs. The doors closed and the train rattled out of the station. Stephens surveyed the platform and found himself alone.

Reaching within his open trenchcoat, double-breasted, blue, he shifted the gun digging into the small of his back. Wedged inside his belt, the nickel-plated .22-caliber revolver was readily accessible. He valued it over any of the pistols he had accumulated from the street over the years. It was accurate and in excellent condition—and unregistered. Before the night was over, it would lie on the bottom of the East River. His regular weapon, a Smith and Wesson .38-caliber revolver, was nestled neatly in a shoulder holster beneath his armpit. That weapon would not be used this night.

The early morning desolation of the subway provided a perfect setting for a shooting. And the noise of a train in motion gave little chance for a shot of a .22 caliber to be heard. The two men would board together. He would shoot Chamber on the train, take his money to make it look like a robbery, get off and be long gone even before the victim was found to be dead. Drunks slumped in their seats were common sights in the subways of New York City. It was a natural setup.

He looked at his watch. It was after one. The minutes passed slowly, but his patience never wavered. Finally, Chamber appeared in his street clothes on the stairway in the middle of the station. Walking casually toward the first deputy, he turned twice to look at the deserted platform.

Stephens' stomach tensed when their eyes locked.

"Any problems losing the tail?" Stephens asked as Chamber joined him.

"None."

The first deputy extended his hands toward the patrolman. "May I?"

Chris knew he would want to frisk him to be sure he was not wired. He nodded.

Stephens tossed him quickly, lingering for a moment by the holstered revolver clipped inside his pants at the hip—it was a likely spot to hide an electronic device. He found nothing. Satisfied, he put his hands in his pockets and resumed a leaning position against the girder. "I have to admit," he said to an obviously apprehensive listener, "the sudden demise of our old friend Stuart Pierce was certainly a coincidence."

"A coincidence in your favor."

"I had nothing to do with it, Chamber. As far as I know, Pierce hung himself. He was a psycho."

Chris was silent.

"But there's nothing we can do about Pierce now, anyway," Stephens added, "so let's forget him."

"How about Sabra?"

"I had to have some offense."

Chris was sorry he had brought her up. He had fallen for her, and it still hurt. A cool breeze announced the coming of a train. Headlights glared in the distance. "And Father Roselli?" He spoke quickly. Soon they would have to talk above the sound of the train.

"The commissioner ordered that without consulting me." He hesitated. "He's a sick man, believe me."

Chris suspected the ploy: that Stephens would make it seem as if the police commissioner were actually calling all the shots.

The train blasted into the station, and the wheels grated to a stop. There were few people; none in the last car. "Let's get on for a quick ride," Stephens said as the doors opened. "It's no good staying in one spot too long."

Chris was puzzled but nodded, and they got aboard.

Stephens had chosen the Independent line because that was the one with which he was most familiar, the one he had ridden so many times as a boy to and from his Brooklyn home. He knew that two stops from 23rd Street the tracks swerved sharply immediately before entering the West 4th Street station. He knew the train would screech its wheels unceasingly for at least fifteen seconds as it rounded the curve. A shot from a .22-caliber revolver would be drowned out completely. And it was unlikely that a passenger would board at the next stop. He looked at his watch. Chamber would be dead in less than five minutes. And whatever trouble he might have caused would die with him.

"We've both got good heads on our shoulders," Stephens said, as they sat down. The train started with a jerk. "And we both know that a solution to the problem confronting us can be worked out." The windows vibrated noisily as the train left the station into the darkness of the tunnel.

[267]

"What problem?" Chris asked above the noise.

Stephens continued, stalling for time. "I feel the first thing that should be established is: what exactly is it that we want?"

"I don't know what you mean."

"Well, I want those tapes. Plain and simple. What do you want in return?"

"I don't know that I want anything anymore. And I don't know if those tapes will ever be available to you."

The train streaked into the first station. The doors opened and closed with no one getting on. Stephens straightened himself as the train started underway.

"Come on now, Chamber. You've got to look at this situation carefully, with an open mind." He paused. "You wouldn't have any intentions of turning those tapes over to another authority, now would you?"

Then Chris saw it. The odd hour, the setting, Stephens' edgy, disjointed conversation of questions that made no sense. It was a setup.

Suddenly, Stephens jumped up from the seat and reached behind his back, withdrawing the nickel-plated revolver. He pointed it at Chamber's heart.

Chris froze and cursed himself for seeing it all too late. "Are you crazy?" he shouted.

The curve was coming up; Stephens knew it. He shifted his eyes from Chamber to the window, then back to Chamber. Any second now the wheels would scrape the rails. Chris's mind spun. What would work? Stall him. Anything. "Listen, I'll give you the tapes. Right now. Let's go get them right now. No tricks." If he lunged, by the time he reached Stephens he'd be dead.

[268]

Stephens waited for the curve. He strained his ears for the first shriek of the wheels. It came and his eyes widened.

Chris glanced up. A red-handled cord dangled above his head. Instinctively he reached his hand skyward and yanked it as Stephens squeezed the trigger. The train's emergency brake locked the metal wheels tight, knocking the first deputy off balance. The gun fired, muffled in the grinding shrill. The bullet struck Chris in the chest, knocking him to the floor. The jerk of the train sent Stephens reeling backward, hurtling uncontrollably. He reached his hand out to grab something but found nothing. He was helpless, stumbling backward through the car faster and faster. Abruptly, violently, the back of his neck cracked against an unyielding enamel pole with tremendous force. The gun dropped from his hand and slid to the door as his body hit the floor.

The train, hissing steadily, had reached the station before coming to a stop. Chris had been thrown beneath a seat. His chest burned terribly and throbbed in pain, but he instinctively pulled his gun and forced himself to his knees, ready for combat. He aimed the revolver in Stephens' direction. The deputy commissioner had recovered his gun and swung toward Chris. Chris fired three times and Stephens fell forward, his face smashing hard against the floor.

For a few seconds Chris did not move. The pain in his chest forced him to slouch, but he stayed ready. He eyed the motionless body lying in a heap against the pole. His mind raced, trying to piece everything together. It had all happened so quickly. The doors opened. Any second there would be someone in the car to help. He relaxed and his mind blurred.

The white paper shades were drawn shut and a round incandescent bulb shone from the center of the ceiling. The room was small, cluttered with emergency medical equipment. Chris had no remembrance of the great effort to save his life. The last thing he remembered was the train. But he had been told he would be all right with plenty of rest in the next few months. He was vaguely pleased with the thought of a lengthy vacation. The mayor, tall and square-chinned, stood beside the bed. He had made certain no one talked to Chris before he did.

". . . And that's just about it," Chris said. "I've got the tapes to back me up."

The mayor needed little convincing at this point. All the pieces fit. Ballistics tests would undoubtedly confirm the fact that the bullet taken from Chamber's chest was fired from the twenty-two found in Stephens' hand.

"You have to admit," the mayor said, "the story is fantastic. I believe it. Every word. But the first deputy commissioner trying to murder one of his own men! And the police commissioner himself involved in . . ." He shook his head. "There's no telling what repercussions this might have if we give it to the press." Already he was thinking of his political future. The scandal made public would blow him right out of office. Chris watched him as he stared in thought at the floor. In a few minutes the mayor spoke again and now there was a different tone in his voice, quiet, appealing. "Can you see the problems we will face if this gets out, Chris? Can you see that many innocent people might get hurt?" Chris was silent. "I'll need your cooperation. We must attack this problem tactfully."

Suddenly the mayor was speaking as if they were old friends, Chris thought. He was alert for the politician's forte: persuasion. He could sense what was coming, but he would not be *forced* into anything. He would listen, but ultimately the decision lay in *his* hands.

"We need a different story for the press," said the mayor. "It's as simple as that."

"I'm listening," Chris said.

"An attempted robbery. You were just sitting there, talking. The only other person in the car was a Negro. He got up, walked straight toward you and pulled the twenty-two. He said: 'Empty your pockets or you're dead,' or something like that . . . and waved the gun under your noses. Before you knew it Stephens jumped up and pulled the emergency cord. The three of you went flying. The black did all the shooting. The fact that Stephens was killed with a thirty-eight will present no problem."

Why? Chris thought. Why let Stephens get away without a mark against him? Joe Hummel flashed to mind. The same feelings that had overcome Chris when explaining Joe Hummel's death to the inspector that night in the Corinthian overcame him now. Stephens was dead. What good would the scandal do? What would Chris gain? The mayor was right: many innocent people might suffer, including, and most important, the men of the Police

Department as a whole. Sensation-seeking newspapers and other media would play the scandal up big, and the shock would be felt by everyone who wore a badge. The question "Why?" turned to "Why not?"

"What about Windsor?" Chris asked. He believed that Windsor knew nothing of the murder attempt, but it made no difference; Chris was disgusted by this imitation man. He did not belong in the office of the police commissioner.

The mayor thought for only a second. "He resigns."

It might work, Chris thought. But would it be best? "How do I explain my riding the subway at 1 A.M with the first deputy commissioner?" Chris asked.

The mayor was ready. "Stephens was not just your boss, you were friends. That's not too farfetched. I can back it up, if necessary. And Windsor will back it up, too. He's smart enough to know that getting out of this cleanly means he says what we want him to say. Your recent visits to Stephens' office will serve as a good basis for confirmation in case anyone has doubts. You can say truthfully that you were talking to him about getting transferred to the Police Academy pool. You know yourself that taking care of your friends is by no means an uncommon practice in the Police Department. Friendship is as difficult to disprove as it is to prove. And who will doubt you, anyhow? You're a hero. What possible reason could you have for not telling the truth? You've done nothing wrong."

Oh, the irony of it, Chris thought: he and Stephens, good friends.

The mayor continued, "You had just finished up a

[272]

four to twelve and he met you by the stationhouse. He had had some business in the precinct and knew you were getting off, so he stopped by. You were going for coffee and a snack down in Times Square, but first he wanted to pick up his car. It was at his office. It's hard enough to find one parking spot in Times Square, so you left your car at the Two-One."

Chris reflected on the dilemma. He would have to make a decision in a very short time. The mayor's story would work. The description of the fabricated Negro who got away would be so vague it would fit half a million people in New York City.

The mayor looked to Chris with inquiring eyes. "What do you say?"

Chris nodded.

Epilogue

ON a sunlit afternoon in the summer of the following year two hundred guests ringed the steps of City Hall to witness the annual Police Department Medal Day Ceremony. Sandy Chamber, her two children, Barney Monaghan and Father Frank Roselli watched from their front-row-center seats as, one by one, thirty-two men were honored by the mayor and the newly appointed police commissioner for outstanding work and bravery in the line of duty.

Chris sat in full-dress uniform on the side of the podium. He thought about the past year. He thought about the Corinthian; about Joe Hummel; about First Deputy Commissioner Stephens. He remembered vividly the day, about a month after Stephens' funeral, when he had sat in his living room reading the newspaper. The

[275]

headlines had been explicit: "POLICE COMMIS-
SIONER RESIGNS; SUDDEN DECISION TAKES
MAYOR BY SURPRISE; SUCCESSOR SOUGHT."
"WINDSOR TO HEAD UP RACE TRACK SECU-
RITY." He remembered the feeling of satisfaction. He
had done it. His initial intent notwithstanding, he had
done it. The Police Department and, in effect, the people
of New York City had been rid of their two most corrupt officials. Everyone had gained by his action; even
his fellow police officers, who unknowingly had avoided
a major scandal that certainly would have pushed morale
to an all-time low.

The highest and most prestigious award, the last
presentation of the day, was preceded by a recap of
events. All the crowd listened in hushed silence as the
circumstances surrounding the shootout at the Corinthian Hotel were described. The last facts mentioned
were that all the participants in the robbery had been
apprehended and that most of the stolen jewelry had
been recovered. On cue, Chris stepped to the center of
the podium.

The mayor's voice crackled with pride as he pinned
the medal to Chris's chest. ". . . In view of the alert, intelligent and decisive performance of this individual, whose
actions were in the highest tradition of the Police Department, I hereby award him, Police Officer Christopher
Chamber, this Medal of Honor."

The crowd applauded.

From the age of seven Edward F. Droge, Jr., knew he wanted to be a cop. When he became a police officer, he was cited eleven times for excellent and meritorious service. Then came the Knapp Commission and Droge made headlines with his testimony about police corruption. In The Patrolman: A Cop's Story *he told the whole blunt, hard-nosed truth about himself and the system that made and broke him. He now lives with his wife and three children in Brooklyn and attends Yale University.* In the Highest Tradition *is his first novel.*